I0541606

INTO THE
GREEN PRISM

By
A. HYATT VERRILL

Illustrated by
Frank R. Paul

ARMCHAIR FICTION
PO Box 4369, Medford, Oregon 97504

*The original text of this novel was first
published by Experimenter Publishing*

Armchair Edition, Copyright 2015 by Gregory Luce
All Rights Reserved

*For more information about Armchair Books and products, visit our
website at…*

www.armchairfiction.com

Or email us at…

armchairfiction@yahoo.com

AN INCREDIBLE GATEWAY TO ANOTHER WORLD!

Two scientists, Don Alfeo and Ramon Amador, plunged headlong into the wilds of Ecuador to conduct various scientific studies on the ancient Manabi Indian tribe. There in the Ecuadorian wilds they found a strange substance near the remains of an ancient meteorite. It was a green semi-transparent material that one might easily cast aside as a bit of a broken green glass bottle. But the two experts soon discovered that this strange emerald-like material contained properties more fantastic than the world of science had ever known. In fact, within this astounding green substance was the doorway to another world.

A. Hyatt Verrill was one of the best known authors during the early years of the classic science fiction magazine, Amazing Stories. *He was a true ace when it came to "hard science" tales. "Into the Green Prism" is one of the best examples of his superb story-telling prowess.*

FOR A COMPLETE SECOND NOVEL, TURN TO PAGE 153

CAST OF CHARACTERS

DON ALFEO

He was an anthropologist by trade, but his joint experiments in the world of physics would soon shock the scientific world.

RAMON AMADOR

A hardcore physicist on the surface, but his inner soul felt the calling of something far beyond the realm of science.

KORA

To say she was the most beautiful woman on Earth might be an understatement, even if she was smaller than the tiniest pinhead.

THE HIGH-PRIEST

He was the strong, religious leader of a lost tribe of Manabi Indians—a tribe that had all but vanished centuries before.

THE CHOLOS

They were hard-working servants, often kept in line by the fear of the results of Alfeo and Amador's "witchcraft" science.

THE CUR

A simple, mangy mutt, unable to conceive of his crucial role in the most daring scientific experiment ever undertaken.

CHAPTER ONE

IT is rather a difficult matter for a scientist to write intelligently and interestingly of a science with which he is not thoroughly familiar, and it is still harder for one who is accustomed to dealing with hard facts and purely scientific truths to record matters that, to those who have never come into contact with them, must appear purely imaginary and highly improbable. Hence it is with the greatest hesitation, and only after long consideration and innumerable urgings from my fellow scientists, that I have decided to relate the truly remarkable story of the astonishing discoveries, and the incredible incidents that resulted therefrom, that were made by my friend, Professor Ramon Amador, while he was associated with me in South America.

As I think the matter over, I feel convinced that Professor Amador without doubt made the most notable and revolutionary discovery in physics that has been made in the last two centuries. Not only did it completely upset many supposed laws and theories that had been held as scientific truths for years, but in addition, it divulged entirely new and undreamed of forces and laws, both in the realm of physics and in optics. I may even go further and state unequivocally that his discovery threw an entirely new light upon our accepted ideas of matter, ether waves, the atomic theory, gravitational force, and even life itself. Had it been developed and brought to the attention of the world it might—and unquestionably would—have been of inconceivable benefit to mankind, although on the other hand it might have proved a curse.

But, as has been the case with not a few epochal discoveries in the world of science, my friend's discovery was completely lost almost as soon as it was made, and with its loss the world—as we know it—lost one of its most brilliant scientists, and I lost—temporarily at least—a most steadfast, cherished and esteemed friend.

Professor Ramon Amador, as no doubt most of my readers are aware, was a Peruvian by birth, a citizen of the United States by choice, and an internationally recognized authority on physics and optics. He was a graduate of Santo Domingo and San Marcos Universities in Cuzco and Lima, a Ph.D. of Harvard, a post-graduate of Princeton and Columbia, and he had taken degrees at several European colleges. Being the fortunate possessor of a comfortable income from profitable investments in his native land, he was able to devote all of his time to study and investigations in his chosen line of science, and while he held the chair of Applied Physics at Moulton University, and delivered courses of lectures on physics and optics at numerous seats of learning both in this country and abroad, he steadfastly refused to accept any permanent appointment where he would be tied down to routine work and would not be free to follow his own inclinations and researches.

I first met Ramon while I was in Peru conducting archeological studies in and about Cuzco, the ancient Incan capital. Like myself, he was making an intensive study of the cyclopean structures of the pre-Incas, but from an entirely different angle—and for a totally distinct purpose. His interest in the ruins of a mysterious vanished race was wholly centered upon the physics and mechanics of the stupendous works, while mine was as equally centered upon the human or anthropological features. Hence our interests never clashed, and from time to time, each of us made discoveries or evolved theories that helped the other, so that we got on famously. But even under any circumstances we would have become steadfast friends.

Amador was a most charming and likable man, once you came to know him well, although to a casual acquaintance he appeared reserved, a bit stand-off-ish—if I may use the term—rather self-sufficient, unemotional, and at times even abrupt and discourteous. But these characteristics were due largely to a latent shyness and self-consciousness that he could never quite overcome, and to a subconscious feeling that other men were not in the least interested in him or his work. But once his friendship and interest were won, he revealed himself as an entirely different character.

His mobile face, usually rather grave and with that indescribable but typical expression of sadness or pathos almost universal among Peruvians, became animated; his lips parted in a delightful boyish smile, his fine eyes sparkled, he talked volubly and entertainingly on almost any subject, and he joked, laughed, and related numberless interesting and amusing stories. Possibly his most outstanding characteristics, and those that made him most loved by those who knew him intimately like myself, were his great gentleness, kindness, and tenderness; his charity and ability to forgive; his optimism regarding his fellow men and women; his poetic and artistic temperament, and his deep respect—amounting almost to reverence—for women. Unquestionably his Spanish blood was responsible for many of these characteristics, but Incan blood also ran in his veins and accounted for some of his most admirable traits. Although by no means Indian in appearance—for he was no darker than myself, yet at times, he seemed almost wholly Indian in temperament and, despite his scientific training, his devotion to his chosen science and his marvelous powers of deduction and matter-of-fact reasoning, there was a great deal of the aboriginal mysticism, imagination and romance in his makeup.

All this rather lengthy dissertation upon the character of Professor Amador may seem dull, uninteresting and of no real consequence, but it is really highly important, for it throws a light upon subsequent events and, without a knowledge of my dear friend's personality, his actions, his psychology, his final end would seem incredible, unnatural, and inexplicable.

DURING the time that we were thrown together at Cuzco—and later at Tiahuanaco in Bolivia—Ramon was a constant source of knowledge and inspiration in my archeological work. Being a native of the country and familiar with the Quichua and Aimara dialects, and with a dash of aboriginal blood besides, he met the native Indians on their own ground, won their confidence and enabled me to secure myths, fables, folk lore and priceless information which they had never before divulged to strangers. Also, these oppressed descendants of the Incans guided us to many hitherto unknown ruins of their ancestors, and while I studied the archeological features of the remains, my friend carried on his measurements and computations, or spent hours, staring at some monolithic structure, a vacant far-away expression in his eyes, as if gazing into the past and visualizing the means by which the forgotten races accomplished feats that were inexplicable to him, even with his knowledge of physical laws. Often, too, his trained eyes and brain noted certain features of the structures that escaped me, and to my utter amazement I soon discovered that Professor Amador held most revolutionary and unscientific views regarding the mysterious structures of the district.

As he came to know me better, he confessed that he was convinced that the ancient Peruvians and Bolivians had possessed knowledge of forces and of natural laws that are unknown to us and that, if they could be rediscovered, they would revolutionize the industries, arts and even the life of our civilization. Not that he regarded them as supernatural—for despite his Indian-Latin blood, Ramon was utterly lacking in superstition—but as he put it quite logically, as the works could not be explained by any known physical laws, and as they could not be duplicated, even with our advanced mechanical knowledge, they must have been accomplished by some unknown method and a knowledge of unknown laws or forces.

It was in hopes of discovering some clue or key to these that he had visited the district, but at the end of several months, when I was compelled to leave for other fields, he confessed that he was no nearer a solution than he was before.

It was not until the following year that I again met Professor Amador. I had recently returned from Ecuador where, in the Manabí district. I had been engaged in making extensive archeological researches, and where I had made some truly epochal discoveries of remains of a hitherto unknown but highly cultured prehistoric race. I had scarcely been able to scratch the surface, so to say, when I had been forced to abandon work owing to the rainy season, and I planned to return to the new field as soon as the weather permitted. But even in the short time I had been on the ground I had obtained some most interesting specimens. Prominent among these were a number of most remarkable gold beads and ornaments unlike anything hitherto known. Viewed with the naked eye, they appeared to be merely grains, or tiny nuggets of gold—for which, as a matter of fact, they were mistaken when they were first found—few of them larger than the head of a common pin. During examination under a powerful lens, they were revealed as hand-wrought, perfectly formed beads, chased, carved, decorated and perforated. Many, indeed, were composed of several almost microscopic portions, soldered or welded together.*

The moment I showed these truly amazing examples of prehistoric handiwork to Professor Amador, he became intensely interested and excited.

"Marvelous!" he exclaimed, as he examined the minute golden beads with his pocket lens. "The most astonishing examples of human handicraft I have ever seen. The very antithesis of the stupendous works of the trans-Andean regions! My friend, I believe your discovery of these may lead to the ultimate solution of all the mysteries of physics that I have vainly tried to solve. Think of it! On the one hand structures composed of stones weighing upwards of one hundred tons, cut, fitted, raised to great heights, and transported hundreds of miles** squared and beveled with mathematical accuracy, sculptured elaborately, hewn into immense doorways and portals as though the refractory pyritic rock were as soft as cheese. Then on the other hand, these minute, almost invisible

---

* Such beads were actually found at Manabí, Ecuador, by Prof. Marshall Saville of the Museum of the American Indian Heye Foundation, and are on exhibition at the museum in New York City.

** In Bolivia and Peru are monolithic stone idols of gigantic size (one measuring fifty feet in length by twelve feet in diameter) which are composed of a rock known only in Ecuador, in a district nearly fifteen hundred miles from where the idols were found.

golden beads, carved, built up, perforated as perfectly, as beautifully as though they were inches in diameter or—perhaps better—as though they had been made by the hands of midgets—elves or fairies—no larger than a mouse! There you have the two extremes; and both, I feel sure, are the result of a knowledge of the same lost physical laws.

"In one case we have normal handiwork exaggerated, enlarged thousands of times; in the other equally normal handicraft reduced in an equal degree. It is…" Here he laughed merrily at the comparison. "…it is like viewing objects through the opposite ends of a telescope; seemingly magnifying them one way; apparently reducing them the other!"

Then, suddenly: *"Caramba!"* he cried, leaping to his feet and relapsing into his mother tongue as he always did when greatly excited. "That is an idea, an inspiration! My friend, these golden beads must have been fashioned by means of a lens! No human being of normal size could have accomplished the feat otherwise, and we know they are the work of normal sized men, for you tell me the other objects are of ordinary size and that the skeletal fragments you have unearthed are those of ordinary human beings. Ah! We must discover those lenses. Even if I cannot solve the puzzle of the laws and forces that enabled the pre-Incas to cut and erect their titanic structures, still I may make epochal discoveries in the line of optics.

"With your permission, Don Alfeo, I shall accompany you when you return to Esmeraldas. Somewhere in the district we must find the lenses—such things are imperishable—and I am not sure—no, I dare not mention such an insane thought—I am not sure, but that the key to the mysteries may be revealed, when we find those prehistoric magnifying glasses."

THAT my friend had some new theory in his fertile brain, I felt sure. His imagination had been fired, had leaped ahead and had seized upon some clue or detail or some feature that had escaped me, and had visualized some possible solution of the puzzles he had so long been trying to solve.

Personally I could see no connection between the cyclopean stone work of the interior and these minute gold objects from the coast. They were as far apart as the antipodes, the work of two distinct races, objects of totally different materials, and, for all I or anyone else knew, of different periods—perhaps hundreds, even thousands of years apart. Archeologically and anthropologically the beads were most interesting as revealing new features of a cultural center, and while they had aroused my wonder and interest, yet how they were made was a problem that, strictly speaking, was scarcely an archeological matter.

The thought had crossed my mind that the makers of the beads must have possessed most remarkable eyesight and extraordinarily deft and delicate fingers, and for a moment I, too, had wondered, if by any possibility, they had possessed lenses of some sort. But, as far as known, no prehistoric American race had even a remote or rudimentary knowledge of optics, and I dismissed the idea as unreasonable, fanciful and outside the realm of scientific reasoning.

I had seen living Indians—such as the Mapuches of Chile— weave horsehair into extremely small forms. I had seen purblind squaws of the Pima tribe weave nests of perfectly-formed baskets, the largest barely an inch in diameter and the smallest scarcely a quarter of an inch square, and I deemed it not at all impossible that the ancient inhabitants of Manabí might have carved and soldered grains of gold with the unaided eye, even if a white man, with the degenerate eyesight resulting from centuries of civilization, artificial light and lack of training, would have found such a feat utterly impossible.

But Amador, as I have said, possessed a vivid imagination, a love of the mysterious and mystical, a vast amount of romance, and, as was quite natural, even necessary I might say, considering the science to which he was devoted, he was a trained, expert theorist.

Here I might fittingly explain that there is a very wide gulf between the two sciences we represented. Archeology and anthropology are sciences built upon facts. The archeologist—

and, as well, the anthropologist—make discoveries, reveal incontrovertible facts, and from the material and data obtained, formulate theories and hypotheses to dovetail with the facts.

The physicist, on the contrary, works out abstract theories, formulates problematical laws and mathematical equations, and, from these, endeavors to prove facts and to demonstrate the accuracy of his calculations. Amador, to be sure, was not entirely a theoretical scientist, but realized that, in many cases, facts should come first and theories later. In fact I had often jokingly told him that the world had lost a most brilliant archeologist when he had turned to physics as a life study, for his remarkable powers of observation, his interest in his prehistoric ancestors, and his powers of deduction would have enabled him to have reached the topmost pinnacle in that science.

But to return to more concrete matters. Ramon, of course, accompanied me a few months later when I set sail for South America, and in due course of time we found ourselves in Ecuador.

I had thought that my own equipment was very complete and, much as I regretted it, far too bulky and voluminous for traveling in a crude and somewhat wild district. But in comparison with the impedimenta of my friend, my luggage was insignificant. Not only did he carry the most complete and up-to-date field equipment, consisting of the latest of tents, camp furniture, cooking outfit, etc., together with clothing, arms, food supplies, and enough to supply a large party for months of tropical exploration; but in addition, he had brought along a most elaborate scientific laboratory, with a complete chemical and mechanical plant for conducting tests and experiments in optics and physics.

I gazed with dismay upon the innumerable boxes, cases, bundles, baskets, trunks, bags and other packages bearing Amador's name, which were disgorged from the steamer's hold and were dropped upon the rickety dock at Guayaquil.

And I foresaw no little difficulty in transporting this mountain of dunnage up the coast to the jungle-covered shores of the river at Manabí.

But I had reckoned without my friend's resourcefulness and familiarity with local conditions. I had prided myself upon my experience and knowledge of Latin America and Latin Americans, upon my ability to accomplish great things when dealing with the natives; but, beside Ramon, I was a veritable amateur. Browbeating, joking, cajoling, flattering, cursing, praising the tattered Mestizo peons, the uniformed officials, the slouching stevedores, the sailors and the innumerable hangers-on by turn, he soon had them laughing, working like demons, obeying him instantly, vying with one another to please him, and, in an incredibly short time, all our baggage was stowed in the dirty coasting schooner and we were ready for the long and weary voyage up the coast.

CHAPTER TWO

WE reached our destination in due time and, having arrived at the location where I had secured the specimens the preceding season and had done my excavatory work, Professor Amador's laboratory and outfit were soon unpacked and set up, forming quite an imposing nucleus of civilization in the midst of the wilderness. Meanwhile, I had arranged my own much humbler and simpler headquarters, had set my men to work clearing the jungle that had sprung up like magic since my last visit, and busied myself searching for the most promising spot in which to recommence my field work.

Ramon, once he had established himself, donned old bush clothes, fell to work with the rest of us, and soon proved himself as adaptable to roughing it as any old hand. He showed the most intense interest in the locality, asked innumerable questions, watched everything I did, and in an astonishingly short time acquired a remarkable knowledge of archeological work.

He possessed the keenest eyes of any man I ever met, and was most amazingly observant. Several times he discovered valuable and interesting specimens, which I had completely overlooked. As the excavations proceeded, he watched each shovelful of earth like a hawk, and would swoop upon every fragment of potsherd or chipped stone that was revealed.

The spot where we were working was on a fairly level, alluvial plain between two streams—a sort of tongue or cape, which obviously had frequently been flooded in times past. That it had also been occupied by a populous village or town was evident, for all along the steep river banks, potsherds, stone implements and remains of fires were to be seen.

Evidently, too, the site had been occupied for a long time, for the traces of human occupancy extended from a few feet below the surface to a depth of more than twenty feet. And as the soil was literally filled with potsherds, digging was slow work. Each time a fragment of pottery was disclosed it was necessary to proceed very carefully; often we worked for hours with a small trowel and a whisk broom in order to secure some fragment without completely destroying it. And as we found no traces of gold ornaments and no traces of any material which might have served as a lens, after several days' work, Professor. Amador grew tired of watching the apparently fruitless labors of the peons and wandered off up the narrow, pebbly beach beside the stream.

It was in the stream itself that I had discovered the minute gold beads, and knowing they must have been washed out from the banks, I had assumed that they had come from the village site. Armed with a baiea or gold pan, Ramon busied himself washing out the gravel in the stream and grew quite excited and enthusiastic when he, too, secured several dozen of the beads. But he was interested only in finding the means by which the ancient Manabís had fashioned the bits of ornamented gold, and when, on the second day of his panning, he shouted lustily to me, I felt sure he had made a discovery. I was not mistaken. From the river gravel he had washed out a fragment of semi-transparent green material which, had I come upon it, I should have cast aside as a bit of a green glass bottle, the remains of one of my own discarded bottles of the previous season. But Ramon, who was busily examining the fragment with his pocket lens, declared that it was not glass.

"Hmm, perhaps an emerald," I suggested, half-jokingly.

"No, it is not beryl,"* he replied, his eyes still squinting through his glass. "It is exceedingly light—much lighter than aluminum, I should judge. But…" With a deep sigh of disappointment. "…it is far too small to be of any use."

I laughed. "What use did you hope to put it to?" I asked.

He looked up, a surprised expression in his fine eyes. "Use?" he repeated. "Why to experiment with, to be sure! This might prove to be the material these prehistoric people used for making lenses." It would be almost perfectly transparent—if it were not roughened and worn by the action of water and sand."'

I could not refrain from smiling incredulously. "Hardly," I declared. "I do not think that even primitive man would select material of that color when there is plenty of clear transparent quartz in the country here about. No, Ramon, if these people ever did use lenses, I'll wager they made them from transparent quartz."

"No use arguing," he said with finality in his tones. "But somehow, by some sort of premonition or hunch or something, I have felt all along that we are going to make an epochal discovery here. Perhaps that is why I am over-elated and interested at everything unusual. And this bit of green mineral is unusual. I wonder whence it came."

Leaving him still pondering on this matter, I returned to my peons, who, the instant my back was turned, had promptly quit working.

BUSY at the excavatory work, I thought nothing more of my friend and his bit of green mineral, until the men stopped work

---

* Beryl is the mineral, especially fine samples of which are called emeralds

at noon and I went to my lunch and found the Professor had not returned. Even then I was not troubled, for I assumed Ramon was still busy washing out gravel and searching for fragments of the green stone. I sent Louis, our camp-boy, to summon him, and went ahead with my midday meal. When Louis returned and stated that he could not find Ramon, I did become a bit anxious. In fact I was about to start off to search for him myself, when he appeared, arriving from the opposite direction from which he had been going when I had last seen him.

"You may be an expert archeologist," he announced with a grin, as he came into camp, "but you've made a great mistake in wasting time digging here. What do you think of this?"

As he spoke, he reached in his haversack and produced a beautifully sculptured figurine of lapis-lazuli.

I was speechless with surprise. It was the most perfect piece of prehistoric American stone-carving I had ever seen. It was far superior to any Maya, Aztec or Inca work; a human figure about ten inches in height and showing a squatting man, his hands resting on his knees, his head topped by an elaborate headdress of unique design.

"Where on earth did you find this?" I cried at last. He chuckled as he helped himself to the food Louis set before him. "Up the stream a way," he replied as he gnawed at a wild turkey's leg. "I suggest," he continued, "that we move to the spot after lunch, and abandon this wasteful digging of broken cook-pots. The locality where I secured the little idol is the spot whence the gold beads came. There are quite extensive ruins there. I found a number of stone columns projecting above the earth and sticking out of the bank, and I picked up the little blue god from where he had tumbled down to the beach. I do not claim to know anything about your line of work, *amigo mio,* but if I am not mistaken, the place I found was a temple or something of the sort. It seems to me that there we will have a much greater chance of coming upon the key to the puzzle—perhaps the very lenses these people used. And," he added as if in afterthought, "if you will examine the little god with your pocket-lens, you will discover that the apparently uniformly smooth surface of the stone is completely covered with intricate carving, invisible to the unaided eye."

Ramon was right. To my utter amazement, I found that the most beautiful and delicate ornamental pattern had been deeply engraved over the surface of the lapis lazuli, although, to my naked eye, the surface seemed scarcely roughened. It was even more astonishing than the almost microscopic gold beads. I could not imagine any human being with eyes and touch, that would enable him to carve the refractory stone in this manner, even had he possessed a lens.

But the indisputable proof was before me, and I plied Ramon with queries about the new site he had so fortunately discovered. He could add but little to the meager information he had already given. But from that little I was convinced that the new site was most promising and, lunch over, orders were given to break camp and move upstream. This was slow work and the sun had set in a blaze of glory behind the palm trees in the west before our camps. Ramon's laboratory and equipment and all our paraphernalia had been moved to a delightfully situated spot on a low hill above the river some five miles from our first location.

My friend had not exaggerated. Rather, he had understated the importance of his discovery. Everywhere, over an extensive area, there were the extremities of great stone columns projecting above the earth; some were plain, others sculptured, and as we cleared the jungle away, we came upon numerous masses of cut and sculptured stone, and not a few monolithic stone images or idols.

As Professor Amador had thought, the place had obviously been used as a great temple or place for ceremonials, and here, if anywhere, we might expect to come upon archeological treasures and—I might add—the means by which the ancient occupants had manufactured their microscopic beads and engraved their invisible designs on stone.

I would like to describe in detail the progress of our work, the finds we made, the remarkable artifacts we secured. But that has no place in this record of Professor Amador's discovery and disappearance. Suffice to say that we had stumbled upon an archeological treasure-house, the very nucleus of the prehistoric civilization of the Manabís, and daily, as my work proceeded and my specimens accumulated; matters which hitherto had been puzzling and mysterious were explained.

The strange carved stone seats typical of this culture were numerous and of all sizes; stone idols and the remarkable carved stone slabs described by Saville were innumerable; we came upon countless numbers of the peculiar elliptical, beautifully-wrought pottery vessels known only from this culture, and in addition to these objects already well-known to science, we secured priceless specimens in the form of wrought and carved beads, ornaments and figures in precious and semi-precious stones. Agate, carnelian, jade, lapis-lazuli, malachite, quartz, garnet, amethyst, beryl, topaz, even a few emeralds and sapphires had been cut, perforated, polished and covered with microscopic engraving by the Manabís, and judging from their abundance, with almost as little effort as though the refractory minerals had been so much soft limestone.

Also, and most interesting of all to me, were many objects of copper and silver plated with gold. How the ancient artisans coated the baser metals with gold was a mystery, and Ramon was almost as deeply interested in solving this riddle as in his quest for his theoretical lens. In his search for this he was tireless. From the very commencement we had found the microscopic gold beads, as well as others equally small, made from the hardest stones; and in several instances we had found hundreds and thousands of these cached in pottery vessels. I truly believe that Amador averaged less than an hour's sleep a night for weeks. At the close of the day's work he would go to his laboratory, and throughout the night, would devote himself to making intensive studies and working out long and involved calculations based upon the beautiful specimens of miniature handiwork we had obtained. His idea, as he explained it, was to determine how great a magnification the artisans must have secured in order to have engraved and perforated the objects by hand.

"If I can determine that point," he declared. "I will know whether they had any knowledge of advanced or rudimentary optics, and possibly I may be able to establish the type of lens they used and even the material from which it was made. Given the magnification it is not impossible to work out the size, curvature, and other details of a lens."

I MUST confess, it seemed a hopeless waste of time and energy, from my point of view. If the Manabís ever used lenses, then, I felt sure, we would find them eventually. And if they did not, then all of my friend's labors would have been for nothing. I am afraid I have little patience—or rather I should say, I *had* little at that time—with abstract theories based wholly upon assumptions. Had we found a lens I could have well understood Ramon wishing to work out its details and properties, but I could not understand his point in determining details of a lens, which very possibly, in fact probably, had never existed. But that was Professor Amador's affair, not mine, and I suppose he saw just as little use in my accumulating thousands of specimens and in my endeavoring to reconstruct the lives, customs, religion and what-not of a long extinct race of fellow men and women.

Then, one morning, he appeared with an elated, triumphant expression on his face.

"I have made a great discovery," he announced. "I have completed my calculations and I am convinced that the lens—or apparatus—used by these people was totally different from anything known to modern optics or physics. No known material and no known form of lens would magnify an article sufficiently to enable a human being to execute work as minute as we have found."

"Hmm," I muttered. "I cannot see, my friend, how that helps matters—even if you are right. Unless you can ascertain what they used—if they used anything—you haven't come any nearer solving your problem. And I admit I *am* a bit skeptical. How can you be sure that it is not possible to grind a glass or quartz lens to magnify to any desired extent? We have microscope objectives that will magnify hundreds—thousands of diameters."

Ramon smiled. "You forget, *amigo mio,* that such high-powered objectives have an exceedingly short focus. Your knowledge of optical laws are, I fear, very rudimentary. The greater the magnification, the shorter the focal length, or to reverse the equation and to point out the truth of my argument, the closer the lens must be to the object to be magnified.

"My calculations prove beyond the shadow of a doubt that, to enable human beings to incise the carved designs upon these precious-stone objects, the surface must have been magnified at least two hundred and fifty diameters.

"Now, my good friend, any known form of lens that is capable of a magnification of that amount would have a field of less than one-eighth of an inch diameter—approximately three millimeters. In order to focus such a lens sharply, it would have to be placed within one one-hundredth of an inch of the surface to be magnified—in fact it would have to be an oil-immersion lens—and hence it would be absolutely impossible for any human being to use a tool between the lens and the surface upon which it was focused. And," he added with finality, "even assuming that a lens could be made to fulfill the requirements of the case, you must remember that the tip or edge of the tool used in cutting the stone or metal would be equally magnified and would appear gigantic and coarse. It would in fact be somewhat similar to using a pickaxe for engraving a copper plate for a visiting card."

There was nothing I could say in rebuttal. If his statements were correct, and I knew him far too well to question them, then it would seem that his deductions were logical. I was accustomed to using a microscope myself, and although in my work I had never been obliged to resort to very high powers, still, when I came to think of it, I remembered that even a comparatively low power objective *did* have a short focus and a small field and had to be most carefully adjusted to within a very short distance of the object being examined. And I also remembered that I had been warned by my biology professor at college to use great care not to crack the microscope slides by screwing the lens against them. Ramon, then, must be right, at least in some of his conclusions. But to my mind he was still working on false or at least unsubstantiated premises.

"Even so," I objected at last, "it isn't necessary to assume that the Manabís possessed lenses of unknown material or design. Their eyes may have been different from ours, or…" I added half-banteringly, "…they may have possessed some mechanical device, some machine that would produce the results that are so mystifying. We have machinery that can engrave steel and other materials in much finer designs than any of those we have found here."

"You are straining at a gnat and swallowing a camel," laughed Ramon. "You are perfectly aware that the prehistoric races had no knowledge of mechanics, no knowledge whatever of the wheel, without which mechanical devices are quite impossible. You simply do not wish to admit that pure out-and-out theories can be right, that mathematical problems can solve matters of which we have no true knowledge, or that anything can be assumed to have existed unless concrete evidences of its existence are found."

"But," he finished confidently, "I am convinced that before you have completed excavations here, you *will* find such concrete evidences and that when they are found, they will bear out my theories and my calculations."

A FEW days later he again mentioned the matter. This time, he admitted he was merely theorizing. "I have been thinking deeply on this matter," he announced as we breakfasted together. "And I have almost come to the conclusion that there is some connection between the minute beads and microscopic carving and the gold-plated objects. I might even go farther and state that in the back of my mind is a feeling that there is a direct connection between all these and the titanic stone work of the Andean regions. You may recollect that when I first saw the gold beads, I remarked that they and the pre-Incan stonework were like looking at objects through the two ends of a telescope. Is it beyond the bounds of possibility that the same means these Manabís used for executing work that is invisible to the unaided eye, might not have been reversed to enable the pre-Incans to perform work which seemingly is that of giants?"

I laughed outright. "My dear Ramon," I cried, "how would visually reducing a fifty-ton stone affect its physical properties? It would still remain a huge rock and would still weigh fifty tons, even if, to the eye of the observer through 'the wrong end of the telescope,' as you put it, it appeared an insignificant pebble? You might as well suggest that the stones were really small and after being cut and placed were treated by some sort of magic, which caused them to expand and remain enlarged, or that these gold beads were cut and made and chased when a foot or two in diameter, and were then—by some occult means—reduced to their present size. No, no, Ramon, I admit the possibility, though not the probability, of a lens having been used—though it was probably a crude, accidentally-made flake of quartz crystal—but I cannot admit, even for the sake of argument, that the prehistoric Americans possessed the power of altering the proportions of non-organic matter."

Professor Amador merely smiled. "Ten, twenty, fifty years ago, that might have been conceded," he replied thoughtfully. "But today we know of a certainty that non-organic matter—and organic as well—is not the fixed, solid unalterable material our ancestors assumed it to be; All matter, as you are well aware; everything, ourselves included, is composed of protons and electrons; independent bodies, movable, transferable, changeable. Certain combinations or groupings of protons and electrons produce certain effects. Such groupings may remain unchanged indefinitely or they may change constantly. A rock may remain unaltered for countless centuries or, under other conditions, it may completely vanish as a rock in a short time. Why? You say by erosion, by weathering, by some one cause or another. Very true. But it is the alteration of the electronic grouping that causes the rock to vanish even though the weather or the elements may produce or incite the electronic alterations.

"A seed sprouts and grows into a tree. Why? Because the atoms which its molecules contain, alter their arrangement and numbers; air, water and sun and their own vitality cause them to change. We can take a huge mass of wood, of leather, of metal, and reduce it to a fraction of its former size and it will remain reduced, merely because we have forced its component atoms to assume a different combination. If we wish, we can increase material in the same manner. It all depends upon the groupings of electrons and upon vibratory waves. What happens when the tobacco in the pipe you are smoking is burned? Do you, a scientist, mean to tell me that the tobacco has actually been destroyed, that by puffing at your pipe you have eliminated a portion of the matter of the universe? No, you have merely altered an electronic combination. Your tobacco still exists though in changed form. You have produced ash, gases, smoke, liquids, solids, by forcing, through the medium of fire and air, the protons and electrons of the original tobacco to assume new combinations and forms.

"Even the human body and the bodies of animals of all kinds are in the same sense indestructible. Upon death the electronic combinations and vibratory waves, which give us our living bodies, become altered. By degrees they take on new and unrecognizable forms. Some become gases; others solids, others liquids, and in time these change still more. They become loam, plants, vegetables. Again they alter and become component parts of new creatures, even of other men and women. For all we know, even our mentality, our spirits or souls, are merely forms of electronic or vibratory wave energy;

for all we know these same forms of energy may, either rarely or commonly, reassume their former combinations and produce reincarnated beings having the same thoughts, the same ideals, the same reactions, the same loves and hates as those who died hundreds or thousands of years ago.

"In the light of present-day science, nothing is impossible, *amigo mio*. What seems impossible or at least highly improbable today may be commonplace tomorrow. Is it any more remarkable to imagine a small pebble increased to a gigantic monolith, or to think of a life-sized statue reduced to miniature, than to conceive of the human voice—the living, speaking image of a human being—being transmitted through the empty air for hundreds thousands of miles? Mind you, I do not say positively that these prehistoric people possessed some power, unknown to us, of permanently altering the proportions of objects. But we must admit, or else discredit the testimony of our five senses, that they possessed some knowledge of which we are woefully ignorant. And I should not be at all surprised if, when we hit upon the secret, we will find that it was along the lines I have suggested."

"Whew!" I exclaimed. "No wonder you hold the reputation of being the most forceful lecturer on physics in the world. Yes, I admit all that you say is incontrovertible truth as admitted by science. In fact, I might add quite a few facts and examples in proof of it. But it doesn't prove anything, and until you can either discover this lost wizardry or can work out a theory that can be proved by repeating the magic, you are no nearer a solution of the puzzle. And," I added, as, I rose to start my peons at their digging, "I suppose you suggest that the copper objects were plated with gold by the Manabís' ability to transform a portion of the copper to gold by some unknown and lost power that would have made the ancient alchemists green with envy."

CHAPTER THREE

IT was only a few days later that we came upon a great find, the find that Professor Amador had hoped for and had foreseen, and which was the direct cause of all the truly amazing and incredible events that followed, and which culminated with the disappearance of my friend.

The "find" itself seemed insignificant. Merely a number of fragments of the same transparent greenish mineral, such as Professor Amador had found in the bed of the stream weeks before. But to him the bits of green material—scarcely one of which was half an inch in diameter—were far more precious than emeralds. The instant the first piece was revealed, he leaped into the pit, shooed away the amused peons, and on hands and knees, began searching for fragments. Not until every shovelful of earth had been carefully sifted and no more pieces of the mineral could be found, did he cease. The result of his labors was a handful of the green slivers, but he was as excited and enthusiastic as though he had discovered a living Manabí, and he hurried to his laboratory with his treasure-trove.

In the course of the day we came upon several more deposits of similar fragments, and wishing to further my friend's work as much as possible, I had all the fragments in each separate lot carefully preserved and kept together, I did not see Ramon until the following day, but a light was burning in his field laboratory all night, and he admitted that he had not slept. But he had a body and nerves of steel and seemed never to tire, never to be exhausted, never to be in need of sleep, so I had long before given up warning him of the danger of not sleeping enough.

This morning he was jubilant. "I was right!" he exclaimed. "These people *did* use lenses, and lenses of a material hitherto unknown—of that green mineral substance. Although," he qualified, "I am convinced it is an artificial material, not a natural mineral formation."

"Good!" I applauded. "I suppose you have reconstructed a lens and have discovered that it is not so very remarkable and that it will magnify enough to solve the mystery."

"Yes, and no," he declared. "After no little trouble and perseverance, I matched up enough of the fragmentary remains to establish the fact that they were shattered splinters of what was once a lens. The rounded surfaces and the obvious indications of grinding and polishing amply prove that fact. But it would be impossible to reconstruct a lens from the splinters that I have. And even if they were cemented together, the resultant lens would be worthless in as far as testing its optical peculiarities is concerned. But, I shall endeavor to make an exhaustive test to establish the refractive index of the mineral or material, and shall sacrifice a small quantity of it—always of course with your permission—in an effort to melt it. If I succeed, I may try to recast the material and manufacture a new lens."

"You can use all of the stuff you want in any way you see fit," I assured him. "We found a lot more after you left yesterday—I should say we have eight or ten pounds of it now. So go ahead and I wish you every success. But I shall not be convinced until you have made a lens and have proved your case. You see, Ramon, in this case I am from Missouri, as the saying is. The fragments may have rounded surfaces, they may have been cut and polished, but I'll wager they are portions of some ornament, some vessel or some ceremonial object, and not parts of any lens. Why should they be broken? Why should a lens have been shattered—or rather, why should half a dozen lenses have been shattered?"

"Humph!" he snorted. "Why should a dish, an ornament, a ceremonial object—or several of them—have been shattered? Answer that, *amigo mio,* and I will answer *your* question."

"That's easy," I assured him. "Virtually all archeologists— and most ethnologists—who have studied American aboriginal races, know that it was and is a widespread custom of the Indians to 'kill' their most prized possessions upon certain occasions. During funerals it is often done, at the dedication of temples the custom is followed, and it also forms a portion of the religious ceremonies of some tribes. There are abundant evidences that the Manabís practiced the custom. Many of the broken stone artifacts—the *metates** and chairs, the idols—as well as much of the pottery I have found, were obviously broken intentionally. I have secured several pots shattered by stones which still remain among the fragments; I have found others resting against the stone columns with smears of their color showing where they were dashed against the stone. The Indians' idea is that by 'killing,' or as we would say sacrificing, an article they prevent evil spirits or devils from taking possession of it.

"And, as a usual thing, the objects most commonly sacrificed are those of a ceremonial character. If you had observed, you would have noticed that, in every case, the plain pottery and ordinary stone artifacts in this site are entire, whereas the objects of a ceremonial or symbolic type have been intentionally broken. Now if these people had very sacred ceremonial objects composed of your green glass or whatever it is, they would be the first to be sacrificed."

"I take off my hat to you as a lecturer," he laughed. "Thanks for the scientific and highly interesting information. But, let me point out, your explanation answers your own question. Admitting that all you say is so, then if these Manabís possessed lenses, they unquestionably would have looked upon them as sacred or mysterious or ceremonial, and they too, would have been sacrificed."

I WAS floored. His argument was logical. Still I was not convinced and I told him so. But he pointed out that not one of the fragments was so shaped that it could have formed a

---

* A curved or hollowed stone used by the Indians in grinding corn. It was a sort of basin in shape.

portion of any dish, figure or ornament, and he insisted that the splinters represented some form of lenses.

"If we could only discover the site whence the material was obtained," he remarked, "we might be able to construct a lens and prove my theory."

"But I thought you said you believed the material an artificial product," I reminded him. "Surely, if that is so, you should be able to analyze it and reproduce it. You are an excellent inorganic chemist, I know, and you have a very complete chemical laboratory with you."

"My very dear, good friend," he said, "chemistry is a most remarkable and exact science to be sure. It will be comparatively easy to analyze the material; but it is an entirely different matter to imitate it. It may prove to be possible as you suggest, but it is just as liable to be utterly impossible. Many materials may be analyzed but not duplicated. And some cannot even be analyzed. Take Bakelite, for example. It is, as you know, a material made by combining formaldehyde and carbolic acid with some filler and coloring matter added. And yet, if some man, say a few thousand years from now, should discover a slab of Bakelite and should try to determine its way of manufacture by analysis, he would find it absolutely impossible. And I could name a hundred—yes fully one thousand—well-known and common substances which, though readily analyzed and their various component parts identified, cannot be duplicated unless the secret of their manufacture is known.

"We can analyze diamonds, granite, mica, innumerable minerals, but we cannot make identical substances artificially, and while I do not mean to state positively that I may not be able to produce material identical with this green mineral-like substance; I am not counting much upon being able to do so.

"As regards to my suggestion that it is artificial, I assume that if that is the case, the Manabís discovered the secret of its manufacture by accident—perhaps by building a fire where its various elements occurred, and fusing them together, just as the ancients discovered how to make glass by kindling a fire on a sandy shore where blocks of crude soda surrounded the fire. And if we could find the spot, we should probably find the crude material, for I should imagine that the aborigines, probably regarding the material as sacred or of divine origin, would invariably have sought the same spot when they desired the composition, never realizing that the various elements could be transported elsewhere and then combined."

"Perhaps you are right," I admitted. "But to find the spot would be like searching the proverbial haystack for the equally proverbial needle. It may be within a few yards of where we stand, and then again it may be anywhere within a radius of several thousand miles. You must remember, Ramon, that the Indians—"

"Yes, I know what you are about to say," he interrupted. "That the aborigines transported articles for immense distances, that they bartered and traded from ocean to ocean and from the Arctic to the Antarctic. I am quite aware of that, my friend. I have often examined those mysterious monolithic idols that are abandoned near Lake Titicaca, but are made from stone that, as far as is known, can be found only near Quito in Ecuador— nearly two thousand miles distant. That, *amigo mio,* is one of the puzzles in prehistoric physics that I have tried and am still trying to solve.

"But in this case I doubt if the deposits of materials I seek are far from here. Your own and Saville's investigations have demonstrated that the Manabís were restricted to a comparatively small area, that savage, uncivilized tribes surrounded them, and hence they were, in a large measure, self-contained. Yes, unless they received the materials by water, the deposit is close at hand, and I intend to search diligently for it. Can I borrow one of your peons to accompany me on my search?"

Of course, I gladly gave the permission, and for the days following, Ramon made trips into the surrounding jungle, covering an allotted and predetermined area each day, and carefully searching every foot of the ground in his hopeless and, to me, endless quest.

BUT Ramon Amador had the perseverance, the dogged determination or instinct of the Indians, whose blood ran in his veins, and he seemed never discouraged nor downcast by his constant failures. I must also add that he had tried in vain to analyze the green material. He learned that it contained certain well-known elements—such as silica, aluminum and sodium, but it also contained several elements and the oxide of at least two metals, which baffled all his attempts at identification. I must also add that we had found several more fragments of the material, and these, being larger than those discovered hitherto, were a great puzzle to my friend. Like the others, they showed signs of having been cut and polished, but Ramon's careful and painstaking measurements convinced him that the cut surfaces had not and could not have formed a curved, lens-like surface.

Of course, I teased him when he admitted this, arguing that my theory, that the fragments were the remains of some ceremonial object, was correct, and asking him how he could longer argue that the green substance had been used as a lens, if his own calculations and tests proved it had not been made into a lens form. Ramon, however, could be as non-committal as a full-blooded aborigine. He merely grunted and refused to reply or to suggest any information, but I knew, from his preoccupied manner and his expression, that he had formulated some theory, and that his active and most brilliant brain was busy searching this theory for possible flaws.

It must not be thought by my readers that I belittled Professor Amador's theories or his knowledge of his special branches of science. On the contrary, I admired him intensely. I had the deepest respect for his knowledge, his attainments and his mastery of what are perhaps the most abstruse and difficult of the recognized sciences. But as I have said, we were most intimate friends; we could argue and discuss matters and could jolly and tease each other unmercifully, without losing our tempers, and very often, either one of us would deliberately assume an attitude and maintain a stand that we did not feel, merely in order to bring about a discussion and to draw the other out. Although in the beginning I actually had no faith in his theory of the Manabís having used the green material for lenses, even though I could not account for the minute work, they accomplished on any hypothesis other than the use of lenses of some sort, yet as time went on and Ramon's indisputably correct calculations and formulas were developed, I became more or less convinced that, in the main points of his theories at least, he was correct.

I had, in fact, quietly, and I confess secretly; done a little in the line of experimenting myself. With infinite labor I had fitted bits of the green material together, and I had convinced myself that they had never formed any portion of any utensil, vessel or image. In fact, from what I could determine, they were portions of most irregular and remarkably shaped objects, and had it not been for the obvious evidences of having been artificially formed, I should have deemed them bits of some natural mineral mass or cluster of crystals.

Indeed, I was rapidly becoming almost as deeply interested in the solution of the mystery of the green substance as was Professor Amador, and I constantly found myself speculating on its purposes and its origin and neglecting my archeological interests.

But of one thing I felt positive. Whatever the origin of the material, my friend had less than one chance in a million of finding it by wandering blindly over the adjacent territory. I well knew how extremely difficult—almost impossible—it is to find anything in a tropical jungle. I had myself searched for weeks for Maya ruins in Central America, for the remains of vast, massive temples and immense stone monuments, and had often passed and repassed within a few yards of them without suspecting their presence. And I had heard the same story from numerous mining engineers and prospectors, who had fruitlessly searched for months for the outcrops of mineral veins that—

from float samples—they knew existed within a very restricted area.

Of course there was the remote possibility of Ramon stumbling upon the deposit by sheer luck, and had there been any inhabitants in the district—either Indians or mestizos—enquiries among them might have given him a clue. But the district was uninhabited; none of my peons were familiar with the territory, and much as I wished my friend every success, I still felt that his quest was merely a waste of time and energy.

According to my notebooks and field-diary, it was three weeks after Ramon had commenced his search that he returned at the end of the day, so highly elated, so evidently filled with excitement, that I knew his efforts must have been crowned with success.

"Congratulate me, *amigo!*" he cried. "I *have* found it at last! It is marvelous, astounding! No, I shall not tell you; I shall not describe it. You must see it for yourself; you must come with me tomorrow. And it is near—not three miles from where we sit! I stumbled upon it by accident. And I *was* right. The material is artificial. But it is not the handiwork of any human being!"

"How on earth can that be?" I demanded. "How can any substance be artificial yet not the result of man's handiwork? For heaven's sake, man, make yourself clear or I shall begin to doubt everything and shall think you have gone crazy on the subject."

But he merely laughed, maintained his air of secrecy, and refused to explain anything. Naturally my curiosity was aroused, the more so when, to prove he had found the deposit, he produced a good-sized lump of the green material, a peculiar, somewhat irregular mass perhaps four inches in diameter and with one side roughly convex.

"But this *has* been worked!" I exclaimed, as I examined it. "By Jove! I believe you *are* right and that this *is* a lens in the making."

Ramon grinned. "Yes, in the rough," he admitted. "But not worked by human hands."

"Piffle!" I cried. "You mean to stand here and try to convince me this mass of mineral hasn't been cut or chipped into form! Why try to make mysteries out of nothing? It's remarkable enough to discover that the Manabís had lenses, without trying to add to the wonder of it."

"Nevertheless it is the truth," he insisted. "But I won't say another word until you see what I have discovered. Then, my friend, the laugh will be on you."

NEEDLESS to say I was as anxious to visit my friend's find as was he, and on the following morning, as soon as we had finished our coffee, we started off. For a space we pushed through the jungle, a most unpleasant place in the early morning before the sun had dried the moisture from the leaves. Then we went along the bank of a small stream, across a ridge, until we came to one of those tongues of barren rocky desert; which, along this coast, extend down from the mountains almost to the sea. Here was a bowl-like depression in the ridge, a crater-like pit perhaps fifty feet in diameter and twenty feet in depth, and surrounded by a rim of fine sand, which caused it to stand out prominently from the dark pyroxene rocks and reddish-brown tufa.

"Behold!" cried Ramon, dramatically indicating the depression with a gesture.

I stared into the pit. In the center of the bottom was a roughly-rounded blackish mass, and gleaming in the sunlight amid the sand of the pit's circumference, were numberless masses of the peculiar green material I have described.

I scrambled into the hollow and examined them. There was no doubt about it. They were the same, and varied in size from a few inches across to masses a yard or more in diameter.

My companion was grinning delightedly. "Now do you understand?" he cried. "Was I not right when I said it was artificial, but not the work of man?"

"Not as far as I can see," I replied. "Quite obviously the mineral is not the result of human handiwork, but equally obviously it is *not* artificial."

"For a scientist, you are not a keen observer," commented Ramon, who had joined me in the pit. "I do not claim to be a geologist and yet the whole affair was plain to me almost as soon as I discovered this spot. Have you examined that black mass beside you? You will find it a meteorite. This pit is the crater it formed in striking the earth, and this green substance is a compound formed by the terrific heat and pressure of the meteor's impact, which fused certain elements and produced the material that has been a mystery."

I realized that Ramon was right. There was no doubt about the immense mass of material being a meteorite, and a closer examination of the green stuff revealed indications of its having been fused. But there was one thing that puzzled me. When I picked up one of the lumps of substance I found one surface roughly convex, exactly as was the piece Ramon had brought in to camp the night previous.

"Ah!" I ejaculated. "I see the Manabís *have* been at work here. It is strange they should have attempted to manufacture their lenses in such a place."

Professor Amador smiled. "Mistaken again," he chuckled. "No human hands have touched that before yours. The Manabís had nature on their side. If you examine the meteorite carefully you will find that its surface is made up of slightly concave facets or depressions. And if you place the piece of material in your hand upon the surface of the aerolite you will discover that it fits perfectly into some one of those depressions. Undoubtedly, when the meteorite fell and fused the minerals where it struck, the molten matter formed a coating or shell about it. In time, owing perhaps to weathering, perhaps to the shrinkage as the material cooled, the fused matter broke off and fell from the meteor, each piece being molded convex on one side where it had been cast into form, as I might say. No doubt the Manabís, finding these rather attractive bits of semi-transparent material, polished the surfaces and by accident discovered that they possessed lenses."

While he was speaking I had been most painstakingly examining both the meteor and the mineral I had picked up.

"I admit your explanation sounds plausible," I replied. "But, as you just admitted, you are not a geologist. Neither am I for that matter, although I did take a special course in that science when at Yale. And I am afraid I must quote your own words of a short time ago and inform you, my very dear friend, that you are not a keen observer. You have, to make use of a time-honored saying, put the cart before the horse in a way. You are no doubt correct in regard to the meteorite generating heat and pressure when it struck; possibly it may have fused certain portions of the rock and sand here.

"But your green mineral substance is not the result of that. On the contrary, it is the crystalline form of the meteorite itself. The mass, of course, was incandescent as it passed through our atmosphere. Probably, in fact unquestionably, when it fell this area was under water, and the sudden cooling, perhaps combined with chemical reactions if it was salt water, as it prob-ably was, caused the outer surface of the meteor to crystallize.

"If you question the accuracy of my deductions, you have only to examine both the meteor and the green substance. You will find that under a lens, minute crystals of the same character are everywhere distributed in the mass of the meteorite."

"Hmmm, I admit you may be right," muttered Ramon, after he had followed my suggestion. "But," he added triumphantly, "that does not in any way affect my statement. Whether the material was formed from molten sand or rock, or whether it was produced from the aerolite itself, is merely a technical question. The main point is that it was produced by a meteorite falling upon our planet, and was not fabricated by man, and that the crude lenses were formed by nature in the way I have explained. But," he continued thoughtfully, "your discovery explains why I could not analyze the material. Meteorites, I understand, contain some remarkable and perhaps unknown elements. No wonder I could not identify them! And, *amigo mio,*" he cried excitedly, "we may be on the verge of an astounding discovery! For all we know the material brought to us from the heavens, from another planet, may possess characters—optical or otherwise—that are wholly undreamed of—totally unknown! *Carramba!* I am impatient to experiment, to solve the secrets, the mysteries of this celestial substance. And I stand here idly talking, wasting precious moments!"

I laughed. "Considering that this meteor and the green material has been here for several thousand, probably several hundred-thousand years, a few minutes delay is of no great consequence," I reminded him. "But, all joking aside, I do not blame you for your impatience. I am almost as deeply interested in it as you are. I shall await the outcome of your experiments with the greatest interest, Ramon. And I most heartily congratulate you upon your great good fortune in discovering this most astonishing source of the material, brought, as you say, from another world, another planet."

CHAPTER FOUR

IT was indeed fortunate that Professor Amador had had the foresight to bring a completely equipped laboratory and workshop with him. Had he been forced to return to the United States in order to conduct his experiments I truly believe he would have gone mad with impatience, and he might never have made the most astonishing discovery of all. Moreover, had he carried out his experimental work in the States, very serious and regrettable results might have followed. And yet, on the other hand, had he not brought such a complete outfit along, he might still be with us, and the final results that I am about to narrate might not—in fact could not—have transpired.

Having taken a number of the best pieces of the new material (which Ramon named Manabinite) to his laboratory, he busied himself day and night experimenting with small specimens of the mineral, covering sheets of paper with abstract and involved mathematical calculations, conducting exhaustive physical and chemical tests and cutting, grinding and polishing the strange material.

"It's almost as hard as sapphire," he informed me. "But, it has a most remarkable property of cleaving on the plane of its rounded surface when it is struck in certain spots, or of cleaving at right angles to its axis if struck on another spot. I have not fully worked out its optical properties yet, but I should say off-hand that its refractive index is fully equal if not in excess of that of the diamond. A lens composed of it should, theoretically, magnify an object fully fifty times more than a glass lens of the same formula.

"Think of it, my friend! Think what that means to science, to optics, to humanity! Think what wonders of biology and nature may be revealed when we have microscope objectives capable of enlarging an object fifty times more than any lens yet produced! Think what it will mean in astronomy! Why, *amigo mio,* with a telescope lens of this material, no larger than any of the great objectives already in use, we should be able to view the trees, the houses upon Mars!"

"Provided," I reminded him, "that your theories are borne out, that the Manabinite is sufficiently transparent to be used as powerful lenses, and provided that you can obtain masses large enough for manufacturing such lenses. You forget, Ramon, that as far as we have reason to believe, the entire world's supply of Manabinite is in that miniature meteor crater. I cannot say how much is there, but I should hazard a guess that the quantity is exceedingly limited, and that the largest piece is far too small to be transformed into a telescope objective for studying the planets."

Ramon's face fell. "Yes, that is so," he grudgingly admitted. "I have searched the pit thoroughly—have dug deep into the surrounding sand and rocks, have even gone several feet below the meteor itself, and have gathered every fragment and flake I can find. The total amount is woefully small. In fact I might say it is inadequate for carrying on as many experiments as I would wish. Yes, unless we can discover another deposit—which is practically impossible under the conditions—or unless I can discover how to imitate Manabinite artificially, then I fear very much that my discovery—our discovery—will be of little real value to the world. But," he cried, once more enthusiastic, "it is going to solve the problem of Manabí art and, who knows, perhaps the mystery of Tiahuanaco and other cyclopean works as well."

"Just what *have* you accomplished so far?" I asked him. "Have you started making a lens yet? It seems to me that the first and most important step would be to make a small lens and test it out. You may find the darned thing won't work at all."

"It will work, all right," he assured me. "Yes, I have been busy a goodly portion of the time, grinding a lens from a small mass of Manabinite. I have worked along rather revolutionary lines and am grinding the lens to conform to the formula worked out by a determination of its refractive qualities. By tomorrow I hope to have it completed. Then, *amigo mio,* for the great test."

Of course we were both keyed up when, on the following day, Ramon announced that the lens was completed, and that he would like to have me present when he made his first test. It was very thoughtful of him to do this, and I fully appreciated how great a sacrifice it had been for him to refrain from satisfying his desire and curiosity until I could be with him.

I must admit that he had done a most beautiful piece of work. The lens was as beautiful as a polished emerald, and seemed actually to glow with internal fires.

"There is one thing certain," I laughed, as I admired it. "Even if this Manabinite is worthless for lenses you can make a fortune selling it for gems. It is harder than emeralds, you say, and to my mind much more beautiful. And, best of all, there is such a limited quantity that the market will never be flooded."

Ramon smiled. "No doubt," he agreed. "But let us defer any such matters until after we have had a look through this lens. Here, my friend, if it had not been for you, I never should have come here nor made this discovery. It is your right and privilege to be the first to look through a lens of Manabinite."

IN VAIN I protested. Ramon insisted and; grasping the glorious green lens, I held it between my eyes and the little pile of golden grains that Ramon had placed upon the table. For a moment I could see only a marvelous, vastly deep, apparently fathomless, green light. It seemed like looking into the very depth of a tropical sea. And then suddenly, unexpectedly, an object seemed to rush towards me, to burst through the wondrous green, to hurl it aside, and I involuntarily uttered a sharp, surprised exclamation.

But the next instant my cry changed to one of utter amazement and incredulity. The object had come to rest, a great dull-yellow mass like a submerged mountain, a mass, the surface of which was scored, cut, incised with deep rough furrows, ravines, valleys, and canyons. But I recognized them instantly. They were orderly arranged, they followed definite lines, and I knew that I was gazing upon the immensely enlarged surface of one of the minute gold beads upon the table-top.

"It is marvelous, amazing, absolutely incredible!" I cried, handing the lens reluctantly to Ramon. "No wonder the Manabís could manufacture such beads, could engrave a lapis-lazuli idol with microscopic designs. Why, man, that bead looks as big as a mountain! It must be magnified hundreds-thousands of diameters!"

But I doubt very much if Ramon even heard my voice. He, too, had seen, and entirely forgetting his surroundings, he was exclaiming, enthusing, almost shouting in his native Spanish.

At last he tore his eyes from the seemingly magic lens, and, with a deep sigh, dropped limply into a chair.

"It is true. It is as I thought, as I hoped!" he cried. "Success has come at last! Ah, *amigo mio,* if you only knew the fears, the doubts that I have had. If you only realized the blow it would have been had all my calculations, my theories and my labors come to nothing. I would have been crushed, discouraged and—do you know, my dear good friend—your ridicule would have been the hardest of all to bear? But now!" he jumped up, filled with energy and life. "Now, I have proved everything. *What* a lens! Do you not agree, *amigo?*"

"Ramon," I said, seizing his hand and looking into his eyes. "I never dreamed that you took my bantering seriously. Come, old man, forgive me, won't you? But I realized what work and life you have put into this thing. You have overdone. You must take a rest. You have triumphed, mightily, beyond my words to express. You have revolutionized optics, my friend. What more do you want?"

Ramon's lips parted in that happy, boyish smile I loved. "Now *you* are taking *me* too seriously!" he cried. "You forget I am a temperamental Latin with the Indian tendency to enjoy a bit of martyrdom and serf-pity. No, I never actually took your raillery seriously. I believed all along that, in the bottom of your heart, you thought much as I did. But I cannot rest yet. I have only commenced. This is merely a beginning. Why, *amigo,* that tiny lens is simply a crude experiment. It is not perfectly ground, its curvature is largely guesswork, and it is made from an imperfect piece of Manabinite. Wait until I make a really good lens and see what you will see."

But when, after a number of days' incessant labor; my friend had made a second lens—or rather had remade the first—to exactly conform with his ideas, his formula and his theories, I could not see that it was very much superior to the first. I admitted that it was slightly clearer, that it magnified the objects beneath to a greater extent, but it was no more remarkable than first lens which, to me, was still a veritable marvel.

And Ramon was bitterly disappointed. He had accomplished wonders, his deductions and theories had been borne out, but somewhere he had made some error and he completely lost sight of the fact that he had apparently solved the mystery of the Manabís' secret in his failure to accomplish what he had hoped for. The discovery of some new optical or physical law.

"There is nothing new or revolutionary about it," he declared, when we were discussing the matter one day. "To be sure, Manabinite possesses most remarkable qualities of magnification, but that is due to its refractive index, not to any new law. Very probably an immense diamond might prove to possess most unusual powers as a lens, although there is something else, some elusive hidden peculiarity of the composition, the crystallization or the color of Manabinite that adds to its power. But that does not mean anything really new.

"And there is another thing that perhaps you have not noticed. This lens, or rather these lenses I have made, possess very little depth of focus—almost none at all, in fact. Outside of a very small portion of the object brought under them, in a necessarily restricted area all within the same plane, nothing is magnified, nothing is clear. In fact the rest of the object is practically invisible. That is why you were so surprised when the gold bead seemed to leap at you when you first looked through the lens. Until the bead was within the very shallow focal plane of the lens, you saw nothing, then, as you brought a portion of its surface into focus, it sprang into view. With an ordinary lens, even where there is little depth of focus, there is a blurred, but visible image of the entire object under the glass, even of surrounding objects, for the glass is transparent.

"But with the Manabinite lens, everything, but the small portion actually sharply focused, is shut off as if by a screen. That puzzles me, and I cannot solve the mystery. Just as soon as an object is within focus, the lens seems to become perfectly transparent—even the green tint vanishes—but as far as everything else is concerned, the lens might as well be opaque. And for that reason, *amigo,* I am sure I have not yet solved the problem of how the Manabís made their minute beads and carved their invisible designs."

"What?" I cried. "You mean you do not believe they used Manabinite lenses? You mean you have cast aside all your assumptions and theories? Good heavens, Ramon, you *are* queer! Just when you have convinced me you were right, you turn about and claim you were wrong. Why, man, you must be taking leave of your senses. Here you have absolutely proved your theories, have proved that the Manabís had lenses capable of magnifying objects hundreds of times, and then you tell me you haven't solved the problem!"

RAMON shook his head. "For a man who always boasts that nothing is proved until it is demonstrated, you take a most remarkable attitude," he replied. "You say I *have* proved the Manabís used lenses of Manabinite when performing their feats of sculpture and handicraft. But I have done nothing of the sort. I have proved that Manabinite possesses unique powers of magnification. I proved nothing more. And I have proved to my own satisfaction that, when it was used in the form of an ordinary lens, Manabinite would have been almost, if not quite useless to the aborigines who occupied this site.

"Suppose, just to demonstrate your assumption, that you try to do a little work upon some object while it is viewed by your eyes through the lens. *I* have tried it and I have found it utterly impossible. It is hopeless, an impossibility, to keep the tool used and the surface upon which it is used in focus at the same time. And it is equally hopeless to try to follow out a design or a pattern upon any object when only a very limited portion of that object is visible. If you doubt me, try to make a drawing of some very simple form—one of your prehistoric pots or a human being or a pig—anything, in fact, by cutting a round hole in a sheet of paper, placing this over another sheet and drawing the object bit by bit upon the surface of the paper visible through the hole. I'll wager that when you have finished, the result of your labors will be utterly unrecognizable.

"No, my friend, if the Manabís fashioned their miniature objects by means of a lens, it was a lens through which they could see the entire surface of the object upon which they worked. But," he added vehemently, "there *must* be an answer, there *is* a solution. I am positive they used Manabinite. I am equally positive they did *not* use it in the form of an ordinary lens, and, *gracias da Dios,* I am going to discover what they *did* use. And when I do, *amigo mio,* I will discover the *great* secret, the unknown law of optics or physics or both. I shall do it even if I spend the rest of my life at it!"

I was almost dumbfounded. What Ramon had told me—and now I realized it was all true—came as something of a shock. I was convinced that the Manabís could never have worked under a lens with the properties of the lenses that Ramon had made, and all the smug satisfaction I had felt because my friend had solved the riddle had been ruthlessly destroyed by his words. The lenses had been so astonishing in their magnifying powers, that I had overlooked their shortcomings. Now I was fully aware of them.

"Possibly," I ventured after a time, "the Manabís may have treated the lenses in some way. Isn't it possible that Manabinite might be changed by heating or tempering or something? I have always understood that glass may be greatly altered by annealing."

Ramon shook his head. "I have tried," he declared, "but without any result. Moreover, I have compared the fragments of lenses found here with the crude materials. As far as I can determine, the two are identical in every way. No, I must look farther for the answer. And, do you know, I have a feeling, a hunch, as you would call it, that the answer is not so far off. Do you remember those fragments we found that so greatly puzzled me? Those pieces with angular surfaces where there should have been curves? I have been racking my brains, trying to figure out what they were, what they meant, and I believe that therein lies the key to the whole matter."

"I remember them well," I told him. "But to me they appeared more like natural crystalline forms than hand-made. But whatever you do must be done very soon, my friend. The rainy season is not far off, and when the rains set in, this locality is no place for civilized human beings."

"If I have not completed my work by then, I shall continue my experiments in the United States," he declared, as he disappeared in his laboratory.

Three days later, Ramon dashed from his workshop, wild-eyed, disheveled, gasping for breath. Never before had I seen him in such a state. He seemed frightened, terrified, and for a brief moment I thought he had gone raving mad. But his first words were reassuring. "I have found it!" he fairly yelled. "It's marvelous, astounding, miraculous! And by accident, by chance, I came upon it! It was last night," he continued, striving to control himself and speak intelligibly. "Last night I dropped the lens just before retiring. It broke—splintered; you remember I told you the Manabinite had a peculiar cleavage. Disgusted, discouraged, I gathered up the splinters—they would be bad things to tread upon with bare feet, and throwing the smaller fragments aside, I laid the largest piece upon my table and went to bed.

"I arose this morning, remembered the accident of last night, and glanced ruefully towards the spot where I had placed the remains of all my labors. *Santa Maria!* How I stared, speechless, startled, even terrified. The Manabinite had vanished, and in its place I saw a monster, a huge, a gigantic insect; an enormous bug! His great cold eyes seemed fixed upon me balefully, his hairy legs seemed poised, tensed, ready to spring. I could scarcely believe my eyes. Never had mortal eyes gazed upon such a creature. Cautiously, grasping a stout stick, my curiosity overcoming my first fright, I stepped toward the table the better to examine the giant insect. Then the incredible happened!

"The huge insect vanished before my eyes, disappeared completely, instantly, and in his place, just where I had left it, was the piece of Manabinite! I rubbed my eyes, speechless, unbelieving, fearing I had gone mad! Then as I gazed, I noticed a minute dark speck beside the shattered lens. I bent close to examine it. Then I understood. Then like a flash all was clear. The wonder of wonders. The tiny speck was an insect, a minute thrips, the Lilliputian counterpart of the giant bug I had seen. I stepped back, gazing fixedly at the lump of green mineral. One, two, three steps. As though dissolved in air, the Manabinite vanished and there, once more, was the ugly, horrible, giant insect! It was impossible, incredible, but true. Chance, accident, fate, perhaps the good God himself, had produced the results I had labored in vain to achieve. The shattered bit of Manabinite had taken on the form that enabled it to project a stupendously magnified image of an object near it. And, most marvelous, most wonderful of all, in doing so, it became itself invisible! Come with me, *amigo,* come to my laboratory and see for yourself. Observe the miracle, the wonder of it! I have not dared to touch it."

AMAZED, hardly able to grasp the meaning of his words, I hurried with Ramon to his laboratory. All he had related had not prepared me for the amazing, unbelievable thing I saw. As I entered, my eyes turned to his writing table. Resting upon it was a roughly angular piece of Manabinite. Then, as my friend led me to one side, my eyes still fixed upon the green material, I gasped, stared, for as far as I could see the table top was bare; the Manabinite had vanished as if by magic. Ramon's voice brought me to my senses.

"Que lastima?" ("What a misfortune") he cried. "The thrips has gone; you cannot see the ogre that greeted me. But wait. Keep your eyes focused as they are."

Hurrying forward, he reached toward the table, and as though conjured from the air, a huge, gleaming golden ball lay upon the table before my amazed eyes!

Instantly I recognized it. It was one of the almost microscopic gold beads, but appearing the size of a football, its chased design, every detail of its surface, clearly defined. But of the fragment of Manabinite that produced this miracle, there was no visible trace. Still keeping my eyes upon the glorious golden ball, I stepped forward, extended my hand, and touched the hard, glass-like surface of the Manabinite. Still without removing my gaze, I moved slowly to one side. Like a flash the gold ball had vanished, and beneath my fingers was the green, semi-transparent piece of mineral! I gasped, and sank into Ramon's chair. It was too much, too startling, too utterly incredible for my brain to assimilate.

Ramon was wild with excitement, mad with delight. He fairly danced; he chattered in Spanish, he babbled in English.

"Do you not understand, *amigo mio!*" he cried. "'Do you not grasp the reason for this miracle? Do you not realize what a discovery this is?"

I shook my head. "I realize it *is* so," I replied. "But why, how, by what uncanny means this miracle, as you call it, is brought about, is beyond me."

"There are many things, many phenomena, which I myself do not as yet understand," he confessed. "But already—*pronto,* in a flash—I have grasped much, have understood much. It is the action of a prism, not of a lens. By the merest chance, by its natural cleavage, this bit of Manabinite assumed a prismatic form. By another chance—or guided by Fate or God—I placed this prism upon my table in such a position that a tiny thrips—a humble, despised plant-louse, came into its refractive field. Otherwise, my dear friend, I never would have known; I should have thrown the broken lens aside, and never would we have solved the mystery or witnessed this miracle. But how the miracle is accomplished, why the crystal itself vanishes when it magnifies an object, what becomes of its color, what the optical principles and laws that govern it may be—these are all unsolved mysteries, matters to be worked out. And they are all new, wonderful, revolutionary. But, now the matter is simple. I shall make more prisms, shall improve them, shall polish the surfaces, and shall devote myself to determining all the secrets of the astounding material and its properties. But we now know how the Manabís performed their wonderful feats of carving and of handiwork. And the puzzle of those bits of Manabinite with angular surfaces, is solved. They, too, were fragments of prisms. But—" his face fell and an expression so lugubrious swept across his features that I laughed. "But," he lamented, "my discovery—our discovery, will be of no value to the world, although it should be of the greatest. There is no more Manabinite besides the negligible quantity in our possession."

CHAPTER FIVE

BUT if Professor Amador was pessimistic in regard to the benefit his discovery might prove to the world; his interest in the remarkable material and its even more remarkable properties was not abated. In fact it was vastly increased, and for days, and nights. He worked feverishly in his laboratory, appearing only for his meals, which he gulped down hurriedly.

"Now that I have the key to the optical peculiarities of Manabinite," he declared, a few days after his amazing demonstration, "I have definite lines upon which to work. You thought that fragment of the mineral gave astounding results, but that was merely a crude, an accidentally formed prism. I shall make a real one, a cut, ground and polished prism, mathematically constructed from the data obtainable from that fragment. Then, *amigo mio,* we shall see what we shall see."

And when, after the most intensive work, Ramon produced his beautifully finished Manabinite prism, it proved as much superior to the prismatic fragment as a high-powered microscope objective is superior to a twenty-five cent reading-glass.

Viewed through it, the tiny golden beads appeared as two-foot spheres of gleaming intricately-engraved metal. Innumerable beautifully-chased designs, which had been hitherto invisible, could be traced between the grooves of the coarser carving, and as I studied these I became convinced that they formed inscriptions in some unknown form of glyphs. The sculptured designs upon the lapis-lazuli idol proved to be of the same character, but words cannot express the marvelous beauty and incredibly fine work upon this. What the amount of the magnifying power of the prism was, I cannot say precisely, but I should judge it to have been roughly about five hundred diameters. But unlike a powerful lens of the conventional type, the prism possessed a tremendous depth of focus and a very wide field. Objects were sharp and clear when placed anywhere from a few inches to several yards from the prism, and their magnified images were as perfect when the observer was yards from the prism as when he was within a few inches of it.

Indeed, there was no effect of gazing into a lens. The magnified image appeared like the real thing, actually and physically enlarged, an illusion that was due largely, no doubt, to the amazing property of the Manabinite losing its visible color and seeming to vanish completely when viewed from a certain angle. I mentioned these matters to Ramon, who smiled knowingly.

"Not being familiar with the laws of physics and optics," he replied, "you cannot differentiate between the two. From a technical and scientific viewpoint Manabinite possesses no peculiarities worth mentioning; its optical qualities, in fact, are no better than ordinary crystal—"

"Nonsense," I interrupted. "Could you make any crystal prism or lens to approach, not to mention equal, this of Manabinite?"

Ramon shook his head. "I could not; neither could anyone else. But that is not because of the optical peculiarities of the mineral. If you will allow me to explain, possibly I may make my meaning clear, my friend. As I said, Manabinite has no unusual optical qualities. But it *does* possess the most remarkable, amazing and hitherto unknown physical peculiarities.

"I have convinced myself that the apparent magnification that you witness is not what you and I at first thought it. Magnification, in the ordinary sense of the term and as brought about by lenses, is due to the refraction of light rays, so bent, or rather so altered, in their angles of incidence, by passing through the lens, that they project an image of larger size. Moreover, a lens, if the curvatures are reversed, will reduce the image of an object. But my most exhaustive tests with Manabinite prove that reversing the prism, or even the lens from the material, will not project a reduced image.

"In fact, you may test this for yourself. Viewed from the opposite direction, the prism appears as an almost opaque mass of green mineral and nothing is visible through it. No, *amigo mio,* the magnified image projected by Manabinite is not produced by the alteration of light rays, or more properly speaking, light waves, but by means of some other form of vibratory waves. For some unknown and undeterminable reason, Manabinite, when formed into a certain combination of angles or facets, absorbs the vibratory waves or the movements of electrons present in the matter within the sphere of its influence, and throws them off at an entirely different vibratory speed, or a distinct electronic motion. It—"

"That all sounds very learned, but also very complicated and even somewhat contradictory and abstruse," I remarked. "Do you—"

"Pardon me for interrupting your question," he continued. "I shall try to make my meaning clear by some comparisons. You are, perhaps, slightly familiar with the practice or the theory of 'stepping-up' electrical voltage."

I assented.

"And you, as a radio enthusiast, must understand the principles of so-called amplification."

"Yes," I agreed.

"Very well," he proceeded. "I might compare the Manabinite prism—if it may be called such, to a transformer or an amplifier. Just as the amplifying units of a radio receiving set pick up the inaudible vibratory waves—which as you know are merely ether movements—and emit them as vastly increased sound waves in air, so the Manabinite prism I have made picks up visible light waves and throws them off tremendously increased."

I shook my head hopelessly. "Perhaps I *am* unusually dense," I confessed, "but I cannot understand how a light wave—which is very distinct from an electromagnetic wave, can be increased by physical means."

PROFESSOR AMADOR snorted and muttered some Spanish expletive. "It is fortunate that I am a very patient man," he declared, his merry smile proving that he was by no means as out of patience with my stupidity as his words implied. "As you know perfectly well, or as any man of your intelligence, education and scientific training *should* know, the so-called electro-magnetic waves, the light, even the heat waves are all closely related, if not identical, the only differences between them lying in the speed of their vibrations or their so-called 'wave-lengths.'

"If you heat a piece of metal, you produce heat waves emanating from it which will burn your fingers, but which you cannot detect by sight. If you heat it more, until it becomes red-hot, you transform the invisible heat rays to light rays that *are* visible. And it is merely a matter of heating it still further until you produce, or rather transform the red rays, to light rays at the opposite end of the spectrum—the violet rays.

"Our poor eyesight does not permit us to 'tune in' on any light rays below red or above violet, yet we know that there is a long range of light-waves at both ends of the spectrum, among them the infra-red, the ultra-violet, the Roentgen, etc. We really know very little about these, and we know still less about various other waves, the vibratory waves that produce scent, for example, the waves that guide various birds, mammals, reptiles and even insects from place to place, the sound waves beyond the range of the human ear, etc. But we *do* know that all of the waves first mentioned are merely the result of the ether moving or shifting about.

"By crowding more than the normal quota of electrons into any object, or by forcing some of the normal quota out, we produce various waves—heat, light, radio, X-rays and what not. And my experiments and my exhaustive calculations have proved, to my own satisfaction at least, that Manabinite, when in the form I have made, has the power of altering the normal movements of electrons in objects placed in a certain relation to it and of reforming these electrons to produce a greatly enlarged replica of the object. Also, I know that in so doing, the Manabinite itself is reduced to electronic movements and actually becomes a portion, an integral part of the increased object."

"But," I objected, "you infer that the object itself is enlarged, and that what we look upon as an image, a product of light and shade, is a *bona fide* object, the same object—increased in size! Why, man alive, in that case, we could touch and handle the magnified edition of the object. Utter nonsense, Ramon, that is absolutely impossible!"

He laughed. "Nothing is impossible," he declared. "A few years ago many matters that are everyday affairs to us would have been deemed impossible.

"We can and do transmit pictures—visible moving reproductions of people and other things—for hundreds and thousands of miles through space by means of television apparatus. You may see a miniature man or woman on the screen of your television receiver. But that does not mean that the actual person has been transported bodily and reduced in size. The original at the transmitting end is still intact, living and unaffected.

"And neither can you touch, handle or feel the image before you. Is the result brought about by Manabinite any more remarkable, any more impossible?"

I had to admit that it was not. And yet, somehow, I could not grasp it. I could not quite conceive of a bit of semi-transparent mineral capable of accomplishing such seeming miracles. I had to have another look, and I took an even greater interest in the prism than before. But I could see Ramon's point when he demonstrated it to me. By very simple diagrams and equations he proved that it would contradict and upset all recognized and established optical laws for a lens to magnify to such an extent and yet have such a depth of focus and such a wide field. I learned that the relationship between magnification, focal-plane, depth of focus, field, and the size and form of a lens, were all fixed, unalterable and could be most accurately worked out.

And when I raised the objection that the established laws had been fixed on the basis of materials with certain refractive powers—thus thinking I was showing a great deal of cleverness and knowledge—my friend quickly proved that the refractive index of Manabinite had been calculated and proven by himself, and that, working from it, it would still be impossible to account for the remarkable features of the case on a basis of optics. Moreover, by sketching a plan of the prism-like mass he had made, and then bringing optical laws to bear upon it, he convinced me that it would be utterly impossible for such a form to serve the purpose of a lens.

"But," I again objected. "I remember, when studying biology, that I had to make many drawings through a microscope, using a camera-lucida for the purpose. The arrangement I used consisted of a small prism, and virtually reflected the image of the object on the slide upon a sheet of paper upon the table, so that I could see my pencil and the image at the same time, and merely had to draw the lines and fill in the details as though tracing a picture already there. Isn't it possible that this Manabinite prism acts as an exaggerated camera-lucida?"

Ramon smiled indulgently, half pityingly. "You forget," he replied, "that the camera-lucida of your microscope did *not* magnify the object you were studying. The objective or lens did that, and the camera merely shifted the image in the eyepiece to a paper below it.

"Now here is another most remarkable quality or property of this Manabinite prism. The ordinary lens, even the camera-lucida you mentioned, is a projector. If you place a sheet of paper back of a lens—at the same distance from it where your eye would secure a focal image, a refracted or projected image will appear upon the paper. But, in this case, no such projected image appears. See here!"

As he spoke, he held a sheet of writing paper back of the Manabinite, moving it backwards and forwards, but it remained white, with no trace of the image I could so plainly see with my eyes.

I ACTUALLY gasped. But more astonishing revelations were to come. "Now please stand back of the paper," said Ramon. "You are convinced that no image is projected upon the sheet; but what do you see now?"

"Good Heavens!" I ejaculated. "The paper has vanished! I can see the image; I can see your hand. But what's become of the paper?"

"That," chuckled Professor Amador, "is more than I can tell you. All I know is that certain tissues—mostly inorganic, but a few of organic origin, seem to vanish when placed within the range of the projected waves or lines of electronic movement produced by the prism. My hand or yours, our bodies, leather, almost any animal matter in fact, remains unchanged no matter where it is placed. But paper, wood, any metal or mineral I have tried, cloth, and numerous other substances, become as transparent—or as invisible—as glass or even air.

"The phenomenon, of course, has a direct connection with the interruption and alteration of waves of electronic force, but just why some materials should be affected and others not, is something of a problem. However, it is not without precedent. Radium for example, or rather its radioactive emanations, pass through nearly all substances, but do not pass through lead. Metals, water, etc., are so-called conductors of electricity, but rubber, wood and other substances insulate it. Water will pass through cloth, paper, even through wood, but not through metals, rubber and other materials. Even—"

"Here, here!" I exclaimed. "That's an entirely different matter. The cloth, paper, etc., are porous—loosely put together, as I might say, and the water passes through the minute openings between the fibers."

"Exactly," chuckled Ramon. "Exactly for the same reason that electricity passes through some substances and not through others; exactly as light passes through some materials and is excluded by others; exactly as heat passes through some objects and not through others. And why? Merely because the materials which allow electrical, light, heat, or other waves to pass through them are, as you put it 'porous' or loosely put together, in so far as their electronical arrangement is concerned, whereas others that bar the same waves are too dense in their electronical compositions to permit the waves passing between the electrons or atoms.

"Perhaps I may make myself more easily understood if I take the liberty of comparing, say a sheet of hard rubber, to a wall built up of loose but closely fitted stones; while a similar wall, composed of large irregular stones with large spaces between them, may represent the sheet of copper. Now, if we compare an electrical current, or more properly an electrical discharge, to a charge of shot, and fire this at the wall of closely-fitted stones, none of the shot will pass through the barrier. But, if it is fired at the other wall, the shot will pass through between the stones. In each case, I might add, the stones and the shot are analogous with electrons.

"Now, *amigo mio,* my theory—mind you, it is a theory and nothing else—is that the emanations of electrons absorbed and thrown out in magnified form by this Manabinite prism, are so altered that the properties of ordinary electrons, as we understand them, are completely upset. In other words, the ratio of the electrons to other substances when issuing from the prism is not the same as the ratio of the electrons to similar substances under normal conditions. And—you will no doubt scoff at this—I firmly believe that, with a little more experimenting, I can devise a Manabinite prism which will so magnify the electronical waves, that an atom will be made visible!"

"Now, I am sure your overwork has affected your brain," I declared. "For Heaven's sake, Ramon, drop all this. Be satisfied with what you have accomplished and don't let the thing get you. How can any invisible thing be made visible? You're talking nonsense, man."

"A week or two ago," said Ramon slowly and thoughtfully, "I should have considered any man mad who dared state that the results we see before us would be possible. And when you speak of things as 'invisible' you are talking from a circumscribed and narrow viewpoint, and in comparative terms only. Unquestionably many things invisible to human beings are plainly visible to other creatures—the infra-red and ultra-violet rays for example. Our eyes are very crude, very inadequate and generally degenerated organs, and yet we have the effrontery to declare that anything that our poor, purblind eyes cannot discern is invisible!

"Why, *amigo mio,*" he continued, "what is visible to one man may be totally invisible to another. We do not even know if you and I see the same thing when we look at the same object. You state an object is green, I agree with you; but no one can be sure that green as I call it looks the same to me as does the green you see. Nothing in human senses varies much more than eyesight and yet, so egotistical, so self-important, so cocksure of himself is man, that he cannot believe in what he does not see, and declares, like yourself, that anything—an atom for instance, is invisible.

"And I would like you to explain, if you can, why or how an atom—even an electron—can be invisible in the true sense of the word? Every substance, as you must admit in the light of latter-day science, is composed of electrons and protons. If protons and electrons are truly, scientifically, invisible, how can any number of invisible atoms form a visible mass? No, no, my archeological friend, we cannot see atoms or electrons merely for the very excellent reason that, individually, they are too minute for our eyes to detect. But magnify them ten thousand, fifty thousand, one hundred thousand diameters and who can say they will not be visible.

"And I see no reason why, with a little labor and experimenting, perhaps by a series of step-ups, so to say, perhaps by altering the angles, a Manabinite prism may not be made that *will* render atoms visible.

"To accomplish that marvel shall be my object in life henceforth. If the rainy season arrives, I shall continue my experiments in the United States. But we have at least a month more here. Before the expiration of that time, I hope to be able to prove to you that I am as sane as ever, and I hope to let you view the atomic structure of some well-known object."

"Ramon," I said, slapping him on the back. "You *are* a wonder. You are, without doubt, the greatest physicist in the world. You have made a most astounding discovery. But I am afraid that you have undertaken more than you bargained for this time. However, I wish you the best of luck. And," I added with a laugh, "when you succeed, let me have a peep at a real live atom."

CHAPTER SIX

MANY a true word is spoken in jest, as I soon learned and little did I dream how soon I should be permitted to look upon a living atom. But I am getting ahead of my story.

The time was rapidly approaching when we would be forced to leave, I had already ceased my excavatory work and was busy with my peons packing my accumulated, specimens and preparing for our departure, when Ramon, his wide eyes and his excited mien speaking at some great event, rushed to me, seized me by the arm, and fairly dragged me to his laboratory.

"At last!!" he cried. "*Gracias a Dios, amigo mio,* I am successful. At last, at the eleventh hour at the very moment when I had abandoned hope, I accomplished the miracle! It terrifies me; it is too wonderful, too amazing! But you shall see for yourself!"

Unable to believe him, thinking he was grossly exaggerating his progress, I entered his workshop.

Resting upon a specially devised stand upon his table was a large mass of Manabinite, a much larger piece than I had thought existed. I learned later that this was formed by fitting together a number of smaller pieces. Its form was that of the prism (I call it prism for want of a better term, though it was a many-angled, complex form in reality) and even in the brief glance I took, I noticed that it seemed to be surrounded with a peculiar nimbus or haze that, while it could not be called visible, was still discernible, (a rather paradoxical statement) and which was similar in its appearance to the undulating masses of heated air that one sees rising above hot roads or sands. It was, in fact, exactly as if the Manabinite was almost red hot. But I scarcely had time to note this and I had no time to give it any thought or attention, for Ramon had dragged me to a spot back of the apparatus.

"Look!" he cried excitedly. "Look, my friend, and gaze at what no other living man but myself has ever seen!"

At first I could see nothing, nothing but that same waving, undulating vapors and then slowly, as though a thin veil or a film of smoke was being drawn aside, I saw a startling sight. Before my wondering unbelieving eyes was a deep unfathomable blue, composed of thousands, millions, trillions perhaps, of pale-blue globular objects; translucent, with radiating internal lines; objects that reminded me of globular jelly-fishes, and each and every one whirling, rotating upon its axis and about each of its fellows. Never have I seen or dreamed of such motion, such a mad turmoil, such an inextricable, confused rush of bodies. And yet as I gazed transfixed, wondering what marvel I was seeing, I noticed that there was no confusion, no variation in the movements of the things; they never collided, never touched, never varied a millionth of an inch from their courses. Ramon was fairly dancing with delight at my evident amazement.

"*Now* do you say 'impossible'?" he shouted. "Now do you say the atom is invisible?"

"Do you mean those creatures are atoms?" I demanded, without shifting my eyes from the fascinating scene before me. "To me they appear more like the highly magnified inhabitants of a drop of swamp water."

"Scoffer, unbeliever!" he cackled. "You are looking upon atoms—upon the atoms composing a bit of blue cloth. I chose cloth because the atomic arrangement is fairly open. In a denser material—in stone or metal—I feared the atoms might not be visible. But I know now it makes no difference how they are arranged. And watch!" he cried. "Behold the wonder of atomic behavior!"

As he spoke, he picked up a large reading glass and focused the sun upon the table in front of the Manabinite. Instantly the strange moving blue globules redoubled their speed. Like a flock of birds striving to escape from a swooping hawk, they rushed madly hither and thither. Rapidly, before my staring eyes, they began to vanish, until their numbers had been reduced to at least half, and there were wide voids between those that remained.

"That is the result of heat," cried Ramon. "I heated the cloth slightly and its fibers 'expanded' as we so crudely put it. And now for the opposite extreme. Watch the result of cooling."

As if by magic, the globules—or atoms, as I must call them, for I could no longer doubt my friend's assertions—materialized from nowhere, came rushing into view, until in a few seconds they were so closely packed, that I expected momentarily to witness a collision; I held my breath, for somewhere, in some forgotten corner of my brain, I remembered that scientists averred the collision of two atoms might disrupt the world. Now the atoms were moving more slowly, slipping past one another, rotating around one another so closely packed that no visible spaces lay between them.

Was it possible, I thought, that my own flesh, my own body, the table beside me, my clothing—everything—was really made up of these tiny, globular Jellyfish like objects? It seemed incredible, impossible, despite my companion's rapid-fire explanations, exclamations and dissertations. My mind was detached, I scarcely heard, and certainly did not comprehend, what he was saying, and my every sense was centered on the amazing sight before me and I was striving to convince myself, to believe that I actually was looking at atoms.

But there are some things that the ordinary human mind cannot grasp all at once, and my mind—which I flatter myself is slightly above the average—could not assimilate this marvel. Despite Ramon's assurances, despite the evidence of my own senses, I could not help feeling that it was unreal, that I was looking at some fantastic, imaginary picture.

FOR hours we two watched with breathless interest as Professor Amador experimented with various substances before his astonishing apparatus. We observed the atomic structures of stones, wood, metal, paper; but, for some inexplicable reason, which Ramon confessed was utterly beyond his comprehension, the prisms failed to reveal the atoms in any substance of animal origin. Ramon's hand, when placed before the prism, showed merely as an enormously magnified hand. Leather remained leather, though the minute pits left by the hairs appeared like the craters of extinct volcanoes, and where there were woolen threads in a bit of cloth, there were great vacant opaque spaces between the gyrating atoms of the cotton threads. In fact, just as the first prism had failed to project the images of anything of an animal nature, although it would project the image of almost anything else, so this remarkable apparatus failed to develop its astonishing properties when animal matter was placed before it.

"It has something to do with the vibratory waves of animal tissue," declared Ramon, when at last we wearied of our experiments. "But," he added, "I will solve that puzzle also. And I am going much farther, my friend. There are no limits, no bounds to the possibilities of my discovery. I said I would render atoms visible. I have done so. Before I finish, I shall render electrons visible, too."

In vain I argued with him. He had, figuratively speaking, gone mad on the subject and like most scientific men, nothing would satisfy him until he had pursued his experiments to the very limit. By that I do not mean to scoff at or belittle scientists. I am, or consider myself, a scientist also, but archeology is a comparatively exact science, and experiments do not enter into it, whereas in Ramon's case—and in the case of various other branches of science—experimental work is the predominant factor. Had Ramon been content to rest on his laurels, to be satisfied with the discoveries he had made—which Heaven knows were marvelous and astounding enough—the events that followed never would have occurred, and Professor Amador would still have been with us.

I knew that it was high time for us to be leaving, yet I could not desert my companion, and as the rains appeared to be holding off, I decided to be patient, to humor Ramon for a time in the hopes that he would soon weary of his fruitless attempts, or would come to his senses, and I occupied my time very profitably by writing up my notes, drafting a summary of my observations and conclusions, and preparing my monograph on the Manabí cultural development.

Meanwhile Ramon worked under his usual high pressure, but from what I could gather from the rather meager information he volunteered, he made no progress towards his goal.

He did, however, make another discovery that he considered of great importance, namely that by slightly altering the planes or angles of his prism, he could greatly vary the magnifying power of the Manabinite. The same piece of mineral, or rather the combined pieces, could in this way be made to reveal atoms or could be used to magnify an object only a few diameters, at will. Every grade of magnification between the two extremes was possible, and Ramon had contrived a very delicate and ingenious device for altering the magnifying powers of his prism. In other words, the prism was, when equipped with this apparatus, capable of being focused. At least that was what it amounted to, although he gave it some other technical term that has slipped my mind. But, try as he would, he could not devise a method of increasing the magnifying powers beyond a certain point; the point, in fact, at which the atoms became visible.

"But it can be done," he insisted. "If the power of Manabinite can be increased from almost nil to hundreds of thousands of diameters, there is no scientific reason why that power should not be capable of being increased still farther—to an unlimited extent even."

I snorted. "There may be no scientific reason," I remarked. "But neither is there any scientific reason why the Manabinite should not reveal atoms in animal matter as well as in other materials. Yet it does not."

"The trouble with you is," I continued, "that you are trying to apply the ordinary laws of nature and of science to a substance that—from my own observations and from yours—is most obviously extraordinary and is quite outside the pale of ordinary science or physics. Now for Heaven's sake, drop your fruitless experiments, Ramon. Pack up your outfit and your amazing prism, gather up every bit of Manabinite there is, and come out of this. Then, if you wish, go on with your experiments in the States, or in your own Peru if you wish, and spend the rest of your life at it if it will make you any happier."

"I suppose you're right," he admitted regretfully.

"But somehow, *amigo mio,* I have a strange, unaccountable and inexplicable feeling that if I leave here I shall never succeed. I suppose it's pure nonsense, but over and over again I have been on the point of packing up; and each time was seized with a real fear, a dread, almost a terror—a premonition perhaps—that if I left this spot, a terrible disappointment—a catastrophe in fact, would result. You see..." He smiled in that charming way of his. "...the Indian blood in my veins is superstitious, or perhaps psychic, and at times it gains ascendency over my common sense. However, I have made up my mind, I shall begin packing at once."

CHAPTER SEVEN

STRANGELY enough, it was his preparations for departure that led to the most astonishing, the most amazing and the most incredible discovery of all, and resulted in the mysterious, hitherto inexplicable, disappearance of my dear friend and companion.

In order that it might be quite safe while he was packing, Ramon asked me to take charge of the prism. As I was carrying it towards my own quarters, a whim seized me to have a last look at something. Idly wondering how an ordinary landscape would appear when viewed through the apparatus, I carried it to a little knoll a short distance from camp, and pointing it toward a sandy area beyond, stepped behind it. Only a faint, hazy, indefinite outline appeared, and very carefully and slowly, I manipulated the adjustments, which were designed to alter its magnifying powers or "focus" as I called it.

Quickly the sand, pebbles and rocks took shape. They became enlarged, seemingly detached from everything else and appeared as if they were floating in the air in the peculiar manner to which I was now accustomed. The image was not tremendously magnified but was sufficiently enlarged to make each grain of sand appear like a pebble, each pebble like a boulder, each boulder like a mountain.

It was a fascinating sight, and anxious to see the effect of greater magnification, I continued to move the adjustments. Slowly the grains of sand, the pebbles and the rocks grew before my eyes. A tiny blade of grass was transformed into a lofty, rough-stemmed, palm-like tree. An ant, scurrying across the field of vision, appeared like some gigantic, prehistoric monster. Larger became the minute grains of sand; the pebbles had become enormous, rough-sided, rock masses, seamed and scarred and pitted.

The pieces of rock were now too vast to be within the field, and rose like stupendous precipices. And then I stared, gasped, unable to believe my eyes. In a deep ravine, which I knew was merely the space between two tiny grains of sand, I had caught a glimpse of movement, of some living creature. What could it be, what form of animal life could be so small, so microscopic that it appeared a mere speck under such enormous magnification?

The next instant I gave vent to an involuntary yell of incredulous, almost terrified amazement. The creature had reappeared. It was standing, clearly revealed beside a gleaming mass of pink quartz, and it was a human being—a man!

I felt I must be going mad. I felt like one in a dream, in a nightmare. Chills ran up and down my back. Either I was suffering from dementia, from an optical illusion or else—no, that was utterly impossible—or else I was gazing upon a miniature human being, a fellow man, who was less than one thousandth of an inch in height, who was smaller than an amoeba, who was microscopic in size!

I was brought back to earth by Ramon, who, aroused by my shout, had come hurrying towards me.

"What's wrong?" he cried. "Have you smashed it?" I was too dazed, too overcome to reply, even to speak. I could only point at the Manabinite prism. My expression and features must have told Ramon that something amazing had happened. But nothing had prepared him for the wonder of it. As he glanced into the prism, his jaw sagged, his eyes dilated, his face paled. "Santisima Madre!" he gasped, crossing himself. "My God!" he ejaculated in English, "it's a man! But it cannot be, it's impossible, supernatural!"

"But true!" I managed to exclaim in a hoarse voice.

"Thank God, Ramon, you see him too! I was afraid I had gone mad; that my brain was affected."

"There's another!" almost screamed Ramon. "Oh, *Dios,* what does it mean? Are we both mad?"

Now I, too, was gazing at the image revealed by the prism. Beside the first figure there was a second. Both were men, both were perfectly formed, stalwart fellows, dark-skinned, with long floating hair, their bodies clad in elaborately-colored poncho-like cloaks, both with staffs or clubs in their hands.

"They are Indians!" I whispered, unconsciously lowering my voice as if fearing they might hear me. "What does it mean, Ramon? Do such beings exist? Are they really there? Or are we seeing something that is an illusion, a mirage, the reduced images of men somewhere else? What do you make of it?"

For a moment Ramon was silent. Then, very slowly, as if weighing every word he spoke, *"Amigo mio,"* he said. "We are gazing upon the most incredible things that human eyes have ever seen. Those two beings are real, they are alive, they are as human as we are. Mirages, illusions, phantasms, ghosts, fairies cast no shadows. Those men do. Down there among those grains of sand, under our feet, is a race of humans infinitely minute. God alone knows who or what they are. God alone knows how many of our fellow men and women we may have crushed beneath our blundering feet. *Amigo mio,* we have, that is, *you* have made a discovery that will startle the world. All of my discoveries are nothing compared with it. Unsuspected, unknown, undreamed of, absolutely incredible as it is, you have discovered a new, a microscopic race of men!"

"But—but, my heavens, man!" I cried, my voice shaking with the excitement and wonder of it all. "It's impossible! Why, we've been walking here, digging, working over this very spot. If such beings existed—and that's a preposterous idea—we would have destroyed them, buried them, crushed them as you say! No, no, Ramon! There's some explanation, some sane, sensible reason for what we see!"

"Hush!" admonished Ramon. "They're moving. They're going on. We must watch them, must follow them, must find out if there are more of them. Perhaps they have—yes, they must have—houses, villages. They—"

I burst into maniacal, nervous laughter. "Follow them!" I cried derisively. "How can you follow a man scarcely larger than an atom?"

"With this prism," snapped Ramon. "You forget that its depth of focus, as you will persist in calling it, is fully fifty feet. To those infinitesimal men among the grains of sand, fifty feet would be the breadth of a contingent. To them a few inches would be a day's journey—perhaps a month's tramp. You desired to see a 'living atom' as you expressed it. You have seen two. Ah, there they go! They are hurrying, *Santissima Virgen!* I see it! There is a house, a village! Scores, hundreds of people!"

CHAPTER EIGHT

EVEN now, when the excitement, the wonder, the weird, dreamlike, incredulous amazement of it has passed; when I can think of it calmly and dispassionately; when, looking back, I can think of that day and re-visualize every moment, every detail, every word as though I was reading it from a printed page; even now; I say, I cannot well describe our feelings, our sensations as, with staring, wondering, unbelieving eyes, we gazed into that bit of crystal and found ourselves looking into another world. We simply could not credit our senses.

There before us, as plain, as clear, as natural as though we were gazing at any other community of Indians, were the throngs of people. There were their houses, their village. But that they were minute, microscopic, so small that the ordinary grains of sand were like good-sized hills beside them, seemed so utterly preposterous, so unnatural, so scientifically impossible, that we could not force ourselves to believe in their reality. No, to us, to our senses, we were looking upon some Indian settlement at a distance. To us, it seemed that by some freak of optics or physics, the images of normal-sized beings had been reflected, refracted (like the images in a mirage), to where we stood, and had been picked up by the prism.

In fact the illusion was so perfect and complete, that I found myself far more interested in studying the people themselves than I was in the marvel of the prism, and temporarily at least, felt that I was watching perfectly normal-sized Indians. That they were Indians was obvious, but they were totally distinct from any Indians I had ever seen before.

Their color was a light ochre or olive, scarcely darker than tanned white men or than Professor Amador. Their hair, worn long by both men and women, was a tawny-brown, and their features were regular, well-formed, and denoted a high grade of intellect.

The men were dressed in poncho-like garments of some material that glistened like metal, or I might better say, fish-scales. They wore sandals upon their feet, their hair was confined by fillets of bright colors, and they wore various ornaments in the form of necklaces, etc. I am now describing the first two individuals we had seen, but I noticed, among the throng at which we were now gazing, that there were obviously several classes or castes among the people. Among the men these were marked by the apparel, some wearing ponchos of dull-colored material, others merely loin-cloths; the ones with the iridescent, metallic garments were in the minority.

Among the women, the castes were marked not only by costume but by the color of the skin. Some were almost white, others were quite dark. The latter were nude to the waist and wore skirt-like garments of some fiber, while the others wore skirts of the same material as the ponchos of the first men and had cape-like garments fastened across the chest, covering the shoulders and back.

It was no doubt largely due to the fact that they were so typically Indian that we could not realize or believe that they were not normal in size. Had we suddenly discovered some minute beings of weird, monstrous or wholly new forms; if they had two heads or four legs; had they been green, blue or scarlet; had they been transcendingly beautiful and fairy-like or as repulsively ugly as Calibans, then no doubt we might have been able to convince ourselves that we were gazing at microscopic beings. But here we were, watching human beings that were not only normal in every respect except size, but were, in addition, typical Indians.

Even the village and the houses were scarcely different from those of ordinary aborigines. The houses were low, domed or beehive-shaped, apparently constructed of adobe or clay, and among them were several larger buildings, the whole surrounded by a thick, high wall.

I noticed, too, that the men, when carrying anything, bore bows and arrows, long slender spears and short stone-headed clubs. The two new arrivals, whom we had first detected, had apparently been on a hunting trip, for, as they entered the village, I noticed that one of them carried the body of a dead creature. At first I took it for a small deer, but, as the hunter threw it down before one of the houses, I saw to my surprise that it was not a vertebrate but some unknown creature, apparently an insect, for it had six legs.

I also saw that its skin, hair, fur or whatever its covering, was like metal and iridescent, and I assumed that the ponchos of the men were made from the skin or covering of the creature. But whether they were woven from the material, or whether the entire hide was used, I could not determine.

Here let me call attention to another peculiar sensation I had—and which I found later was shared by my companion. As we watched these people, we had an almost irresistible temptation to reach out and touch them. As I saw the strange animal, I forgot for the moment that I was merely watching the thing through the prism, and unconsciously, I extended my hand with the idea of picking up the creature and examining it.

INSTANTLY the scene was blotted out—people and village vanished, and in their place was a wall, brown, seamed, scarred, pitted. An exclamation of mingled amazement and impatience came from Ramon. I stared, speechless with amazement. What had happened? What new miracle was this?

Then, as suddenly as they had vanished, the people were before us again, and the wall had disappeared. I broke into hysterical laughter. I had withdrawn my hand; the wall that had blotted out the view had been a portion of my own hand vastly magnified!

For the first time since we had first seen the men, full realization of their size came to us. For the first time we were fully able to believe that the Indians before us were Lilliputians that would have made the denizens of Gulliver's Lilliput appear like enormous giants; people so small that, by comparison, even the smallest ant would appear as gigantic a monster as a dinosaur would to an ordinary human being.

It seemed beyond the bounds of reason, and had not Ramon seen exactly what I saw, I should have felt sure I was mad or that my senses were playing me false. How *could* such beings exist? How *could* there be living men and women so minute that they were invisible to the unaided eye? How could they survive? How could they escape being trampled and crushed underfoot? How could they avoid being utterly destroyed by the first rain, by the first puff of wind, by the first handful of drifting sand or dislodged gravel?

Such were the thoughts that raced through my mind as I watched the people in the village before me.

Then a remarkable thing happened. The scene before us was darkened. Twilight fell upon the village. Above the heads of the people some dense cloud was drifting. Involuntarily, I glanced at the sky. It was almost cloudless. Without thinking, I turned my eyes towards the spot where the Indian village had been, momentarily forgetting that it would be invisible. There was the bare stretch of sand, and crawling across it, was a tiny green lizard. I gasped as a sudden thought, a sudden idea swept through my mind. I sprang to the prism. There was the village; light was beginning to shine upon it once more. Again I glanced upward to see the lizard moving away. It was a wild, an insane thought, but a fact. The lizard had crawled *directly over* the Indians, but so far above their heads that he appeared merely as a dark cloud! So minute were they that the ordinary grains of sand were like what the loftiest mountains are to us.

What we—looking through the prism—had mistaken for the sand grains, were particles of impalpable dust! Any ordinary thing, any normal creature, would pass over them, far up in their sky, leaving them unharmed, protected by their surrounding sand-grain mountains! They were as safe, as protected between grains of sand as ordinary human beings would be in some narrow canyon between the highest peaks of the Andes. Even Ramon and myself, walking across the sand, would not harm them. Our gigantic feet, treading the sand, would merely appear like dense black clouds.

Something of this I managed to babble to my companion. "Of course," he snapped back a bit impatiently. "You can't crush a molecule or an atom, can you? Those beings are scarcely larger than atoms. Good heavens, man! Don't you realize how small they are? Why, you could put a whole family of them on a microscope slide, place a cover-glass over them, press it down as tightly as you could, and they'd have plenty of room to walk about and be comfortable! Good Lord, *amigo mio*, what a train of thought this leads to! They probably imagine they are full-sized men and women. They feel themselves just as large as we feel ourselves. What if there are still others as much smaller than they, as they are smaller than us!"

But I scarcely heard him. I had caught sight of a large building, a temple or a palace, and was staring transfixed. It was unmistakable, the counterpart of ancient, pre-Incan temples, and they were being used. Before it there were two stone chairs, chairs of exactly the same form, style and workmanship of those I had found here at the Manabí site! I was dazed, my mind was in a turmoil. What could it mean? Then I began to realize, to note a hundred details. There could be no doubt about it. These Indians, these infinitesimal beings, were the same race as the ancient Manabís. Their sculpture, their chairs, their pottery, their ornaments were identical.

But how, what, why—? The Manabís, as I knew from skeletons and skulls, were normal-sized men and women. Yet here were Manabís of microscopic dimensions, carrying on precisely the same industries, following the same customs, living the same life as the ancient Manabís had lived. Was it possible they were spirits? Was it possible that the uncanny powers of the prism had made visible the wraiths of another world? Were we gazing at the ghosts, the souls of long-dead Manabís? I laughed madly, hysterically, at the thought. But what other explanation could there be?

A raindrop spattered upon my head; another and another fell. In a few seconds it was raining hard, yet we continued to stare, for to both our minds had come the same thought, the same desire to see what happened to those minute people, as the rain poured down upon them.

But we were doomed to disappointment, as we might have known we would be, if we had stopped to think or to reason. Seen through that magical prism, each descending drop of rain was as big as a Zeppelin. Each drop, as it dashed down, completely blotted out everything from view. Each, as it struck the earth, burst like a fifteen-inch shell and sent vast cataracts of water in every direction. In that chaos of flying spray, of gigantic globules, of the torrents released as they burst, the Indians and their village, the temple and the surroundings were as effectually hidden as though behind a mountain range.

There was no sense in our getting drenched. There was nothing more to be seen, and we scurried to the shelter of our camp.

"There won't be anything left of them now," I observed, as we threw off our soaked garments. "This rain will be infinitely worse to them than a Johnstown flood."

RAMON snorted. "My good friend," he exclaimed, "for a scientific man you certainly say and do the most childish things at times. Do you, for one moment, suppose these incredible people have been developed, have lived, have grown to adult men and women, have built villages and temples, and have developed arts and industries all in a day or a month or a year? No, of course not. And yet it has rained here every year, rained harder than at present and steadily—for weeks at a time—and they still exist. This rain will not affect them in the least."

"Nonsense!" I cried heatedly. "You are arguing from the point of view of our own world, on our basis of time. Those minute wondrous people must have everything in proportion to themselves—their lives, their time must be as short in proportion to ours as they are small in proportion to us. For all we know, a second of our time may be a year—several years— to them. In a day of our time they probably go through many generations, perhaps centuries of their time. But even if they didn't, how could they survive a heavy rain? Why, man alive, the spot where they were must be under, an inch of water by now!"

Professor Amador roared with laughter. "There you go again!" he cried, when he could control his merriment. "You have been so amazed, so upset and overcome by finding something that upsets all your preconceived ideas that you do not stop to reason. You assume, because one feature of the case is revolutionary and wholly beyond all preconceived scientific theories and hard facts, that everything connected with it must be as bizarre and miraculous. Your own senses would controvert what you have just said if you stopped to reason about it.

"We were watching those midgets for nearly an hour. Did you notice any flying of time among them? Did they grow old and die? Were children born, grown up and developed into men and women during the seconds, minutes that we watched and which you claim would have been equivalent to centuries to them? Not a bit of it. The men brought in their game, it was being skinned and prepared, and the fellows were still talking about their hunt when the rain began. No, no, *amigo mio,* an hour to us is an hour to them. Moreover, they have the same sunshine, the same hours of darkness as we have. They have no separate planetary system. Hence their time is our time, and you may be sure they have been in existence, living as they do now, for centuries, ages.

"As for being destroyed by this rain, by a few inches of water. Pooh! Water wouldn't affect them any more than that lizard that crawled above their village. We've walked right over them time and time again, but it hasn't destroyed them. Possibly, if there are other villages, we may have buried hundreds of them under dirt thrown out from our excavations. Probably they looked upon it as a convulsion of nature. But rain!"

"I admit your argument as to time is sound," I replied. "But I still fail to see why rain or water would not destroy them. To tread over them is one thing—they are protected by the sand and pebbles and our feet do not press or crush what is beneath and between them. But water permeates everywhere. I can even conceive of a Juggernaut, some gigantic machine or even an imaginary Titan, rolling or striding across New York, crushing the buildings, spanning the city, and yet with the people escaping death in the canyon-like streets. But there would be no hope for them if the city were flooded until the highest buildings were submerged."

"Again you forget the most rudimentary truths of science," chuckled Ramon. "Did you ever dig carefully into sand after a heavy rain? If so, you must have observed that while it appears wet—water-soaked in fact—there is much dry sand.

"And you have forgotten how difficult, how nearly impossible it is to secure perfect adhesion to a dry object. We pick up a stone, a pebble, and it appears wet, to be sure. But, if we examine it under a powerful lens, we will find that what appears a uniform coating of water is, in reality, composed of innumerable tiny drops; that there are appreciable dry spaces between them, and with infinitesimal particles of dust, next to the stone almost immeasurable layer of air, which is usually filled with infinitesimal particles of dust, next to the stone itself. Hence, my dear friend, these microscopic aborigines are quite safe.

"The rain that would soak us to the skin is composed of drops far too large to affect those little people. All they see of the descending torrent is the finest, the most microscopic spray that bounces off the sand grains and pebbles and falls like a gentle shower among the inconceivably minute crevices where they live. And the water that to us appears to cover them 'an inch deep' as you put it, appears to them like a vast dark cloud. Precisely, I might say, as that black cloud above us appears to our eyes.

"That cloud overhead is nothing more or less than water that, could it descend all at one time, would prove a flood many feet in depth. But because we are under that poised mass of water, we do not necessarily suffer. Do you see what I mean, my friend? Do you not understand that those remarkable beings are so inconceivably minute that the molecules of water, which to our eyes and senses appears a homogeneous liquid, are visibly separate, each aqueous molecule appearing to them like a great cloud? No, no, *amigo,* we must entirely reconstruct all our previous ideas and conceptions of humanity, of nature, of a thousand other things.

"It has been too great a revelation, too great a discovery, too revolutionary, too amazing for our poor brains to assimilate all at once. I confess that I, myself, cannot really believe that we have seen what we have seen. Yet, I have always held to the theory that we were purblind, unimaginative, egotistical, self-sufficient and unreasoning beings. That we humans were so bound down by our own ideas of our important place in nature, so limited in our viewpoint by our own exalted opinions of ourselves; and so dull in our perceptive senses, that we have built up, constructed the idea that all humans must be made more or less like ourselves, that the world, as we know it, must be the only world, and that there can be no other world.

"Even our ideas of inhabitants of other planets are always based on our own forms or the forms of creatures familiar to us. Always, as I said, I have held that this was the utmost nonsense, the most short-sighted policy; that for all we know there may be countless other strata—as I might call it—of life all about us. That we may be moving in a world of one particular range of vibratory waves; that above or below our perceptions there may be others, that even within the substance of which we and other bodies are composed, there may be universes teeming with intelligent forms of life that, as far as we are aware, every atom may be a minute planetary body with its own satellites, its own inhabitants, its own individual forms of living organisms, each and all thinking and believing like ourselves that they alone are the only reasoning, intelligent beings in the entire universe.

"And now I find that, in a certain way and to a certain extent, my theory is borne out. We know that under our feet there is a race of men as small as microbes. That they possess much the same forms, features, habits, passions and arts as ordinary mortals. That to them there is no other world, that we are as invisible, as inconceivable to their eyes and their senses, as they arc to ours. And this, my friend, is a most remarkable feature of the case and pleases me immensely. They are Indians—aboriginal Americans—people of my own race and blood."

"What is more," I observed, when he ceased speaking, "they are Manabís—the same race that inhabited this place in prehistoric times, the same tribe that made the stone seats, the slabs and those minute gold beads. I cannot understand it. The Manabís were full-sized people; these microscopic beings are precisely the same except for size.

"Do you know, I have been wondering if by some unknown, some preposterous, improbable means, they gradually diminished in size through the ages—if it is not within the bounds of possibility that the tiny beads that puzzled us were not the work of the Manabís when they had dwindled to say—six inches in height."

"Hardly," replied Ramon. "Of course, I admit that a six-inch gold worker would find making such beads as simple as an ordinary artisan would find the making of beads several inches in diameter. But in the first place we have found no transitory remains—no artifacts showing or indicating a diminution in the size of the Manabís. And, moreover, there is the lapis-lazuli idol. The fine carving would have been simple for a six-inch man, but to cut the images of that size from lapis lazuli would have been a far greater undertaking than for a normal-sized man to sculpture an idol several hundred feet in height from a mountainside."

"But if the theory was true, it would account for the cyclopean stone-work of the pre-Incas," I reminded him. "How do you know but that once upon a time giants as much larger than ourselves as these people are smaller, inhabited this land; that during countless ages they gradually decreased in size. That the Titanic stone work was not the handicraft of the race when they were still giants?"

"For the same reason that you know the ancient Manabís were neither dwarfs nor giants," retorted Ramon. "The fragments of skeletons of the pre-Incas are those of normal-sized men and women. No, *amigo mio,* I cannot accept that idea. But I admit any thing—even the wildest, most insane and preposterous things would not surprise me after what we have discovered."

CHAPTER NINE

ORDINARILY, Professor Amador showed not the least indication that he was Indian. When discussing scientific matters, when conversing with his equals, when mingling with white men and women, he was wholly, absolutely the educated polished white man. In fact, he was far more Anglo Saxon than Latin. He had no trace of an accent and, aside from the use of an occasional Spanish expletive or a Spanish expression now and then—such as his favorite *"amigo mio"* when talking to an intimate friend—no one who did not know him would have suspected that he was of Spanish descent. But often, when he was in uncivilized places, when he was among aborigines, when he was busied with some problem or when he was excited, his Indian blood came to the fore and temporarily, at least he would be entirely Indian. He would sit for hours, as motionless and silent as a stone statue, staring fixedly at some object or into space, oblivious of everything.

He would assume the tone, voice, and manner of the Indian; would speak in their poetic, oratorical, symbolic way, and would relapse into his ancestral Quichua.* He could be as perverse, stubborn and determined as any aborigine, and he was as untiring, as immune to personal discomfort as any of his pure-blooded relatives. Not that I liked him any the less for this. My long association with Indians had taught me to appreciate many of their admirable qualities, and in some ways, I rather liked Ramon better as an Indian than as a Spaniard. Now, however, he had become obviously predominantly Indian once more.

He had been talking like any fellow scientist, discoursing learnedly; but with his final words, he seemed to become suddenly transformed. The thought, the idea that had been suggested, had gripped his imaginative fancy, had appealed to the Indian love of the mysterious, to the Indian's pride of race, and he had become obsessed with the idea. Here were these amazing, these most marvelous of human beings, a race never dreamed of by anyone, and they were Indians! No wonder he was proud that he was of their race. News of their existence, of our startling discovery would set the whole world agog, and word that the smallest of all known organisms were human beings, and that they were Indians, would lift the aboriginal race into prominence above all other races.

Ramon, I knew, was thinking of this. His eyes were fixed, a far-away look in them, his lips were set and he had frozen into immobility. His words, too, had set me to thinking. It was strange, a most remarkable fact that these minute people should be Indians, for—a wild thought had possessed me—was it not probable that they were the most ancient of races on the planet? Was it not possible that from these microscopic beings man had evolved to his present size? Or, was it the other way about?

_____

* A South American Indian language.

Had the Manabís diminished in size until they had become invisible to the naked eye? Or—wilder and wilder thoughts were racing through my brain—were all the various human races represented in atomic-sized individuals? Was there another, a totally distinct sphere of existence going on, unseen and unsuspected all about us, a world of microscopic dimensions, a minute replica of our own?

If so, was it not possible that there were larger spheres, spheres as much bigger than ours as we were bigger than these tiny mites whose world was a patch of sand? My mind was in a turmoil. Within the space of a little more than an hour, all my ideas, my conceptions, my knowledge, my beliefs and convictions of a lifetime had been utterly upset and destroyed. I could make neither head nor tail of it all. If I kept on thinking I should go mad, and heedless of Ramon's detachment I seized his shoulder, shook him into consciousness, and insisted on talking to him.

Of course our conversation was all of the fantastic, miniature Indians we had seen and whom, even now, I could not force myself to believe we had seen.

IT was too unreal, and yet Ramon appeared to have accustomed his mind to their reality. In that way, I admit, he was superior to myself. Or it may be that it was his Indian blood, the superstitious tendency of the aborigine to believe in anything, no matter how impossible or incredible.

My own mind was a chaos. I knew in my heart that we had seen the beings; I knew the impossible had happened, and yet my better reason told me there were no such things, that we had been subjected to a hallucination or an illusion of some sort. Oddly enough, too, I found myself constantly striving to convince myself that this was the case, mentally arguing that the people did not, could not exist, and I began arguing with Ramon on this line.

Wasn't it more sensible, I demanded, to think we had been deceived, to assume that, as I had suggested before, we had been looking at the reflected images of normal Indians at some distant point?

"You forget they are Manabís," Ramon reminded me. "Can you tell me where there are living Manabís?"

"No, but it would be more reasonable, more possible for Manabís to exist and to follow out their arts unknown to us—in some remote mountain or desert retreat—than for microscopic people to exist."

"Granted! Then how do you account for that beast they had killed, that six-legged, shining creature?"

"I don't," I admitted. "But even that would be more within reason if it were of normal size. Possibly there *are* such creatures somewhere in the interior."

Ramon grinned. "And assuming that is so, how about that lizard that crawled over the village and looked like a dark cloud?"

"Illusion," I replied, knowing perfectly well I was arguing against my own convictions. "The lizard was normal, but it was transposed, the reflected image of the village merely *appeared* to be beneath it—something like a double-exposed photographic negative."

"You are perfectly aware it was nothing of the kind," cried Ramon, testily.

"Like all scientific men—and most white men, I might add, you are not willing to admit the existence of anything to which you are not accustomed, which science has not approved, which is outside your hide-bound ideas and conceptions, which you cannot explain by what you term possible or probable rules, laws and beliefs, which are all stuff and nonsense. There the savage, the primitive man is superior to the civilized white man. The aborigine takes things as he finds them. He does not try to reason that they cannot be because they are beyond his comprehension. He does not say this or that is impossible. He believes what he sees and a great deal that he does not see. You call it superstition. A few years ago, belief in radio, in hypnotism, in any one of a thousand things we know today, would have been termed superstition.

"What is superstition? Belief in something one cannot explain, that is not generally accepted by dense, pig-headed tradition-bound men! Yet you cannot explain a lot of things you believe in—electricity, light, the rotation of the earth, the planetary system, the spark of life, the working of the mind. Thank God, *amigo mio, I* have Quichua blood and can believe in anything! I can believe that anything is possible to God, that there are countless things in nature we cannot explain, that matters are transpiring all about us of which we know nothing, of which we do not even dream. But this matter is simpler. We can see these tiny beings. For Heaven's sake, why can't you believe in what you see?

"Why try to convince yourself it is impossible?"

"Good Lord, I *do* believe in them!" I exclaimed. "But do you think for one minute, you or I could make anyone else believe in them? That's the trouble, Ramon. I am thinking of it from the scientific viewpoint. Yet, I must admit, there is nothing scientifically impossible about those people. We know there are innumerable forms of life of microscopic size; undoubtedly there are as many more too minute to be seen even through the most powerful microscope. If one form of life of minute proportions can exist, there is no scientific reason why there should not be others. But vertebrates! Human beings! I don't know. Somehow that makes it different. Somehow, I suppose, it is merely because we are accustomed to it—human beings *must* be of more or less normal size."

"So must ants and insects," said Ramon. "And yet you do not doubt that Dr. Henden lost his life in a district where ants and insects were as large and larger than human beings. You yourself secured his notes telling of his strange experiences. You, yourself published the story. You have told me about it scores of times. Is it any more remarkable, more incredible, that there should be human beings as small as ants— thousands of times smaller than ants—than it is to have ants hundreds, thousands of times larger than ordinary ants?"

"I don't suppose it is," I confessed.

"And do you, a scientist, assume for one moment that our world is the only sphere on which intelligent vertebrate life exists?" he continued.

"No, of course not," I assured him.

"VERY well," Ramon proceeded. "In that case, why should there not be forms of life on electrons? An electron is as much a portion of a planetary system as our globe. Why shouldn't life, intelligent life, exist upon atoms? And why should there be any hard and fast rule limiting the size—and mind you, *amigo mio*, size is a relative term as vague and meaningless as our time— why, I say, should there be any limit to size?"

"Scientifically speaking, there isn't," I agreed. "But the trouble is, these beings are so darned much like anyone else. If they'd been wholly different, it would have simplified matters."

"That, I admit, is a puzzle," he said. "I've been thinking a lot about it, and about your suggestion that the pre-Incans might have been giants. I wonder—no, that's too wild even for the primitive side of my mind. Do you know, these people are exactly like—? They bear the same relation to giants as the Manabí gold beads bear to the titanic works of the pre-Incans. As I said once before, it is like looking at things through the opposite ends of a pair of field-glasses. One way normal things are enlarged; reverse it and they are reduced.

"But there's a lot that puzzles me. You see, *amigo mio*, I am not enough Indian to accept everything without question. My aboriginal and my Iberian blood produce a conflict in my brain. I have the white man's desire for reasoning, cause, and effect, for getting at the bottom of things; but I have the Indian's tendency to accept things as they are. In some ways I wish I had never experimented with that confounded Manabinite. What I didn't know would not have troubled me. But no—" he said, "—now I cannot rest until I have solved a lot of puzzles."

"Neither can I, Ramon," I assured him. "But somewhere, somehow there's an explanation of this phenomenon. I cannot believe those minute beings, who are obviously identical with people who were of normal size, were created in their present form and size. Somewhere lies a mystery. Ethnology or anthropology does not repeat itself. No two distinct races of man are alike in every way. They may borrow one from another. There may be traces of cultural influence. There may be similarities in arts, in costumes, in religions, in anything. But never are two races—even though one or both may be the result of mixtures—never, I say, are two races identical.

"From what I have seen, these minute Indians are identical with the ancient Manabís. Perhaps future observation may lead to the detection of differences, but if they prove to be identical, then they *are* Manabís, and if they *are* Manabís then, my friend, there are but two possible solutions. Either the original Manabís were normal in size and by some hitherto unknown process or cause, have dwindled to microscopic proportions, or else the original Manabís were microscopic and, for some undetermined reason and by some unknown process, developed into ordinary-sized mortals. We know the normal sized Manabís have vanished. We know those of microscopic size still exist. Now, Ramon, I propose to stay here until we learn the secret of these people or are convinced that we never can solve it."

Professor Amador rose and grasped my hand.

"That," he declared, "was almost precisely what I was about to suggest. In view of our amazing discovery what does the rainy season amount to? It will be uncomfortable, and we may be stricken with fever or other sickness. But I for one would consider my life well spent and would gladly succumb, if by so doing I could solve this greatest mystery that has ever faced a scientist. I shall remain until we learn the truth, or have abandoned efforts in despair."

Fortunately, however, we were not doomed to endure as much discomfort and to take such risks as I had feared. The rainy season was late, it was not severe, and often there were sunny days with no rain. But I am anticipating again.

It poured all that afternoon and we chafed with impatience. We slept little or not at all that night. Our minds were too filled with the wonders of the day, and we spent the long hours discussing, arguing, suggesting, theorizing, propounding wild hypotheses, only to find ourselves as much at a loss as ever. We came no nearer an explanation, no nearer a logical theory to account for the existence of the incredible, microscopic people we had seen. And when morning dawned at last, and the sun shone from a clear sky, the whole affair seemed so unreal and fantastic that we both felt as though it were all a dream.

WE could scarcely wait to rush off to the prism, which we had left where we had used it, our sensations—or mine at least—a strange mixture of emotions. One moment I felt sure we would see nothing, that it was all a figment of imagination; the next I was wild with curiosity and interest to see the strange people again; to learn how they had fared during the rain.

Almost breathless, we peered into the prism. And our first glance was enough. There was the village, there were the Indians. The earth about their village was damp. Evidently they, too, had had rain; but there was no indication that they had suffered from too much water. I was more amazed than ever. Despite Ramon's exposition of why they would not be affected by the downpour, it seemed incredible, unbelievable, that they could have survived. Yet there they were, unharmed, though I knew that the spat where they were had been covered with water during the night.

One thing struck me forcibly. I was not yet able to adjust my mental processes to the new facts, I could not conceive as yet how minute these beings really were. They were so perfect in size and proportions, so like ordinary mortals, so wonderfully revealed in the prism, that there was no effect of their being small. That was the greatest difficulty. Until I could adjust my mind to the new conditions—the lizard, the rocks, even the rain, would appear tremendously enlarged and exaggerated.

It struck me mast forcibly, too, that it is a peculiar fact that the human brain finds it easier to appreciate or conceive of gigantic objects than of minute objects, probably because the eye can see and take in objects of large size, whereas those of unusually small size are difficult or even impossible to discern, and must be viewed through a lens, where they immediately lose their minute proportions. All this flashed through my mind as I again watched the miniature Manabís.

Now they were all busy at their various tasks. Some of the men were making weapons, others were twisting ropes, others were building houses or repairing their dwellings, and I saw one gray-haired old fellow chipping away at a partly-finished stone seat. The women, too, were busy. Some were making dresses, others were weaving or spinning, others were grinding some sort of seeds on *metates,* others were preparing food. It was, in fact, precisely the same scene that one might expect to see in any ordinary Indian village.

Presently the people put aside their various utensils and their work, and rising, started across the open space near the houses. It was obviously a concerted movement for every individual joined the procession. Then I discovered that their objective was the temple, and I turned my attention to it. Here was a wonderful, a unique opportunity for an archeologist. The Indians were going to a ceremonial, and I would be able to watch it, to study their religious observances. And I had not the least doubt they would fallow out the same practices as had the ancient Manabís. What an addition to my knowledge of that vanished race! It would solve many an archeological puzzle, would add immeasurably to the world's knowledge of pre-Incan Indian religions and ceremonies.

Then, from a large building near the temple, a second file of people appeared. All were dressed in white, their single, poncho-like garments decorated with gold, and with ornate gold-adorned and bright colored headdresses. First came a group of men, venerable, dignified, each carrying some ceremonial object. One had a huge axe elaborately carved. Another had a mace-like scepter with the head carved in a semi-human face that I instantly recognized as the same as that on the lapis idol. Another was bearing a staff, still another carried a beautifully painted, vase-like urn. Then, following them, came a group of women—young girls—clad also in white and gold. That the men were priests and the girls nuns or vestal virgins, I felt assured, and intently I watched them.

Up the broad temple steps they passed, and formed two lines on either side of the main portal. Then, in the center of the door, the priest bearing the mace took his stand, while before and below him the crowd of villagers stood waiting. And I noticed that instead of facing the temple and the priest, the people faced in our direction, gazing towards us intently, curiously, expectantly. So vivid were their expressions, so near and so natural they appeared, that, for a moment, I thought they saw us, were watching us. The next instant I realized my mistake, understood what they were gazing at. A brilliant patch of light struck upon the earth before them; slowly it crept towards the temple steps. They were awaiting the sun, awaiting the daily vision of their sun-god!

Up the steps crept the light. It struck upon the majestic figure of the high priest. Up, it crept, until with a sudden burst of reflected light, it struck full upon his upraised golden mace. Instantly the people prostrated themselves, raised their arms and, gazing directly into the rays of the sun, their lips moved, I listened intently, expecting—so plain and vivid was the scene—to hear their voices raised in a chant. But of course there was no sound.

I turned for a brief instant to call attention to the illusion to Ramon. I could scarcely believe my eyes. He was prostrate, his arms raised, his face uplifted. Temporarily, unconsciously, he had reverted to the faith of his ancestors! The scene had awakened his old Incan blood. Carried away by the sudden flood of long-dormant beliefs he, too, was making obeisance to the sun-god. I was wise enough not to speak, not to let him see I had noticed him, and I again turned to the prism.

Now the priest had entered the temple followed by the virgins and the people and, so plain was everything, that by the flood of light entering the place of worship I could distinguish the priests gathered about a great stone altar upon which rested an immense golden disk engraved to represent a human face.

But that which held my gaze, that aroused my greatest interest, was the fact that, ranged about the temple walls, were scores of sculptured stone chairs, the counterparts of those that had so puzzled all archeologists, myself included. They were ceremonial, and, a moment later, the priests seated themselves in the chairs while the Virgins of the Sun prostrated themselves about the altar, and raising their arms, placed offerings upon it. I had solved the riddle of the chairs! I was immensely pleased, and I had completely forgotten that I was gazing at an invisible temple, at invisible men and not at a full-sized temple and normal-sized men.

Then a movement at my side attracted my attention. I turned. Ramon had risen. With fixed eyes, with transfigured features, like one in a dream, he was walking forward, hands outstretched. Before I realized what it meant, what had come over him, he dropped on his knees, lifted his hands, and in vivid pantomime, placed an invisible object on an invisible altar. I understood. For the moment he had been transported back for hundreds, thousands of years. To all intents and purposes he was the reincarnated person of some aboriginal ancestor. In one brief moment, all the white blood, all the inheritance of civilized men had been swept from him. Only the Indian remained, the Indian worshipping his ancient gods.

But he had knelt exactly upon the spot where stood the miniature temple! Unwittingly he must have crushed it and its worshipping people beneath him. Involuntarily I shouted a warning. Dazed, as if awakening from a dream, he blinked, turned towards me. A peculiar expression swept over his face, and slowly, as if still in a daze, he rose.

Beset by fears, forgetting everything in my desire to see the devastation he had wrought, I turned to the prism.

I could not credit my senses! I gasped, I think I screamed. Nothing had changed. There was the temple. The people were streaming down the steps; Ramon might never have existed as far as they were concerned!

CHAPTER TEN

"GOOD Lord!" I ejaculated. "You were right over them and they didn't know you were there!"

For a time he remained silent, lost in thought. Then, ignoring my exclamation: "Really," he said. "I don't know exactly *what* happened to me. The last I remember clearly was looking into the prism and seeing the priest in the temple door. Then I heard you shout and found myself out there. I must have been temporarily hypnotized by gazing into the crystal. Did I do anything foolish or ridiculous?"

"No," I lied glibly, feeling he might be embarrassed if I described his strange behavior. "You merely acted as if you were walking in your sleep."

Then, not wishing to let him know my suspicions as to the real cause of his actions, I added: "Probably you are right. Gazing fixedly at any bright object often produces a hypnotic effect. But, man alive, don't you realize the wonder of what I said? You stood on top of the temple and produced no effect upon it!"

"Naturally not," he replied, although I could see that his mind was not on my words. "I was, relatively, as far above the temple as the summits of those snowcapped Andean peaks are above us. Much farther in fact—perhaps as far above it as— well I won't say the moon; but so far above the people and the temple that I was beyond the range of their vision.

"But, *amigo mio,* I have a strange sensation of having seen those people and their ceremonies before now. A vivid impression. I even know the words of their chant. I even feel as if I had been in that temple myself. Of course, I never have seen anything of the sort. I wonder if it is the result of my studying so many of the Incan and pre-Incan remains and reading so much about their ceremonies?"

"Very possibly," I agreed, without taking my eyes from the prism. "But, look, Ramon! Did you notice those stone chairs in the temple? They are exact duplicates of those we find about here. It solves the mystery of their use. And the ceremonial! It proves conclusively that the Incan religion was a direct outcome of the beliefs of these pre-Incan people. Why, man, it's like turning back time for several thousand years and seeing the people as they were forty centuries ago!"

Ramon was beside me, staring into the prism again. I glanced at him. His lips were moving as if he were talking to himself. Then, completely lost to his surroundings, his words became audible. *"Kapak Inti Illariymin"* he muttered in Quicha, and to my amazement, using the ancient Hualla form of the dialect, while through the prism I saw the high priest bowing before the altar. Then *"Puncaho Pakariyrcumen,"* muttered Ramon, as though he was there among the worshipping Indians.

Now the people were dispersing; streaming away from the temple, dancing and singing, until, reaching the open stage or plaza of the village, they gathered in groups and knots as if awaiting some other event.

Ramon was, to all intents and purposes, living in another age, in another sphere.

"The *Taquicamayoc"* (musicians), he exclaimed, as from one of the buildings there appeared a group of nearly one hundred Indians playing upon various instruments. And, as the people commenced dancing and going through the complicated steps of the sun-dance, my companion's lips hummed an Incan or pre-Incan tune. So amazed was I at his actions, at his complete disembodiment, as I might say, that my interest in him exceeded my interest in the people and their actions.

What had come over him? How had it been brought about? How was it that he knew and spoke the ancient Incan or Hualla dialect, recognized each phase of the ceremonies before it occurred, spoke the words of the Incan salutation to the sun-god? Was it possible that he, Professor Amador, the scientist, was the reincarnation of some long-dead Incan or pre-Incan? Had he or his spirit, his soul or whatever it is, lived in the dim past? Had he witnessed and taken part in such ceremonies as were being enacted before us? Did this part of him awaken at sight of the people, and the temple and, for the time, dominate him?

Or was it, as he had suggested, the result of some form of hypnosis? I could not say, but there was no doubt that he was, for the time, a pre-Incan taking, mentally at least, an active part in the pre-Incan ceremonies so strangely revealed to us.

Personally, I was convinced that my friend was actuated by the spirit of some remote ancestor, for despite the ridicule of my fellow ethnologists, I had always stoutly maintained my belief in reincarnation. I was therefore immensely pleased at Ramon's behavior. My theory, I felt sure, was being borne out. Here was proof that man is but the reincarnation of other beings, and I regretted that I did not have others to witness the actions of my friend.

Also, I wondered whose spirit dwelt dormant within my own body, and I regretted somewhat that I, too, was not of Incan ancestry, for I could then perhaps have taken as intimate a part in the scene before us, as had my friend. At all events I could have obtained a much more vivid and intelligent understanding of everything that was taking place. But I realized that, in all probability, Ramon would remember nothing of what had occurred when he again returned to his normal status, and hence any information I might have secured in that manner would have been of no value to science.

Meanwhile I had not failed to continue watching the amazing scene in the plaza, and I remember that my mental processes were somewhat confused and chaotic. I had long since lost all impressions of looking at minute beings through a magnifying medium; my subconscious mind told me I was not witnessing a scene brought by some mysterious means from a distant spot, and I found myself possessed with the feeling that I was actually in the village among the celebrants while, at the same time, there was the feeling that I was watching a most vivid and perfect motion-picture.

This effect was greatly heightened by the absence of sound, although I could see the movements of the Indians' lips, could see the musicians playing upon their Pan's pipes, their flutes and their drums. But no cinematograph film ever portrayed a scene with such detail, such color, such depth and perspective. Intent, fascinated, I gazed; one portion of my brain was filled with Ramon's actions, the other was intent upon the scene before me, and all the time I was feeling that, at any moment, I would awaken to find it all a dream.

A SUDDEN exclamation from Ramon startled me. I glanced at him. Never had I seen such an expression upon his face before. He was transformed. His eyes were wide, fixed, staring, yet filled with such a longing, yearning expression as I have never seen in mortal eyes. His lips were parted, his breath came in short sharp gasps, his face was flushed, and the veins in his temples throbbed visibly.

"*Kora!*" he cried, stretching out his arms. "*Kora! Sumak Nusta!*"

What did he see? What had called forth that cry "Kora! Beautiful Princess!"

Again I peered into the prism. The question was answered. The dancers had parted, had formed a double line across the plaza, and through the lane thus formed came a procession of girls led by the most beautiful woman I have ever seen or hope to see. No wonder Ramon had called her *Sumak Nusta* or Beautiful princess. That she was a princess was evident, even to me. Her every movement was regal. Her robes, of some shimmering materials, gleamed and sparkled with iridescent hues as though sprinkled with diamond-dust. Her long, beautiful hair was confined by a diadem of flashing gems. Over her tiny ears were oval coverings of gold. About her slender graceful neck was a collar of magnificent emeralds and golden-hued topazes. And in her right hand she carried a golden *Champi,* the insignia of a monarch in pre-Incan days.

To describe her person or her face would be impossible. Her figure, partly revealed by the clinging robes, was that of a goddess. Her bare arms and her right shoulder, that was exposed, were of an indescribable golden hue. Her oval face and straight nose were flawless and might have been chiseled from old ivory, had it not been for the vivid warmth of her great lustrous eyes and her red luscious lips.

Had I the descriptive ability of a great novelist, I could devote pages to describing her, to detailing her loveliness; but while I admire a beautiful woman, I am more accustomed to dealing with archeological subjects than with feminine attractions. I confess, though, that I was enthralled; overcome by the beauty of the microscopic princess, the more so as I had never before seen an Indian woman, who could be considered even pretty. Indeed, I must admit to an increase in my slow pulse beats, to a most unusual and novel throbbing, as I gazed at her, and I am not ashamed to admit it, for she was enough to excite the admiration, and to thrill the nerves of any man.

Ramon was babbling, speaking incoherently in Hualla as though by the very force of his utterances he could attract the attention of the princess whom he had called Kora.

Suddenly she halted, turned her head and glanced about, a troubled, puzzled expression in her magnificent eyes. Then she frowned slightly, passed her left hand across her brows, and turned her gaze directly towards me. I could have sworn that she was aware of our presence, that she saw us, yet I know it was impossible. Ramon uttered a sharp exclamation. A cry that was almost a moan. The princess' lips parted in a smile; slowly she turned her head and stepped forward. What followed I cannot say, for I leaped away to grasp Ramon who, staggering back, sank unconscious into my arms.

For a moment I was seized with gripping fear, fear that the strain had been too great, that something in his brain had snapped, that my friend was dead. But to my unbounded relief, I found he still breathed, that his heart still beat. He had merely fainted. For the last half hour he had been under tremendous strain, under tremendous emotional pressure, and the sight of that vision of glorious womanhood, of the *Sumak Nusta,* the Beautiful Princess, had overcome him. He had been in a state of semi-hypnosis, he had been living again through the ceremonies of his ancestors, and, I wondered, as I strove to restore him to consciousness, if it were possible that, in the princess, his spirit had recognized the woman it had loved and lost in remote bygone days.

No doubt, when he came to himself, he would remember nothing of what he had gone through. He had said his actions were blank when he had gone through the pantomime of making an offering to the sun-god. It would be just as well if he failed to remember anything. But I was to be greatly mistaken in my surmises. He was coming to. He opened his eyes, stood up, stared about with a puzzled expression, seemed searching his mind for memory of something.

"Queer!" he exclaimed at last. "What happened? Where am I? I thought—but of course, I see, I understand! It is you, *amigo mio,* I am here at our camp. But I thought—Oh, my friend, where is she? Where is my Kora, my beloved? Have I lost her? Did you see her? Oh, *Madre de Dios,* was it a dream?"

He was staring about wildly, his face drawn, distressed. From the very bottom of my heart I pitied him. "No," I said trying to quiet and comfort him. "It was not a dream, my dear friend. I saw her—the woman you called Kora the Beautiful Princess. She is real, she exists, but she is one of those minute invisible people.

"You have not lost her, for you never had her, unless perhaps, Ramon, you two existed in some former life, some former sphere."

Ramon sprang to the prism, but the next moment turned away and sank dejectedly to the ground. *"Santissima Madre!"* he almost sobbed, bowing his head and covering his eyes with his hands. "Was ever a man in such a predicament? To see the woman one loves, the woman one has loved through the ages. Ah, yes, my dear friend, I know it now. Once, long ago, I lived. Once in the bygone forgotten days my soul loved Kora. To have loved through the ages, I say, to see the woman your spirit has loved, and to know that she is as unattainable as the stars? Ah, *amigo mio,* that *is* bitter, bitter sorrow, indeed!"

Then, suddenly brightening. "But she saw me!" he cried, leaping to his feet. "My love called to her! She saw me! She heard my voice, my cry! Did you see her, *amigo?* Did you see the look of joy in her eyes when she knew I was near?"

"Yes, I saw her look towards us," I replied. "But, Ramon, my good friend, calm yourself; try and be reasonable. Greatly as I would like to help you, to reassure you, I cannot. I do not think the princess saw or heard you. That, you know, if you stop to reason, would be impossible. And do you not see that it would be far better for you both if she did not? Is it not bad enough for you to suffer without causing her suffering as well?

"And, stop to think, Ramon—think how greatly she too would suffer if she knew that you were near and that you were still as remote, and as unattainable to her as she is to you."

RAMON bowed his head and stretching out his hand, grasped mine. "I know," he assented in scarcely audible tones. "You are right. I hope—yes with all my heart and soul, I hope she doesn't know, for I would rather suffer any agonies than have sorrow touch Kora. But, *amigo mio,* I know she saw me or heard me."

"Possibly," I said, as I considered the matter. "Possibly she *sensed* your presence. Although I am a scientist and profess no hard and fast religion, yet I have faith in the Creator and His power to perform miracles that we poor humans cannot explain. And I believe in the soul or spirit and in its immortality.

"Also, I believe, as you know, that the immortal spirit must possess a body and that, in every man and every woman, is a spirit that has occupied the bodies of other men and women for infinite time. I also believe that under certain conditions, the consciousness of the spirit's former incarnations is aroused. That, my friend, has been the case with you. Within your body is the spirit of some ancient being. It was the consciousness of that spirit aroused at sight of old familiar scenes that caused you to act as you have. That gave to your lips the ability to speak the ancient Hualla tongue, that made you recognize the ceremonies—each step, each event, in advance; that caused you to cry out when you saw the princess. And, as you confess, it was that spirit that loved her in the long ago.

"But, my friend, it is impossible that you or your spirit loved or knew this tiny princess herself. Even were she of normal size she could not have existed unchanged for centuries, any more than you yourself. No, no, Ramon, it is her spirit that your spirit recognized, and possibly, very probably, her soul responded to the cry of yours and caused her to turn and look towards you. But that she, with mortal eyes or ears, saw or heard you, is not possible. You must remember that, proportionately, we were as remote from her as the planets from us; that, compared to her, you are as big as our entire globe or even larger. She could no more have seen or heard you, than you or I could hear or see a person on the other side of the world."

"All you say is true, Don Alfeo" said Ramon. "Perhaps I should have told you more about myself before. But I feared you might scoff. Always, *amigo mio*, I have been somewhat this way. Always I have been aware of an inner self or something that at times reveals matters I could never have learned by any ordinary means. Always, when in the presence of the remains of my ancestors, I seem to feel as though I was amid familiar things, as if I had known them long ago.

"Often, by fixing my thoughts upon them I can see—as plainly as in a vision—the ruins reconstructed, and the people who once lived within them. Often I have tried thus to learn the secrets of those pre-Incan cyclopean structures. But in vain. Always I have seemed to see those titanic blocks of stone just as they are today. My strange vision cannot pierce their mysteries.

"But when I came here, though somehow much seemed vaguely familiar, I had no such sensations. And yet, now, since I have looked upon those microscopic Indians and have seen their temple, matters have been plainer, more vivid to me than ever before.

"And then Kora appeared, and over me swept a most marvelous change. No longer were there hazy visions of the past. No, I seemed bodily transported, to be a part of the scene. And though I have never heard her name, though never in my life have I even dreamed that there was such a divine creature, yet, instantly, I knew that I had known her, loved her always. God, how I suffered!

"*Amigo mio* have you ever had a nightmare in which you strain, you strive, you exert every physical and mental effort to reach something, to touch something, to grasp some object to keep yourself from some fearful fate, only to find yourself powerless, bound by some invisible, unaccountable bonds, unable to move? Such were my sensations, *amigo*. My spirit fought to speak, to call to her, to tell her of my love, to hold her fast, to press burning kisses upon her beloved lips. But in vain. I was bound, helpless, as in a nightmare. Can you imagine what I suffered, what agonies I endured? And now, now the awakening is almost as bad, even worse, *amigo mio*. I know she lives. I know she is near me—within reach of my arm—and yet as remote as the stars."

"But you can see her, Ramon," I reminded him. "That should be some comfort; that should give you some happiness."

But I fear I only made matters worse. I was deeply, truly sorry for my dear friend. Had he been young, possibly I would not have been quite so sympathetic. A boyish passion, a youthful love affair would not have appeared so serious. Infatuations of that sort are soon forgotten. But Ramon was no longer young. He was about my own age. He was deeply emotional and, little as I know of affairs of the heart—being a confirmed bachelor myself and never having found either time or opportunity to devote myself to women—still I had seen enough of the world, and was a sufficiently informed student of human nature and human passions, to know that it is no light matter when a man of Ramon's age and type falls madly in love. Moreover, Ramon's passion was not of recent birth or sudden inspiration. Unquestionably, I thought, he and Kora—or better, his soul and Kora's—had loved in the past, hence his present love for the Beautiful Princess was a thing of countless ages.

So, as I have said, I fear I rather muddled matters in my desire to comfort and sympathize with him by suggesting that he could see her.

"Do you think that makes it easier?" he flared. "Do you think a famished man finds his gnawing hunger appeased by being shown food he cannot reach? Almost I had rather shatter that prism, remove forever the possibility of looking upon her. But no, no, no!" he almost screamed. "I cannot! I must see her! And I *shall* find a way. I shall force nature to give way before my love. God, Inti, Kapak, cannot be so cruel as to keep us apart…"

He sprang to the prism. I followed. But Kora and her attendant maidens had disappeared. The temple was deserted. The people had resumed their interrupted labors.

Yet, at any moment the princess might reappear. For hours we remained, silent, gazing into that wondrous bit of crystal, until the failing light forced us to desist.

Reluctantly, Ramon withdrew from the prism. He seemed aged, depressed, utterly forlorn. With bowed head he plodded beside me towards the camp.

"She has gone," he muttered. "But I shall see her again. I shall find a way to be with her. *Amigo mio,* this has been both the happiest and the saddest day of my life."

CHAPTER ELEVEN

AFTER dinner I asked Ramon if he would not spend the evening with me, for I knew that he was depressed, rather miserable, and that companionship might cheer him up a bit.

He shook his head. "No," he said, with a rather wan smile. "Thank you just the same, *amigo;* but if it's the same to you, I'd rather not. I want to be alone tonight—alone with my memories and my thoughts. I know you think I need company, but not tonight, old friend. I want to be free to think, to concentrate by myself. I *must* find a way to be with Kora, to communicate with her. But do you know, *amigo mio,* somehow I feel that she is near me in spirit, if not in person, as if when I am by myself she might appear to me. Perhaps it's ridiculous, and as you know I am no spiritualist, but I have never felt this way before. So, *mi amigo,* I will leave you to yourself this evening."

"That's quite all right," I assured him. "I know how it is—how one wishes to be alone at times. But if you feel a bit lonely or decide to come over for a chat, don't hesitate to do so. I have a lot of notes to write up and shall be up late."

"Thanks," he said. "But I don't think I shall disturb you. I, too, have much to occupy my mind. Good night, old man—*Hasta luego!*"

While I busied myself jotting down my notes on the remarkable occurrences of the day and the amazing things we had seen—and which were of inestimable scientific value, it began to rain. As the big drops rattled like musketry upon the thatched roof of my hut, I found my thoughts wandering to the miniature people and their village. How were they faring in this downpour, and was Kora the Beautiful Princess also listening to the patter of rain? One thought led to another, and, presently, I found myself idle, my eyes half-closed, my mind re-visualizing the scenes I had witnessed.

Again I could see the sun-drenched village, the temple, the figure of the dignified high-priest, the colorful multitude prostrate before him as the rays of the morning sun flashed like fire from his upraised golden mace; once more I visioned the rhythmic figures of the sun-dance; and once again I saw Kora the *Sumak Nusta* in all her glorious beauty at the head of her train of attendant girls. No wonder Ramon loved her! Even to picture her mentally set my blood a-tingle and my heart beat a trifle faster. It was all so vivid, so real and yet so dream-like that I could scarcely believe it merely imagination, and, with an effort, I roused myself and resumed my work.

Gradually, almost unconsciously, I was aware of strains of music penetrating through the swishing roar of the rain, and I realized that Ramon was finding solace with his beloved violin.

I had forgotten to mention that Ramon, like most Peruvians, was passionately fond of music. Also he was an accomplished musician and played a number of instruments to perfection, especially the violin, and he was particularly fond of the haunting, plaintive melodies of the Incas. But when he really wanted to express himself, his favorite instrument was the Quicha flute or *Quena,* the old-time instrument of the Incas, and many a time I had listened to his rendering of *Ollantay, Cuando la India llora* * and other Incan songs that seemed to tear at one's very heart strings.

But tonight the music that came floating across through the slashing rain was different, and I stopped my work and listened intently. I am no musician, I do not know one note from another, and I could not hum or whistle a tune to save my life. But I possess good ears and a most retentive memory. If I hear an air once, I never forget it. And I was sure I had never before heard the tune that Ramon was now playing. In some ways it was reminiscent of Incan music. It held the same pathos, the same inexpressibly pathetic appeal, and yet there was a strain of joyousness, of gaiety running through it as if through sorrow of the moment there were glimpses of a brighter future.

---

*When the Indian woman weeps.

I wonder what it was, why Ramon had never played it before and had it not been raining in torrents. I should have been tempted to run across to my friend's hut to ask him about it, even at risk of disturbing him.

Presently, however, the music ceased, dying out in a final long-drawn despairing wail, and once more I fell to writing my notes, at which, I must confess, I was making little progress.

But I had written scarcely a page in my notebook when once more, the sounds of music mingled with the incessant noise of the descending rain.

It was the same air, but this time the notes were mellow, sonorous, silvery sweet, almost as though some song bird were caroling the air. Ramon had abandoned the violin and was playing upon the Incan Quena. Entranced, I listened. I closed my eyes, charmed, almost hypnotized by the music that was, if anything, enhanced by the accompaniment of the rain. Never before had I been so affected by any music. It conjured up visions, visions of the past, of mighty temples and great palaces, of green fields and vast mountains, of brown-faced, gayly-clad people, of strange ceremonies, of golden images, of dancing Indians, of—I came back to full consciousness with a start.

Suddenly, as if by some revelation, I had recognized the tune! It was the song the people had been singing as they had danced before the temple, while we had watched them through the prism! It was amazing, incredible! How *could* I recognize it? Not a sound had come to us from the lips of those microscopic beings, not a sound from the miniature musicians. And yet I knew, could have sworn, it was the same tune they had played! It was not so astounding that Ramon should have played it. I had abundant proof that, by some mysterious psychological phenomenon, he had been attuned to, if not actually (in spirit of course) a part of the scenes I had witnessed. I had even seen him muttering the words of the chant and songs as if he knew them by heart, and it was no more remarkable that he should have known the tune, should have been able to render it upon his violin or his Quena.

But that I, who had merely seen, to whom everything was strange, new and utterly foreign, should have recognized the music, was little short of miraculous.

But there are many things that happen that are unaccountable, and pondering upon this, I fell again into a brown study while I remained dimly conscious of the distant strains of the music in my ears.

Then, abruptly, the music ceased. The next instant I leaped to my feet, startled, alert. Surely I had heard Ramon call! Or had it been the cry of some nightbird? The next moment my door was burst open and Ramon flung himself into the room, wet, disheveled, wild-eyed, excited.

"Santisima madre de Dios?" he cried, relapsing into Spanish as he always did when greatly excited or under emotional stress. *"Gracias a Dios,* the miracle has happened, *amigo!* It is as good as done! It is accomplished! Tomorrow, if God wills, I shall clasp my Kora in my arms! But come, come instantly, *amigo mio!* Come that you may see the miracle yourself, that you may not think me raving, mad! For the love of God come! *Dios en cielo,* was ever such happiness vouchsafed to man before?"

Seizing me by the arm, babbling in English, Spanish and Quichua, he dragged me to the door, into the drenching rain, towards his hut. Too amazed to resist, too astonished even to think of seizing my rubber poncho or a hat, wondering if he really had gone mad, wondering still more what had occurred, what it was all about, I stumbled, dripping wet, into his shack.

Ramon sprang forward and pointed dramatically at the table. "Behold!" he cried. "Behold the miracle that leads me to eternal happiness and makes Kora mine!"

I gasped, stared wide-eyed, incredulous, and sank speechless into a chair. I was still at a loss to know what Ramon was driving at, yet what I saw was enough to bowl me over. Upon the table, gleaming dully in the dim light of the camp lamp, was a great, spherical, golden object a foot or more in diameter. Covering its entire surface was an elaborate, deeply-incised design, and from side to side it was pierced by a neatly drilled hole. In every way it was the exact duplicate of one of the minute golden beads, but hundreds of times larger.

Where, how, had Ramon secured it? What *did* it mean? What did he refer to when he spoke of the "miracle?" What had this mass of wrought gold to do with Kora?

I WAS not to be left long in doubt. Ramon, wildly excited, was trying to explain.

"It is the Manabinite—the prism!" he cried. "Here, upon this table, was the first small prism I made. It was here, left as it was when last we used it. Before it was a tiny bead of gold no larger than a pin's head.

"Tonight I sat there—where you now sit—playing upon my violin, playing a tune that had come to me, that was humming in my brain. It did not seem right played on the violin; the instrument seemed unsuited to it, so I tried the Quena. And as I played, my thoughts were all of Kora, of our great, eternal love; of my sadness, my hopelessness. There before me lay the prism, in it I could see the golden bead, magnified, enlarged. Slowly over me came hatred, detestation for the thing, for the prism that could bring the image of my *Sumak Nusta* before my eyes to haunt and torture my soul. Perhaps it was the hand of God. Perhaps the emotion in my heart—I know not what—made me forget the tune, which caused me to end the melody with a long-drawn, peculiar note. Dropping my Quena I sprang forward, intent on hurling the accursed crystal aside, maddened at thought of the suffering it had caused me. But as my hand shot forward, I yelled with pain. Where I had thought there was nothing, my hand had struck upon solid matter. *Valgame Dios!* What I had thought was but the image of the tiny bead, was real!"

"You mean?" I demanded. "You—"

Ramon interrupted me. "The miracle had happened!" he repeated. "The magnified image of that tiny bead had materialized! By some magic the bead itself, its very substance, had been transferred, enlarged, magnified bodily. It is incredible, beyond belief—supernatural! But there lies the proof. The little bead has vanished. There is its transformation! And, *amigo mio,* believe it or not, the prism itself has vanished, dissipated into thin air…"

Had Ramon gone mad? Had I heard aright? His statement, uttered jerkily, excitedly, was utterly beyond belief. Yet there was that great sphere of sculptured gold. Unsteadily, not knowing just what to expect, I rose, approached the table and extended my hand towards the gleaming mass. I had half-expected to find nothing, to find it was merely the projected, magnified image of a tiny bead. When I felt solid metal under my fingers, when I was forced to realize the gold was real, I actually trembled with the amazement of the thing. Was it possible that by some weird, unaccountable means the bit of Manabinite had transformed the little bead of gold to the golden ball under my fingers? Speechless with wonder I examined the table, passed my hands over it. Aside from the big gold sphere it was bare. But no, I must qualify that statement. Upon my fingertips was a gritty white powder, perhaps something spilled there by Ramon. But there was no trace of the crystal prism or of the original small bead.

Ramon was watching me intently, breathlessly. "Are you convinced?" he asked, when at last I gave up my search. "Do you believe me now?"

"I must!" I cried. "And yet—yet it is—why a physical impossibility. It is impossible for an object to be transformed to larger size by means of a bit of transparent mineral. It would be impossible by mechanical means. It's a law of nature. There was only an immeasurable amount of gold in that minute bead. In this sphere there are—scores—probably a hundred pounds of metal. Why, man alive, you, a professor of physics, cannot believe that definite amount of matter can be increased a thousand times and more without adding anything to it."

"God knows how it is done," he exclaimed. "'All I know is that it *has* been done. And to me it seems no more impossible than many of the other things we have seen. Is it any more impossible than those tiny people? Any more impossible than to see atoms? And I care not a jot how or why it was brought about as long as it gives me my Kora..."

"Even if it *did* happen, I fail to see how it helps you in your love affair," I said.

"What!" cried Ramon. "You don't see? *Por Dios,* but you *are* stupid! Don't you see, *mi amigo,* that I can do for Kora what I have done for that tiny bead; that I can transform her to a normal-sized woman? Tomorrow, as soon as day dawns, I shall do so. An instant later she will stand beside me, glorious, beautiful—my own forever!"

"In that case you will make her very miserable," I remarked, feeling still that he might be mad, for his words were assuredly those of a madman.

"Do you imagine that she could be happy when all her people—her subjects, remain microscopic, invisible?"

"No, I shall do the same for them all," cried Ramon. "I shall focus the prism upon the village, and by its magic, its miraculous power, bring the people, the village, the temple—everything—to normal size."

"How do you know it will not utterly destroy them?" I asked. "It occurs to me that a human being, suddenly and by some unknown power increased many hundreds of times in size might not withstand the transformation. And how can you control their size? They might be enlarged to gigantic proportions."

"*Madre de Dios;* you are right!" he cried, throwing himself upon the couch, in despair. "I must wait, must experiment, must learn to control the thing. I must test it upon some living creature."

"And now, Ramon, for Heaven's sake, be calm and sensible and tell me just how this 'miracle,' as you call it, happened. We know it is *not* a miracle. It *must* be explicable. We have seen the beads—countless objects—magnified by the prism, but nothing has ever before been bodily enlarged, physically magnified. What brought about this incredible effect?"

"My music!" was his astounding reply. "That last note upon the Quena. And now I know the secret of those cyclopean structures that have always puzzled the world. They were once small—built by normal sized, or possibly miniature, stone blocks. And then, then by means of a prism and a musical note, they were transformed to titanic proportions."

I COULD not restrain my laughter. "Nonsense!" I cried. "This thing has taken possession of your senses. It is marvelous, miraculous enough, and I do not blame you. But to assume that the pre-Incan structures—piffle, man! And how on earth can a musical note bring about such a thing?"

"I cannot say," admitted my friend. "But I assume it was owing to a certain vibration. As I told you long ago, and as you should know, everything in this world—and perhaps in the next as well—is due to vibrations. The Manabinite magnified objects—increased the vibrations of light.

"Is it so astounding, so incredible that, if the molecules, the atoms of the prism—were set into violent motion by the note of the Quena, that the altered, magnified light waves might be fixed, transformed to atomic waves? That would account for the disintegration of the prism. In performing the miracle, it exhausted, expended itself.

"And as for your statement regarding the physical impossibility of increasing matter without adding to it, that, *I* say, is 'piffle.' What *is* matter? An aggregation of atoms, of protons and electrons, nothing more. And how do we know what electrons, protons, atoms, may not be so altered, so increased by such a medium as Manabinite that the so-called matter will be increased?

"But what difference does it make? I'm tired of trying to solve miracles by scientific reasoning. I know it's been done. What has been done once can be repeated. And I intend to repeat it, to win my Kora. Nothing else in the world matters to me."

I had been thinking deeply. If, as I knew, a certain note, a certain vibratory wave of sound, could utterly destroy and disintegrate an object, even a building or a bridge, then after all was it not equally possible that an object could be produced— conjured up so to say—by means of a certain wave? It was a poor rule that did not work both ways, and I for one could not see why such a thing was not within the bounds of scientific reason. Naturally, the object produced must be built up of matter from the object that was destroyed. And was it not possible, even probable, that the Manabinite acted as some sort of an intermediary to transform the molecules of the destroyed object into a new object?

Granted that was so, then if the Manabinite magnified the object so immensely, was it not possible that the new form would be produced in the dimensions of the magnification? After all, as Ramon had so often pointed out, we know very little of the properties of vibratory waves. Light, heat and other waves are merely variations of the same waves producing varying phenomena under varying speeds of vibrations, so was it not possible that the molecular or other waves—whatever they might be called—that were actuated by the note of the Quena, and which destroyed one bead and created another, were the same as the light waves that rendered visible a vastly enlarged image of the bead?

It was all an involved, a hypothetical matter, but the more I thought about it the less preposterous and inexplicable it appeared. And no matter what the solution, no matter what the cause or the effect, the unalterable fact remained that it had occurred. But if, as Ramon thought and as was undoubtedly the case, the phenomenon had been produced by a certain note upon his Quena, could he reproduce that note so as to repeat the phenomenon?

"Do you know what particular note resulted in your miracle?" I asked him.

He smiled. "I do not know which particular note it was," he replied, "but I do know what combination of notes—what bar of music, contained that note. Would you care to hear it?"

"No, no!" I cried hastily, as Ramon reached for his Quena. "Good Lord, man, you must be careful! If you should strike that note when we were in range of the prism, we might be killed or enlarged to giants. For heaven's sake, don't start any experiments without taking every precaution."

Ramon grinned, the happiest expression I had seen on his face since morning. "You forget there's no prism here," he reminded me. "But I realize the truth of what you say. I *must* be very careful. However, as soon as it is daylight, I am going to start experimenting. I shall take that best prism—"

"No, you will not," I interrupted. "If your experiment works, you will lose the prism—it will vanish, as did the one here. Then you could never see Kora, and you'd have no chance to experiment further. If you're bound to experiment, try your tests on the small pieces of Manabinite. If it works on one, it will work on another."

"Thanks, *amigo mio,* for reminding me," he said. "In my excitement, I forgot that the crystal is destroyed. But I must test it upon living creatures—upon ants and bugs. Then, if they survive, I will try it upon small animals—upon vertebrates."

"And if they do *not* survive, even if it is a complete failure as far as living organisms are concerned, you have at least discovered a means of becoming a multimillionaire in a day. Think Ramon—" I laughed at the thought, "think of placing a worthless diamond, a mere chip, before your prism, playing a note on a Quena, and instantly possessing a diamond weighing several pounds! Or of transforming a pennyweight of gold dust to a gunnysack full of nuggets! Talk about the ancient alchemists or Aladdin's lamp! But of course you'd have to acquire your riches all at once. There is no more Manabinite after you have exhausted what we have here."

CHAPTER TWELVE

NEEDLESS to say there was no sleep for us that night. There was far too much to discuss, and we talked over the matter and discussed it from every angle and every viewpoint. For one thing, I was very glad to see that Ramon's scientific interests had been aroused, that he had, temporarily at least, sidetracked his love affair, and that he was no longer morose, miserable, and disheartened. Once more he was his old self— keen, alert, vivacious, thinking and reasoning clearly; once more he was the thoroughly practical scientist.

In a general way his views agreed with my own regarding the explanation of the phenomenon. But he put it slightly differently. "I have felt all along," he declared, "that the magnifying powers of the prism questionably does, then it should magnify approximately five hundred diameters."

"Then for the love of Heaven, don't try it on an ant!" I cried. "An ant five hundred times enlarged—an ant even if only one quarter of an inch in length—would be transformed to a monstrous terrible thing over ten feet in length! No, Ramon, let us proceed carefully, one step at a time, even if you *are* filled with impatience to attain your goal and your happiness. Let us first test the prism on inanimate objects. We know it has worked on gold. Let us try it on a minute grain of sand, on a minute sliver of vegetable matter. Let us be sure you are right about the extent of magnification and then try it upon the most minute and inoffensive creature we can secure—upon a thrips or a soft-bodied larva, for instance."

"I suppose that's sensible," admitted my companion. "But it seems a pity to waste this crystal and a day's work just to repeat a phenomenon."

"It won't be wasted," I assured him. "You must be sure of the note, and it will teach us a great deal."

"Very well," he assented. "But why not combine several objects? We'll try a minute grain of sand, an almost invisible vegetable fibre, and—yes, a speck of gold, just to make sure that your idea that gold alone responds is *not* correct."

I agreed to this, and very soon we had the three almost invisible objects sharply focused in the prism. The grain of sand—a mere speck of impalpable dust, appeared like a large cobblestone; the tiny flake of gold, chipped from one of the gold beads, appeared like a golden shaving from a machine lathe, and the hair-like strand of plant fibre was revealed as a section of a rough, twisted rope.

Then, while I stood to one side and watched the table, the crystal and the practically invisible specks that marked the three objects, as I had never watched anything before, Ramon placed the Quena to his lips. The first few notes were those of the tune he had played the preceding evening. He was feeling about, searching for the final bar.

And then, suddenly, so unexpectedly that I jumped, came the long-drawn wailing finale. I can swear I did not remove my eyes from the table for an instant. I can swear that as far as I could see, nothing happened to the objects there. Almost inaudible, through the notes of the Quena, I heard a peculiar twang, a rather musical sound, more like the sound of snapping a guitar string than anything else.; For perhaps the tenth part of a second the table seemed to be blurred by a faint mist. That was all. I was still gazing at the enlarged, unaltered images of the grain of sand, the bit of fibre, the flake of gold.

"Evidently," I remarked with a laugh, "something is wrong, Ramon. Are you sure you had the right note?"

As I spoke I stepped forward to examine the prism more closely. A sharp cry rose from my lips. I staggered back! The prism had vanished! So had the original grain of sand, the fibre and the gold! In place of the magnified images were the actual, solid enormously enlarged objects themselves! It had worked! The miracle had happened a second time!"

Never have I been so utterly dumbfounded. I had been amazed, staggered by what Ramon had shown me the evening before. But here it had happened again, had taken place under my eyes, under my closest scrutiny, and I had not even been aware of it! There had been no movement, no alteration in anything. It was exactly as though the intangible images of the things had been instantaneously solidified.

RAMON was as excited, as pleased as I was, and more elated. He had every reason to be. Not only had he proved the truth of his assertions, he had demonstrated that he could produce the mysterious magical note. And the test had proved that the properties of the Manabinite prisms were not confined to gold alone.

I believe Ramon worked all that night without cessation. I labored with him until I could remain awake no longer, and I must admit that in the intense interest, the mad desire to experiment with this new discovery, I completely forgot my ethnological studies, my notes and everything else.

When Ramon roused me for breakfast, he announced that a second prism was ready, and declared in most decisive terms that this one was to be used in a test on some living creature.

I agreed to this, for I was really as keen on learning whether any living organism could survive the transformation, as was Ramon. So as soon as we had eaten and had taken another peep at our microscopic Indian village, we searched about for some tiny organism of a harmless character. It was not a very satisfactory collecting ground for a naturalist. Ants there were in abundance, ground-beetles, worms, spiny caterpillars and other good-sized insects; but nothing small enough and inoffensive enough to warrant risking transforming it to the size of a full-grown man. But at last I discovered a colony of tiny land-snails under a stone.

Here were creatures that would be harmless, regardless of size, and I called to Ramon. But he was not satisfied. Snails, he declared, were far too low in the scale of nature to prove anything. They might survive when a more highly constituted creature would not.

"So might an insect," I reminded him. "And there is no vertebrate in existence small enough for our purposes. However, if we can find a thrips, he may answer. If he *is* transformed to a gigantic beast, I believe we could manage him. But it would be a shame to be forced to kill him. Think what a sensation a fifteen-foot thrips would cause in the Bronx Zoo!"

Presently we found the thrips we sought and, selecting the smallest of the lot, proceeded to Ramon's camp and secured the new prism. To try the experiment in his hut would be foolish, for the creatures, if enlarged five hundred times, would more than cover the table, to say nothing of breaking it down with their weight, and it was not pleasant to think of a pulpy, six-legged, elephantine beast, twelve feet or more in length, occupying our restricted quarters.

Hence we decided to make the test out of doors. We placed one of the snails before the prism, and to kill two birds with one stone, as it were, we placed the captive thrips upon the snail. Once more I watched intently as Ramon placed the Quena to his lips. Once again that startling, wailing note issued from the Incan flute. And once more nothing happened.

Fully expecting to find the gigantic image of the snail and the ferocious looking image of the thrips actually alive before me, I stepped forward and hesitatingly touched the surface of the huge snail's shell. My jaw dropped, my eyes stared incredulously. There was nothing there! My hand felt only thin air, then the surface of the prism itself! And there, just where we had placed them, were the tiny snail and the minute thrips. No change had taken place. The test had proved an utter failure!

Ramon was as nonplussed, as chagrined as I was. What was wrong? Why had the experiment failed?

"Are you sure you produced the same note as before?" I asked.

"Absolutely," he assured me.

"Possibly the prism is not precisely the same as the others," I suggested.

"It's within one five-hundredth of an inch of it," he affirmed.

"Hmm, do you suppose it's because it's out of doors?" I asked.

"No," he replied a bit sharply. "That couldn't affect it."

"Well, let's try it again," I said. "Perhaps it takes a stronger vibration in the open than in the hut. Get close to it this time, Ramon."

But the second test was no more successful than the first. Even when we took the prism with the snail and thrips into the hut and made the test again, still there was no result.

Ramon bit his lip. I knew it was a terrible blow to him. He was totally at a loss. Then, slowly, deliberately, he placed a few grains of fine sand beside the snail and again blew that strangely penetrating note upon his Quena. The result was startling. Once more I heard that sharp musical twang. Once more I saw the crystal prism and its surroundings through a faint momentary haze. And, there before us, were three great uneven masses of quartz! Once more the magical prism had transformed the sand grains to boulders. But—that was the most amazing part of it—the tiny snail and its thrips companion remained unaltered, unchanged, still the same minute living organisms as before.

"That is the answer!" cried Ramon, throwing aside his Quena and sinking dejectedly upon his couch. "It works with stone, with metal, with vegetable substances, but it will not work with animate objects. I am lost—there is no chance of my winning Kora!"

Evidently he was right. The properties of the prism, linked with the sound vibration, did not extend to animals. Kora and her people could *not* be transformed to full-sized men and women. I was truly, deeply sorry for Ramon. He had counted so much upon it, had looked forward so confidently to the culmination of his experiments.

But a sudden idea came to me. Almost an inspiration, I might say. It came so suddenly. "Don't give up, old man!" I cried cheerily. "I think we can overcome the difficulty yet."

"How?" he demanded brightening perceptibly.

"This is the way I look upon it," I said. "A certain note or vibration creates a certain reaction or agitation in the prism. You happened to produce the note that aroused the energies that would react on metal.

"The atomic structure or vibrationary structure, or whatever you may call it, of stone, even of vegetable fibres, also responds to that certain note, or more probably to other notes that you included in that one bar from your Quena. But living tissues must of certainty consist of a totally different atomic or vibrationary structure. Somewhere in the range of musical vibrations there *must* be a note that will force the prism to act upon such tissues. All you have to do is to find that note."

RAMON laughed, hoarsely, insanely. "That is so simple!" he cried sarcastically. "Have you considered the number—the range of vibratory musical notes? No, of course you have not! You are not aware that they run into countless, incalculable millions. Even could the human ear differentiate them, could any instrument devised produce them all, it would require a lifetime—several lifetimes—to run through the entire gamut of such notes. And to attempt to find one—the one—at random, would be worse than hopeless."

"Nothing is hopeless," I assured him with far more confidence than I felt. "You found the one by accident. You may find the other the first time you try. Don't give up, Ramon. Think of Kora, think of what it may mean to you both. Remember, there's nothing like trying. And in all probability the desired note is very close to the one that works on stone and other material."

"Oh, I'm willing to try," he declared wearily. "I *know* it is hopeless. But it's my one chance of happiness."

"Fine!" I exclaimed, slapping him on the back. "No time like the present. Let's start now. And," I added, as another thought flashed through my mind, "I may be wrong. Possibly the prism may act on some forms of life and not on others. Perhaps, if we tested it on a warm-blooded creature, on a vertebrate, it might work We might try it on a bird—on a dove for example. Even the most gigantic dove would be quite harmless."

Ramon smiled. His old sense of humor and vivacity was returning. "I don't know about that," he said. "A dove, one hundred feet in length and with a wing spread of three hundred feet, might cause most unpleasant results by perching upon one's house-top."

I chuckled. "Yes," I agreed. "But such birds might solve the question of aerial transportation. Tamed and trained, doves of that size could carry a number of passengers or several tons of freight from place to place."

"And exhaust the grain supplies of the world in six months," Ramon added.

"However, I don't think we need worry. I don't believe a vertebrate will be affected any more than an invertebrate. But we'll try. There are lots of subjects."

To recount all of the tests and experiments we made would be monotonous and of no importance. It is enough to say that we met with utter failure. We tried every form of insects, of mollusks, of crustaceans, even of reptiles that we could find—all without result. Then we decided to try the experiment upon a warm-blooded vertebrate and, after a deal of trouble, we captured a gentle little ground-dove.

"I'm so certain it won't work, that I'd be perfectly willing to stand before the prism myself," declared Ramon, as we tethered our captive and he picked up his Quena.

"You'd be perfectly safe," I told him. "*I* cannot play the Quena!"

All was ready, and, once more, Ramon placed his lips to the flute and again that now familiar note shrilled through the air. But the little dove was still tugging at its tether, no larger than before.

"Didn't I say so?" cried Ramon. "It's no use. Living creatures are immune."

"See here!" I exclaimed. I have an idea. I don't know much about music, but I've learned something from you. Isn't it possible there is not enough power—enough quality or, or what do you call it—penetration—to the notes from the Quena? If I am right, the same note—any note—can be produced upon any properly constructed instrument possessing the same range. Could you produce this same note upon your violin?"

"Of course I can," he declared. "But it would have the same effect. The vibrationary factor would be identical."

"Possibly," I admitted. "But how do you or I know? It won't do any harm to try. Get your fiddle, Ramon, and let's test it out."

Rather reluctantly, he agreed, and produced his violin. As he took up his position, I noticed that one of our burros was grazing near, and in a half-subconscious way I thought what a monstrous thing the jackass would be if he could be enlarged a thousand times or so. Nearby, too, was one of our Cholo laborers watching us at a safe distance, whose thoughts were probably wondering what deviltry we were up to, for our Cholos always regarded our scientific work as a form of witchcraft, and gave us a wide berth, for which we were duly grateful.

Then I turned to watch the result of this new test. Slowly Ramon drew his bow across the strings. Soft, beautiful notes came from the instrument, and then, with a sudden sweep of the bow, the wailing, piercing notes tore the air like a despairing scream.

Instantly there was the loud familiar twang, but far louder than before. Dove and crystal were hidden in a white cloud like a puff of steam. I fairly shouted with delight.

But my cry of triumph was drowned by a terrific yell from the watching Cholo.

"*Madre de Dios!*" he screeched, terror in his tone. "El *burro!* The donkey! The devil has taken him!"

CHAPTER THIRTEEN

I WHEELED. The Cholo was racing off as fast as his feet could carry him, screaming as he went. But the donkey that had been there an instant before was nowhere to be seen. He had vanished completely! What *had* become of him? What *had* the Cholo meant when he said "the devil's gone off with the donkey?" Evidently something had frightened him half out of his wits. But what? It might have been the twanging sound or the vaporous cloud, but neither of those could account for his yell regarding the burro. All these thoughts raced through my mind in the fraction of a second. They were interrupted by a shout from Ramon.

I turned to see him staring, pop-eyed, utter amazement written on his features, at the spot where the prism had been. The next instant I was doing likewise. And no wonder! The prism had completely disappeared, but there, just as we had tethered it, was the ground-dove, exactly the same size as ever!

We were both absolutely speechless with wonder.

Had the dove been transformed into a human being, into a stone idol, into a dinosaur, we could not have been more amazed, more dumbfounded. Everything had happened exactly as I had hoped, as I had expected, as it had always happened when an object was transformed to magnified dimensions. There had been that unmistakable twang, there had been the cloud of vapor; the prism had vanished; but—there was the marvel of it—the dove had remained unaffected! It was beyond me, utterly beyond my reason or my comprehension. Something must have been transformed, my inner brain was telling me, something must have been altered in order to produce that typical twang and that cloud of vapor. And yet—

An excited yell from Ramon shattered my thoughts.

"*Dios mio!*" he cried. "I have it! I know!"

"For Heaven's sake, *what* is it you have? *What* is it you know?" I demanded.

Ramon stooped and released the dove, which fluttered off, mightily relieved at finding itself free once more. "It was the burro!" he exclaimed, his voice betraying his intense excitement despite his effort to speak calmly. "That's what the Cholo yelled about."

"I was quite aware of that," I remarked tersely. "But what has either the Cholo or the burro to do with this confounded prism going to pieces with its customary accompaniments, but without producing any result?"

Ramon burst into a wild, maniacal roar of high-pitched laughter. "Result!" he reiterated. "Result! That was it, that was the result!"

"Look here!" I cried impatiently. "Can't you stop talking in riddles or utter nonsense and explain what you *are* driving at? What *was* the result?"

"That burro, *amigo mio!*" replied Ramon, suppressing his hysterical outburst. "When the note of the violin sounded the prism responded and acted on the donkey."

"Have you gone completely crazy?" I stated bluntly, involuntarily glancing about as if expecting to see a burro of titanic proportions in the vicinity. "If that is the case, where's the enlarged donkey?"

"No, I'm not as crazy as yourself," Ramon shot back. "I don't know *where* the burro is, but he's not far away. Perhaps under your feet! Enlarged! No—just the opposite—he's been reduced. He—why it's as plain, as simple as the nose on your face, *amigo.* The donkey was in line with the prism, in focus, so to say, with the wrong end of it. And instead of the agitated prism enlarging the dove, it reversed the process and reduced the donkey! Don't you understand? Can't you see?"

"By Jove!" I exclaimed, as his meaning dawned upon me. "You mean—but no, that can't be. In the first place we've stood—I've stood behind the prisms time and time again when you produced the note, and *I* haven't been affected. And why wasn't the dove magnified? If the confounded thing works on one animal, it must work on another. I can see, or at least I can conceive that it *might* be possible for the properties of the prism to reverse matters and reduce a normal-sized object to microscopic size, but if it did so, then, at the same time, it would also have enlarged the dove. No, no, Ramon, your reasoning is wrong."

"Is it?" he queried, a note of sarcasm in his tones. "Very well, I'll believe it when you show me that donkey."

Ramon had me there. There was no doubt that the burro had vanished. But I had a card up my sleeve, so to speak. "And," I informed him, "I'll believe you are right when you can show me the donkey in reduced form or can reduce some other creature."

"I might be able to do both," he retorted. "But to find a microscopic and probably terrified burro in this waste of sand is a lot harder than to reduce another one. Just as soon as I can fix up another lens, I'll prove I'm right. And—" he became very serious, "—and, *amigo,* if it works, as it surely will, I shall have found a way to join Kora. I cannot transform her to normal size, but I can and I shall transform myself to her proportions!"

"No!" I almost yelled. "No, Ramon! You'll do nothing of the sort. Why, do you realize what it means? Even if it works, even if by some magic it is possible to reduce a living creature without injury, and you do this thing, you will be dead to the world, to all your friends! You might just as well commit suicide and be done with it. And, even assuming you could do it, think of the risk you take. You cannot control, do not know the powers of the Manabinite. You might reduce yourself to the size of an atom—to a size that would be as invisible to the princess as she is to ordinary mortals."

"All very true," replied Ramon calmly. "Nevertheless, I *shall* take the chance. If I die, if I lose in any way, I shall be no worse off. Without Kora, I shall not care to live. With her, my friends, my world, would be well lost."

As he spoke, a sudden thought came to me and I laughed. "You say you will," I remarked. "But," I asked, *"how* can you do it? Who's going to produce the proper note to reduce you? *I* can't, that's certain."

"What is to prevent me from doing it myself?" he countered. "I shall stand back of the prism, in focus with it, and play the note myself."

"Hmm, possibly," I remarked. "But before we come to loggerheads over the ultimate sacrifice of yourself, wouldn't it be a good idea to make some tests to prove your theory, and what is of more importance, to prove whether or not a living creature still lives after its reduction? If you were to be reduced to a miniature corpse, it wouldn't do much good either to yourself or to Kora."

"Of course I shall experiment," he declared. "And you will find I am right. Tomorrow we will make a test on another burro."

"You will do nothing of that sort, Ramon," I informed him. "We have no burros to waste. Even the loss of one will hamper us when we pack out of here. Moreover, even if yon did reduce another donkey you could prove nothing. He, too, would be forever lost in this place. No, you will have to experiment on something else, on some creature that you can place in your hut. Then, provided you can figure out the spot at which the reduced creature will be delivered, we can determine not only if it is reduced, but whether or not it survives."

"You win," smiled Ramon. "I admit you have more common sense than I have. But we cannot test it on a dove. It would be reduced to such small size, we never could find it. How about a dog? There are two or three mangy curs over at the Cholos' camp.

"A dog should answer your purpose very well," I replied. "But I doubt if you will ever see him after the test is made. In my opinion, the burro was not reduced in size but was absolutely destroyed, shattered into its atomic parts. Now, Ramon, promise me, swear to me, one thing. Promise on your oath that unless we can prove conclusively that a living creature can be reduced without the slightest injury or harm, and that the extent of the reduction can be controlled, you will not insist on carrying out your mad scheme."

FOR a time he hesitated. Then: "Very well," he said at last. "I will make that promise. And now I'm off to make another prism."

At the time it did not occur to me, but later, as I thought over the past and remembered our conversation and our behavior, I realized that the calm matter-of-fact manner in which we discussed the whole affair was really most remarkable. But it only goes to prove how we had come to regard the amazing events we had witnessed. One astonishing thing had followed so closely upon another, that we had grown blasé, accustomed to phenomena that at any other time would have seemed incredible.

Ever since Ramon first discovered the amazing properties of Manabinite everything had moved along by an almost unbroken chain, so to speak, each link of the chain being some new and more astonishing event than those that had preceded it. First there was the lapis idol, then the discovery of the Manabinite about the meteorite; then the lens with its truly marvelous magnifying powers; then the chance discovery of the prism form with its stupendous magnification; then Ramon's clever device for focusing, his building up of a super-prism, and the sight of atoms.

Following close upon that came our discovery of the microscopic people. Then the discovery that when, actuated by a certain note, the image of an object became the actual object itself; the fact that animal life did not respond to this action, and finally the vanishing burro. Any one of these marvels would, by itself, have left us awed, rather incredulous, perhaps in doubt of our own senses. But scarcely had we been thunderstruck at one when something still more astounding followed. Thus by comparison—and nearly everything in life is comparative, as Einstein proved by his Relativity theory—thus by comparison, I repeat, each previous marvel seemed to us almost ordinary and commonplace.

Two or three days earlier we had regarded the bodily enlargement of an object as a miracle, as almost magical, as being akin to the supernatural. But now we had become so accustomed to that, so familiar with it, that it seemed nothing very extraordinary, and even the idea of the prism having the power to reduce an object to infinitesimal size did not, once the first surprise was over, seem either preposterous or miraculous. In fact we took it rather as a matter of course, and went about our preparations for the tests as calmly and deliberately as we would go about any other scientific experiments.

But our interest was indescribable. In fact our interests in the properties of the Manabinite and our desire to determine its limits had become an obsession with us both. I had completely neglected my own work, my notes lay uncompleted where I had dropped them on that evening when Ramon burst into my hut with his amazing discovery. So engrossed had we become, that we scarcely gave any time to watching Kora's people. Each day, to be sure, we took a peep at them.

Once or twice, too, I looked out of my hut at dawn to see Ramon at the prism and—perhaps unconsciously, prostrating himself and muttering the prayers and chants in unison with the people whom he was watching through the prism as they made their daily obeisance to their sun-god. Once or twice, also, we had caught glimpses of Kora, but evidently she seldom appeared in public, and I was glad of that, for each time we saw her ravishing face and figure Ramon was almost beside himself and for hours afterwards was miserable, depressed, morbid and blue beyond words.

Perhaps most significant of all, as proving our overwhelming interest in our experiments, was the fact that we were remaining at the spot despite the imminent danger of the heavy rains setting in. Before we had discovered the little people, I had been impatient to get away. I had insisted upon it, in fact. And yet, here I was, never giving a second thought to the rains, staying on day after day, and quite forgetting that, should the rains come on suddenly, we might be completely cut off, might find the rivers and ravines flooded and impassable, and might be forced to remain in this or some other equally bad spot for six months, or until the next dry season.

That may not sound like such a very great catastrophe. But unless one has experienced a tropical rainy season on an exposed, unsheltered, restricted spot where there are no resources, no game, no inhabitants, one cannot fully realize just what it means.

Of course, if we had planned to stop through the rainy months, and had prepared for such an extended stay, we could have been fairly safe and comfortable. We could have erected permanent, durable houses raised above the ground on posts; we could have provided ourselves with mosquito-netting or wire screens for doors and windows; we could have stocked up with provisions and supplies; and all would have been well enough. But I had planned to remain only until the end of the dry season. In rainy weather, excavatory work was impossible, and I had not foreseen anything else to keep me there. Hence we had not brought any suitable equipment or supplies to last over. So, as I have said, if the rains burst upon us, we would find ourselves in rather desperate circumstances.

Yet I do not think that our danger, or even our possible discomfort once entered my head after we discovered the village of the little princess. And, very fortunately for us, nature was most kind. It rained off and on to be sure—often heavily—but the rains were merely showers, and in every case, they came on in the late afternoon or evening and cleared up after sunrise the next morning. And they were not the precursors of the seasonal rains by any means. I had lived long enough in the tropics to recognize these when they appeared; to know the difference between the short, vicious downpours of great blood-warm drops and the steadily-descending deluge, like a solid wall of water, that falls without cessation or let up for day after day, night after night.

But even had these torrential rains arrived—and they were long past due and might put in an appearance at any time—even had they arrived, I say, I doubt if I could have forced myself to leave as long as Ramon's experiments were uncompleted.

BUT our Cholos held other views. They were impatient, nervous, sulky and insistent. Over and over again they demanded that we clear out, and I had begun to fear open rebellion, or at least desertion, when happily the incident of the burro completely altered matters.

I shall never know precisely what the Cholo who had witnessed the thing told his fellows. No doubt he exaggerated tremendously. Very probably he averred, and swore by all the saints, that he actually saw the devil in person as he seized the donkey and whisked him away. But even if he adhered strictly to the truth and to facts, his story would have been enough. As I have said, the Cholos regarded our scientific work as a form of witchcraft and they probably—in fact, undoubtedly, looked upon us as exponents of the black-art; but as long as nothing particularly terrifying occurred, and they were well paid, well fed and were not molested, they were quite content to work for men who might be in league with the devil, provided the devil did not approach their hut, which was some distance from ours.

But they were not sufficiently superstitious or awed by our supposedly-occult powers to prevent them from becoming a bit threatening when they found themselves facing a danger that was real, and with which they were thoroughly familiar. But when the terrified Cholo reported what he had seen, they changed their minds. Here were white men who, by merely playing on a fiddle, could cause a donkey to vanish before their eyes—and there was ample evidence that the burro had vanished. And, so they reasoned, if playing a fiddle could whisk a burro from sight, was it unreasonable to think that, if the white men so desired, they could do the same with a Cholo? The result was that from that day on, the Cholos were as subservient, as humble and as deferential as anyone could wish, and never so much as mentioned the question of leaving.

But I am forgetting myself. I am wandering from my account of what took place. I must confine myself to the account of those events that had a direct bearing upon the ultimate outcome and Professor Amador's fate.

However, I thought it wise to mention the matter of the rains and of the men in order that my readers might understand how it was that, having been so intent upon leaving before the rains commenced, I stayed on now quite willingly.

But to return to my story. The supply of Manabinite was now getting very low and it was becoming increasingly difficult to obtain a fragment large enough for a prism. In fact, by the time of the disappearance of the burro, Ramon declared that in order to produce a prism that would be practical, he would have to build one up, much as he had constructed the one through which we viewed the miniature Indians. This, by the way, remained where we had placed it when we had first seen the Indians, for we feared that if we moved it or altered it in any way, we might never again be able to locate the village.

Also we had made one or two somewhat important discoveries. We had found that the twanging sound I have described was due to the abrupt disruption of the Manabinite, and Ramon advanced the theory that it was the responsive musical note aroused by the vibration produced by his notes. I do not know if I can make my meaning wholly clear, for I am not a musician and musical terms are as Greek—or worse, for I can read Greek—as far as I am concerned. But from what I could gather from Ramon's somewhat technical exposition of the matter, every musical note has its responsive note. For example, if a tuning-fork is struck and placed near a stringed instrument, a faint responsive note will emanate from the strings. It is in fact a sort of vibratory echo, but instead of the echo being an exact reproduction of the original sound, as in the case of ordinary echoes, the responsive note may be quite different in tone.

To continue: Ramon's theory was that the twang was the responsive note, and that it was this sudden, terrific vibration of the crystal, this abrupt exertion, this throe of the atomic structure, that disrupted the mineral itself and that, in its disruption, the atoms or molecules or electrons reformed themselves—together with those in the object exposed before the prism—in the precise form of the magnified image.

In other words, the vibratory waves that—according to Ramon, for I am quoting him and make no claim to a profound knowledge of physics myself—the vibratory waves, that controlled the atomic structure of both the crystal and the object before it, were so altered in the speed of their vibrations that they vibrated in unison with the vibratory waves that produced the magnified image, and thus solidified it. Perhaps I may, in a manner, compare it to filling some thin receptacle, even a transparent object, such as a toy balloon, with water and then freezing it. Of course that is not an exact simile, but the result was more or less the same.

PROFESSOR AMADOR, however, went much further, much deeper than this. He possessed a most profound, almost uncanny knowledge of physics, and he evolved many theories as he labored at the new prism. But to me most of these were totally incomprehensible, being involved and dependent upon the most abstruse problems and equations in the highest mathematics, and which I never could master, being, I confess, a very poor hand at even the simplest mathematics.

But I could understand how, regardless of the physical phenomena involved, the process of the prism could be reversed, and an object reduced. But even Ramon could not offer any lucid or satisfactory theory as to why the prism should act backward—if I may use the term—on living tissues, and refused to act in the other direction.

We had also proved conclusively that the fine dust, which I mentioned we had found on Ramon's table, was the visible remains of the prism, a residue that, for some reason, was not transferred to the magnified body produced. This, it also developed, was the cause of the peculiar haze or cloud that invariably appeared when the transformation of an object took place. We were both rather curious to learn what the material was, and Ramon wasted some time in attempting to analyze it. But his efforts were without definite results.

"Possibly," he suggested, with a grin. "If we could manage to enlarge a pile of this powder, we might create a piece of Manabinite."

But we had no intention of trying it, and devoted our energies to making the prism that meant so much to both Ramon and myself.

If it worked, if it actually reduced a living, warm-blooded creature—one of the stray curs at the Cholos' camp for instance—and if, after its reduction, the dog remained unharmed, then I knew I was fated to lose my dear, friend forever. But if it failed, if the dog was not reduced or if, when reduced, it was killed or injured, or if it completely vanished, then would I hold Ramon to his promise. And despite my sympathy for him and my real desire to see him happy, even if in a microscopic way, yet I hoped and even prayed that the experiment might prove an utter failure.

Several times, as we worked, Professor Amador tried to induce me to join him on his mad venture. He argued that I would never have such another opportunity; that I would be able to study the habits, the lives, the religion of the miniature Manabís; that I would be content and happy; that I would have the companionship of himself, of Kora and of the high priest, and that, after all, it makes little difference where or how one lives, provided one is content and has an interest in life.

Naturally, I declined. I do not value my life more highly than others; I have many times risked it for the sake of my favorite sciences, but I had no desire to run such a risk as he suggested, even if the advantages he pictured were alluring. It was quite a different matter with him. In the first place, his disposition was very distinctly different from mine. He had the aborigines' utter contempt for life or for danger, and he was as thorough a fatalist as any pure-blooded Quicha. Also, he was absolutely convinced that he was fated to possess Kora, the princess, and his strange and truly remarkably vivid sensation of having met and loved her in some past existence, only made him the more convinced of this. And I could well understand that, with such a prize of loveliness and of love as a reward, he felt that the step he proposed to take, that life itself, was of little importance.

Indeed, I feel rather sure that, had I been younger and had such a vision of glorious womanhood lured me on, I should not have hesitated to have risked my life on the chance of winning her. And Ramon took no chance on the latter score. He loved her madly, devotedly, with every fibre of his being, and he knew, he was as certain as he was of his own existence, that she responded and loved him as deeply as he loved her. Just how he knew, he could not exactly explain. I talked with him a great deal about the matter and about Kora, for somehow as the time for the test drew near, we seemed to grow closer and even more intimate than before. Moreover, it seemed to relieve Ramon to talk to me of his passion and the princess.

"How," I once asked him, "can you be sure Kora loves you? How can you be positive that she even knows you—that she would recognize you if you were to stand before her? I know you *say* that you two loved ages ago, that your spirits have always loved. But is it not possible that you alone are aware of that? Is it not possible that her subconscious self, her soul or spirit, may be reincarnated in another body? Or even if that is not the case; that her spirit or subconsciousness might fail to retain the memory of the dim past as does yours?"

He shook his head and smiled enigmatically. "All those contingencies have occurred to me," he declared. "But I *know* they are not so. *I know,* I feel, that she saw or heard me on that first day. That even if she did not see me with her eyes nor hear me with her ears, still she knew I was near. And her eyes and her wonderful face were aglow with joy and love. Ah yes, Don, she knows, she remembers, she loves me as of old. You will see, my dear good friend. When I have vanished, then you will look through the, prism at the village and you shall see Kora and myself, and shall witness our happiness.

"Yes, *Valgame Dios,* I promise, I swear, that no sooner do I find myself among her people and beside her than I will signal to you. Although I may not be able to see you, yet will I know my great, good and tried friend—a friend larger than a mountain—is watching us, and I shall raise my hand and salute you, for you will see us.

"And I will tell my Kora, my Sumak Nusta of you, *amigo,* and will ask her also to salute you—yes, even, *amigo,* to throw you a kiss from her beloved lips. Then, will you know that all is well, and that I have found happiness beyond words with my Kora. That the love of ages—of ten thousand years—has endured and has met its reward at last.

"Will you promise to look, amigo? Will you swear that you will? And then, my friend, do me one more favor. Destroy the prism, shatter it to bits and destroy all fragments that may remain about the camp. Someday, at some time, someone might discover its secret, and some one more adventurous than yourself might follow in my steps and intrude himself—perhaps intrude a crowd upon my Kora's people. Promise me then unless—" He grinned his boyish, happy grin. "—unless you decide to change your mind and join us."

"I promise that I will destroy it," I assured him. "And of course I shall look through the prism—l could not resist that. But there's no fear of my changing my mind. Moreover, even if I did, I could not join you. You forget I cannot play the violin!"

CHAPTER FOURTEEN

WHEN at last the prism was completed, and the time came to put it to the test, I was a-tingle with excitement. In fact, I had never before felt my nerves so keyed up, so tense. Upon this experiment depended so much. It was the next thing to Ramon testing it upon himself. We had, so he thought, provided for every possible contingency. We had repeatedly tested the focal distances of the prism, in order to determine just where the dog should be placed and just where we might expect to find his reduced body, alive or dead. But we had a great deal of difficulty, and many rather heated arguments, over these details.

Although it had never occurred to us before, yet, when we came to look into the matter, we discovered that the prism did not act as a reducing glass, or in other words that we could not use it reversed as can be done with lenses in a telescope or field-glass.

It worked perfectly as far as magnifying an object was concerned—although its power was only about two hundred diameters—but when an object was placed behind it, and we looked into the opposite end, we saw nothing, but the dull, greenish, semi-translucent Manabinite.

At this impasse, Ramon declared that the only way to determine the locations for our canine experiments and the resultant miniature dog, would be to reverse their positions when magnified. In other words, if a small object placed in front of the mirror was clearly magnified, then the spot where that object rested would be the spot where the reduced subject of the test would be found after the experiment had been made.

"But," I argued, "how do we know that? The image, as you know, is not at any real distance behind the prism. To be sure, it appears to be in mid-air, an actual thing of impalpable wraith-like material. But we cannot touch it, and the nearer we come to the prism, the more it recedes before us, until it seems to be within the Manabinite itself. Where, in that indefinite range, are you going to place the dog?"

"It doesn't make any difference," declared Ramon. "As long as he's in the focal plane of the thing, he'll be reduced."

"You're merely assuming," I argued. "Think of the number of times I have stood back of a prism when you gave the note, and I have not been reduced, as I remarked once before. No, Ramon, I feel sure there is some exact and definite point at which the prism operates. That burro for example. He was at least twenty-five feet from the crystal. To my mind, the subject must be at a considerable distance. The reason I have not been affected is because I have always been close to it."

Ramon grunted. "Then how is it that a portion of the hut— my couch for example—hasn't been reduced?"

"Possibly the reduction process may not work on inanimate substances," I suggested. "If the magnifying process works upon inanimate things but not upon living organisms, why shouldn't the reverse process work on living things and not on others?"

"Something in that," he admitted. "But it's all guesswork. Anyhow, we can try the dog at various distances."

"And if he vanishes, we may not find him afterwards," I reminded him. "It stands to reason that the point at which the reduced object appears must be in direct ratio to where the original object is located."

"We'll get around that difficulty," replied Ramon. "We'll build a sort of pen—an enclosure—in front of the prism, line it with white and then we'll be able to find the microscopic pup easily. But he won't be hard to find. If the prism magnifies two hundred times, it can't reduce to less than one two-hundredth of the original, and that wouldn't be an invisible dog. A little larger than a flea, that's all."

"I wonder if the fleas will be reduced also!" I laughed.

EVERYTHING was soon arranged. We placed a large sheet of white paper before the prism, turning up its edges to form a shallow tray within which we hoped—or at least Ramon hoped—to find the reduced dog after the test. The prism, I might explain, had been placed upon the floor of the hut in order that the dog might come within its focal plane. Then I brought out the victim. We had kept him with us for several days, and never in his life had he been so well fed and cared for. Now he fawned and wagged his stump of a ragged tail in expectation of another feast. In this he was not to be disappointed. We had decided not to tie him up, for if my theory was correct, the prism might not work upon inanimate objects, and complications might ensue if the dog were reduced and his leash remained normal. So, to insure his remaining in one spot, I placed a tin plate of food upon the floor where, as nearly as we could judge, he should be in focus of the prism.

As he wolved greedily at the food, Ramon picked up his violin, while I stood well to one side, my eyes fixed upon the dog. For a moment or two Ramon tuned his instrument with care. He tried a few soft subdued notes, and the next instant the shivering magic note came from beneath his bow. As the weird note rang out, and my ears recorded the peculiar twang from the crystal, I uttered a startled cry and involuntarily leaped back. The dog had vanished before my eyes! One moment he had been there, gulping down his food; the next instant he was gone, he had dissolved, had instantaneously and completely disappeared. And with him had gone the meat, the bones, the grease. Only the empty tin plate remained, unchanged, unmoved, but as clean as though it had been washed and scoured! It was the most astounding, the most incredible thing yet! I felt as if I was in a dream; it was so unreal, so utterly beyond reason.

All this had happened in a breath. All this was over in the fraction of a second. Now Ramon had thrown aside his violin, and was stooping above the white paper examining it, searching it, for the transformed reduced dog he confidently expected to find there. I joined him, shaken, still dazed. But the white surface was bare. Not a trace of anything could be found, aside from the white powder, the remains of the prism that had fallen upon it.

"I must have miscalculated the powers of the prism," muttered my friend. "He was probably reduced to invisible dimensions. I—"

"It is just as I said," I declared, at heart vastly relieved that Ramon had not been successful in his search. "The poor dog was utterly destroyed—reduced to atoms—to impalpable dust.

Now, Ramon, do you see what a terrible risk you would have taken had you not tested the prism on the pup?"

"Possibly you are right," he admitted. "But I do not agree with you. I believe the dog is here somewhere."

As he spoke, he rose, rummaged about, and produced the Manabinite lens he had made. "Now we shall see," he remarked, as he again proceeded to examine the prepared paper tray. But though we went over every inch of the surface, there was no trace of any object, alive or dead.

"Aren't you convinced yet?" I exclaimed. "Aren't you convinced that the dog has been utterly annihilated?"

"No, I am *not,*" he asserted. "I may have made a mistake in my calculations regarding the prism. Even with this lens, the reduced dog might remain invisible. The only way to be certain is to expose the paper to the magnifying powers of our big prism. Come on, *amigo,* we'll carry it over and examine it with the prism. Then, if we cannot discover the dog, I'll admit you must be right."

Willing to humor him, anxious to convince him, and feeling greatly elated at knowing that Ramon would now refrain from his mad design, I helped him pick up the paper tray, covering it with a second sheet of paper to prevent any draft from carrying away its contents, and with him proceeded to the prism that remained focused upon the Indian village in the sand.

"We will have to place it directly above the village," I observed. "'I'm afraid your friends will imagine there is a terrific storm brewing. I hope they are not terrified."

"They will never know the paper is here," declared Ramon, "the interstices between the fibres are large enough, in proportion to themselves, to permit plenty of sun to come through. It may appear like a thin high cloud to them, but nothing more. But I do not intend to place it directly above them. I could not do that without walking over them and somehow—although I *know* it will not affect them in the least— I cannot bring myself to tread over my beloved Kora."

"Then how are you going to see it without moving the prism?" I enquired.

"We will move the prism," he replied. "We will first look through it at the village, and then gradually swing it about, until the outlying huts are just visible. Then we can always swing it back again."

This seemed a good plan, and once more we viewed the village with its people. For an instant we watched them, then, very slowly, we swung the prism about until we could barely distinguish the most outlying houses just within the sphere of vision.

"Now," said Ramon, "we will soon see who is right and who is wrong. Look through the prism while I place the paper. In that way you can direct me so I can place it directly in focus with the prism. All ready?"

Intently I gazed at the apparently vast expanse of terrific mountains and ravines, the deep canyons, the monstrous rock-masses, the wild chaos of boulders, stones and sand that the prism revealed, and which I knew was nothing more than the immeasurably magnified sand before me. What, I wondered, would the paper look like when it came into view? Would I see the microscopic dog? Would he be dead, mutilated, or would he be unhurt, perhaps still munching a bone?

THE next second I uttered a yell as if I had stepped upon a scorpion. "Ramon!" I screamed. "Ramon! Quick! Come here! Am I going mad?"

No wonder I was startled! No wonder I could not believe my own eyes!

As I gazed into the prism, an animal had appeared from behind a mass of rocks. He moved slowly, sniffing suspiciously and cocking his long ears as he proceeded. There was no mistaking him. He was a donkey, a burro! And, instantly, despite my amazement, I recognized him. He was the identical burro that had so mysteriously vanished several days before!

There could be no slightest doubt about it. Even our own brand upon his hip was plainly visible!

Dropping the paper, Ramon sprang to my side. One glance was enough. *"Nombre de Dios!"* he cried. "It is—it *is el Burro!"*

"Then I am not mad!" I exclaimed, relieved to find that it was no figment of an overwrought brain. "You see him the same as I do?"

"Caramba, yes!" he nearly shouted. "The burro, the donkey that vanished before the eyes of the Cholo! Do I not know him? Do I not see the brand? *Gracias a Dios, amigo mio,* now do you believe? *Now* do you scoff! *Now* do you doubt that I, too, can become the size of my Kora's people? *Santissima Madre!* now I *am* happy! Now my life's dream is about to be realized!"

I could no longer doubt, could no longer question. I could not even advance any valid reason why Ramon should not carry out his mad plans. If a donkey could be bodily transformed to microscopic proportions without the least injury, then there was no reason why a human being should be injured by the same process. And as realization of this came to me, I felt a sharp twinge in my heart, a pang at thought of losing Ramon forever.

Meanwhile the donkey was proceeding slowly across the rock-strewn plain. Now and then he stopped, lowered his head, and apparently grazed upon invisible tufts of grass or weeds. Now and then he raised his head and obviously brayed, though no sound issued from his mouth. Indeed, so thoroughly natural were his actions, so familiar his appearance, that I could scarcely force myself to believe he was not still a full-sized burro on a normal stretch of earth.

Evidently, too, he was none the worse for his remarkable experience, for he appeared fat and sleek, though a bit nervous and ill at ease in such strange surroundings. So engrossed had we become in watching the donkey, that momentarily we had forgotten all about the paper and our search for the dog.

I was just on the point of reminding Ramon of the matter, when the donkey halted abruptly, pricked up its ears, wheeled about, sniffed the air, laid back its ridiculous ears, wrinkled its lips to bare its yellow teeth, and showed every unmistakable evidence of asinine anger.

"By Jove!" I exclaimed. "Look at the beast, Ramon! He's all ready to lash out with his hoofs! Being reduced hasn't changed his nature any. I *wonder*—"

The next second I gripped Ramon's arm until he yelled, I uttered a sharp exclamation of utter amazement, and stared incredulously. My half-formed question had been answered in a most astounding way!

Dashing towards the angry burro, leaping over the stones, was a dog? *The* dog! The unmistakable mongrel that, less than half an hour before, had been wagging its tail and munching its food in Ramon's hut!

Somehow I felt faint, weak, almost ill. It was too much, too weird, too much of the supernatural. I tore my eyes from the prism and stared about. No, I was not dreaming. Everything in the vicinity was as it should be. There were the huts, there was the sheet of paper where Ramon had left it. There was he, his eyes glued to the prism. There was no burro, no dog in sight. It must be true, I could no longer doubt it, and I again turned my gaze to the magical prism.

I was just in time to see the burro lash out viciously with his feet. But the Cholo's dog had not been brought up among burros without acquiring knowledge by experience. He dodged the flying hoofs, snapped at the donkey's flank, and, by his actions and attitudes, we knew he was yelping, barking, as he circled about, keeping well out of reach.

Presently the inevitable happened. The burro gave up and sought to evade his tormentor by flight. Away he galloped, the dog at his heels. Again and again he halted, prepared to fight, but each time the dog urged him on. Then, for the first time we noticed that the cur was driving the donkey in a definite direction, and suddenly it dawned upon me. The dog was herding the burro towards the Indian village! He was following out his former instincts, was doing just as—when he had been a normal size dog—he had done hundreds of times before. He had come upon a stray burro, his duty was to drive the donkey to its proper place. He knew that Indians were near at hand and he was seeing to it that the wandering burro returned to where he belonged.

Ramon had realized it also. *"Mira!"* (look) he cried excitedly. "The dog is driving the beast to the village! *Dios!* What will happen? What will the people think? What will they do when they see the burro, when they see the dog? Never, *amigo mio,* have they dreamed that such creatures exist. Quick, quick, *amigo,* turn the prism or we shall miss the fun!"

AS we turned the prism, the donkey, followed by the dog, raced past the outlying houses and dashed pell-mell into the village. If a full grown Megatherium in chase of a Dinosaur should suddenly appear in the center of New York, and should rush down Broadway, it could not create greater consternation and excitement than the unheralded apparitions of the burro and the dog in the Indian village. Never before had the villagers seen such beasts. To their eyes, no doubt, they appeared gigantic, ferocious monsters. With one accord every man, woman, and child in sight dropped whatever they were doing, and screaming—although of course their terrified cries were inaudible to us—they dashed headlong for the temple. Pushing and crowding, tumbling over one another in their panic, heedless of everything but to reach the sacred precincts and the protection of their gods, they streamed from the village, and in an instant the burro and dog were left in sole and undisputed possession of the scene.

We both roared with laughter. It was like a comic movie, and yet I was at heart deeply sorry for the poor people who must have been frightened out of their wits.

Fortunately, however, the two beasts did not take it into their heads to follow the crowd or to approach the temple. Once more amid familiar scenes and in the presence of Indians to whom he was accustomed, the burro halted and, seeing a bundle of some vegetables dropped by the fleeing inhabitants, he at once helped himself and began feeding as unconcernedly as though he had been there all his life. And the dog, now that his mission was done and he had successfully brought the donkey to the village, abandoned the burro and, sniffing about, at last threw himself down in the shade of a house, perfectly at home.

Meanwhile, from their refuge in the temple, the Indians were watching with mingled fear and curiosity to see what the next move of the two creatures would be. And, realizing how the two beasts must have appeared to him, I could not but admire the courage of the high-priest who, pushing his way through the crowd, descended the temple steps and, holding aloft his golden emblem, advanced slowly towards the two animals, as if to exorcise them.

At that moment Kora appeared. I heard Ramon's short, indrawn breath as he caught sight of her, and again I felt the blood rush to my temples as I gazed upon her. For an instant she hesitated, glancing about as if wondering what had caused the excitement. Then she caught sight of the two strange beasts and I saw her start. But there was no terror, no fear in her eyes. Almost at the same instant the dog saw her. His stumpy tail wagged furiously, and springing to his feet, he leaped forward, fawning and barking. To us, familiar with the ways of dogs, he was very obviously intent on making friends with the princess. But to her he must have seemed a very terrible monster about to attack her. But Kora did not shrink, did not retreat. Though her face paled, she stood her ground, and we knew by their attitudes and expressions that a wail of despair arose from the watching people who expected to see their beloved princess torn to bits and devoured before their horrified eyes.

Then a strange, though perfectly natural, thing happened. The dog cowered at her feet, wagging his tail, nuzzling her ankles, rolling on the ground like a playful puppy anxious for a patting, and Kora, as though she had all her life been accustomed to dogs, bent and patted the creature's head.

I would have given a great deal to have been able to hear the shout that must have arisen from the Indians' throats as they saw this seeming miracle. But even if we could not hear them, we could see them as, with one accord, they prostrated themselves in adoration of their princess and her seemingly supernatural powers.

But I doubt if Kora heard or saw them. She glanced once more at the complacently feeding burro and then, as if drawn by some irresistible force, she turned slowly until she faced us, and lifting her face, gazed steadily towards us. Slowly her lips parted in a happy smile, and into her wonderful eyes came a look of ineffable happiness and joy.

"Dios en cielo!" gasped Ramon. "She knows! She sees! Oh, Kora, *Sumak Nusta!* I come—*apecha uarcu cuel tak huam ira oka Kora."*

With a wild longing cry he threw out his arms as though to clasp the princess to his breast. He had forgotten where he was, had forgotten the prism. His arms knocked the crystal to one side, and village, people, Kora and all vanished.

For a space he stood there, silent, intent, his eyes fixed upon the spot where the princess had stood. Then a deep breath that was almost a sob shook him. He ran his hand across his eyes, and slowly, as if coming out of a trance, he came back to earth.

"Now at last do you believe?" he asked in a hoarse half-whisper. "Now do you doubt, *amigo mio?* You have seen. The burro and the dog have survived, unharmed, unchanged except in size. So I, too, shall survive, unharmed, unaltered, except in size. Nothing can now restrain me. Soon I shall be with Kora. And did you see, *amigo?* Did you see her look at me? Can you longer doubt, can you longer question, that she knows I am here, that she is waiting for me, that she loves me?"

I bowed my head to the inevitable. "No," I said slowly. "No, I cannot doubt now. *How* she knows of your presence, *how* she knows you are here, I cannot explain, I do not know. But little as I know of women, yet I know that no woman's eyes, no woman's lips can speak so eloquently of joy and of love save when she knows her beloved one is near and is gazing at her. And I can no longer raise an objection to your determination,

Ramon. I have faith, I *believe* that you can accomplish your desire. But even if I felt you might fail, if I felt you might be destroyed, I would not try to dissuade you. No, Ramon, if I were in your place, if *I* knew that such a glorious being as Kora awaited me and loved me, I, weather-beaten old bachelor as I am, would take the step. May God be with you, Ramon, and may He bless you both."

CHAPTER FIFTEEN

RAMON was a changed man. He seemed to have been given a new lease on life, to have thrown years from his shoulders. He whistled, he sang, he fairly capered. He had been through a terrible strain. He had worked almost beyond human endurance. He had, no doubt, been as worried, as troubled, over the outcome of our experiment as I had been. And now that it was over, now that it had proved successful, now that he felt assured that he could reduce himself to the minute dimensions of Kora's people, the reaction was terrific.

He gabbled and chattered incessantly. He talked English, Spanish and Hualla by turn, and, had I not known it was an impossibility, I should have thought he was slightly intoxicated. For that matter, he was no doubt intoxicated with excitement, with joy, with love, and not with alcohol.

"At once I must prepare the prism," he declared, as he calmed down a bit. "I must make it with extreme care. But did you see, did you notice, that the dog and the burro were of precisely the right proportions compared with the people?"

I had, and I had vaguely wondered at it, and now that Ramon brought the matter up, I wondered still more. It was certainly remarkable that he had so calculated an unknown factor that both the animals had been reduced to precisely the right size, both in relation to each other and to the minute Indians.

"Yes," I replied, "you did that most cleverly—or was it just luck?"

Ramon laughed. "Neither, *amigo,*" he declared. "Do you not remember that the prism we used for the dog was of only two hundred diameters' power, whereas that which operated upon the burro was over five hundred? No, there is a feature of the prism that you do not yet grasp, that I knew nothing of, but that I now know, and that makes all much easier, much simpler, much surer. The fact is, my friend, that the Manabinite can reduce objects only to one definite size, to one hard and fast fraction of the original size. There is the secret, the wonder of it!"

"You mean," I demanded, "that, no matter what the, size of the prism may be, the result is the same as far as the dimensions of the reduced object are concerned?"

"Not the same dimensions," chuckled Ramon. "But the proportionate dimensions. No matter what sized or what powered prism we might have used, the dog in his reduced form would have been exactly the same size—a certain definite proportion to his original natural size, I feel sure of it. It could not be otherwise. And that is why my last doubts, my last fears are cast aside.

"Now there is no question of any miscalculation, no question of my being reduced too much or not enough. I will be exactly the same size in proportion to my present size as Kora and her people are in proportion to normal people. And, *amigo,* I feel sure of another thing. It will amaze you, astonish you; it may arouse your ridicule and your doubts. But I feel it is a fact. Those Indians—those microscopic people—were once normal; they were reduced by the same means with which I shall use to reduce myself."

I halted in my tracks and stared at Professor Amador in utter astonishment. "Now you *are* mad!" I declared. "Why, you know as well as I do that they are still living—in the same way as did the Manabís hundreds—thousands of years ago; that they could never have existed as normal-sized Indians. What got that insane notion into your head?"

"You don't understand," he grinned. "I do not mean that those particular individuals—Kora included—were ever normal in size and were reduced. But their ancestors were. I can see it all now; I can understand everything. They knew the use of Manabinite. They used prisms of the mineral for making their gold beads, for doing their astounding sculptures. Perhaps they possessed vast quantities of it, perhaps they worshipped it and had a huge mass of it in their temple. Then, one day, probably by accident, the note that causes the Manabinite to exert its strange powers was made by some flute or some pipe, and instantly every person in the focal plane was reduced.

"Possibly many escaped. Very probably only comparatively few were transformed to microscopic midgets. But those that remained were terrified. Their friends had vanished before their eyes. Also, their mass of Manabinite had vanished. To them the place was bewitched, filled with devils. Nothing could induce them to remain. They left, wandered far and wide, died out or were absorbed by other tribes, while all unknown to them their fellows remained here, invisible but unharmed.

"No doubt they had a hard time of it at first. All their metal objects, their stone implements had been left behind, for you have seen, *amigo,* that only animal matter is affected. The dog's pan was left behind, the rope with which we had thought of fastening him remained. So, as I say, they must have had a hard time of it. They had no tools, no weapons, no implements— probably no garments except their feathers, their rawhide sandals and perhaps woolen ponchos.

"But they retained their knowledge of their arts, their religion, their civilization, and with Indian stoicism and dogged determination, they went at it. For some reason—I do not pretend to say what—the reduced size was inherited, and so, through the ages, they have gone on, decreasing or increasing perhaps, but living, dying, being born microscopic Manabís. That, *amigo mio,* is the explanation; at least that is my theory. Have you a better one?"

"No, I have not," I admitted. "Possibly you may be right. I cannot conceive of any human beings created so minute. And since I have witnessed the incredible happenings here, nothing seems too fantastic or remarkable. Personally I do not see any reason why it should not have been as you say. The only point is, whether a condition brought about by such artificial means is perpetuated by inheritance.

"Still it must have been if the people were originally normal and were reduced as you assume. It would be manifestly impossible for microscopic women to give birth to full-sized children, and preposterous to think of microscopic infants growing up to normal-sized adults. And, if your theory is correct, it might also account for the scarcity of the Manabinite and the absence of finished prisms."

THINKING it over now, in my present surroundings, here in my library among my books, my papers and my pictures, looking back upon it while the roar of New York's traffic comes to my ears, with the phantasmal forms of great skyscrapers and vast apartment houses like dream-castles in the summer haze, with the honk of motor-horns sounding from the street below, the whole affair seems dreamy, unreal, almost ridiculous. To imagine myself calmly, seriously discussing the probability of men and women being bodily transformed to minute, invisible beings; to think of arguing on the chances of a fellow scientist being able to reduce himself to the same size, savors of a deranged mind and utter nonsense.

At times I can scarcely convince myself that anything of the sort ever occurred, or that I personally ever actually witnessed the things I have described. But there is Ramon's violin, there is his beloved Quena, there is the ingenious device he made for focusing and adjusting the Manabinite prism through which we viewed the princess and her people. There also, locked in the safe-deposit vault of the museum, is that great golden bead, and finally, there is the fact that Professor Amador has disappeared from the sight of men.

But I am getting ahead of my story, am anticipating, though, after all, it makes little difference, for everyone knows he has gone, and my narrative was undertaken with the avowed intention of explaining his disappearance.

But to resume. Though it all appears so dim, so unreal, so visionary now, yet at the time it seemed quite natural and matter-of-fact to discuss Ramon's theory. As I have said, we had become accustomed to weird, incredible things, and nothing seemed either impossible or improbable.

At all events, whether or not he was right in his surmises, it really made little difference. The all-important matter, the tremendous, the dramatic feature of it all was Ramon's intended sacrifice; if such I may call it.

And, for the next few days, all his efforts and attentions were centered on making his preparations for the climax of his lifetime. I aided him as much as possible—despite my innermost desire to hinder, to prevent him from carrying out his plans. But even when I was not devoting my services to his cause, I could not put my mind to anything else. I was restless, nervous, uneasy. I was about to lose a very dear and valued friend, no matter what happened.

Regardless of what the ultimate result might be to him, there could be but one result as far as I was concerned. I had not the least doubt that he would vanish. To be sure, if after he had gone I looked through the prism and saw him happy and content with the princess, I need not grieve for him. But suppose I did not see him, never learned his fate? Even so, worrying would do no good, and though I could not control my uneasiness, my nerves, yet I did manage to put my worries and my pessimistic fears aside. After all, death is not the worst thing that can befall a man, and Ramon would not be the first to die for science or for love of a woman.

He, however, was absolutely confident and was not in the least nervous. The only thing that troubled him was the necessary delay in making the prism. Although he insisted—and offered what I admitted were undeniable proofs—that neither the size nor the power of the prisms affected the size of the reduced objects, yet for some reason or other he was determined to make a large prism, the largest, in fact, of any, with the exception of the one through which we viewed the Indians. Indeed, he cast covetous eyes upon this, and even hinted that he might use it. But here I was adamant. I was bound that I would follow out my promise to see if he attained his goal, and I felt that I was warranted in insisting that I should at least have the satisfaction of knowing whether or not he survived his experiment.

Besides, I could not see the sense in destroying the prism just to make a larger one, when, according to his own statements, a small prism would serve his purposes just as well.

But, as I have said, Ramon at times could be obstinate and set in his ways, and this was one of those times. He had made up his mind to have a large prism and have it he would, even though he raved and ranted and complained over the time that slipped by. So much of the Manabinite had already been exhausted in our numerous tests that comparatively little remained. But there was the lens he had made, there were a number of small fragments, and very patiently and skillfully Ramon cut, ground and polished these, fitting the angular pieces together to form one prism, until at last he had produced a prism almost as large as the one we had preserved.

"If you are wrong in your theory," I declared, "you will have made a great mistake in constructing a device of that size. Of course, if the power of magnification bears no relation to the power of reduction, then you are quite all right. But, Ramon, if you have erred, if there is any ratio between the two, then you will be reduced far too much for Kora ever to see you."

"I am not worrying over that," he assured me. "In the first place I am convinced that the size and power has no bearing on the scale of reduction, as I pointed out days ago. And in the second place, although this prism is larger than the others, its magnifying power is certainly no greater—possibly less. The quality of the mineral is inferior—I have foolishly used the best in my experiments—and a compound prism does not possess the power of a prism made from a single mass of mineral."

"Well, it's your affair, not mine," I said resignedly. "But I am anxious to see you successful and to know that you and the princess are happy. When do you expect to take the final step?"

"Tomorrow," he announced. "I shall attempt it just after the birth of the sun ceremony, when Kora appears in the plaza."

"I'm afraid you'll terrify the people as much as did the burro and the dog," I said. "And are you sure about your clothing? It would be rather embarrassing, to say the least, if you suddenly appeared before the princess and her maidens in a state of nature."

RAMON laughed. "Don't think I haven't foreseen that," he assured me. "Animal matter of any kind responds to the prism, and I shall wear nothing but wool. In fact, I have decided to attire myself as nearly as possible like the Indians. I shall wear my Quichua poncho, my sandals, and a woven woolen *llauto* or headband. My great regret is that I must leave my violin behind. That, I feel sure, will not be reduced."

Of course, during all this time, we had not failed to watch our friends of Kora's village. In fact, since the arrival of the donkey and the dog, we had been intensely interested in events that transpired there. As soon as the princess had demonstrated that the dog was friendly, the people had evidently taken courage, for when we next looked into the prism, we found them once again in their village, working and playing as usual, with the donkey near at hand and the dog frolicking among them.

But we had to laugh at the transformation of the two, particularly the burro. Whether the people regarded the donkey as a deity or a gift from the gods, I do not know. But he was obviously looked upon as sacred. From head to tail he had been glorified. Brilliant feathers or objects resembling feathers, which I strongly suspected were the scales from the wings of some minute *microlepidoptero* (butterflies), adorned his ears. His head was almost concealed under gold ornaments; golden bands were around his legs; his brushy little tail was wound with bright-colored strings, and his shaggy burro body was clothed in a shimmering iridescent blanket. The dog was not so elaborately attired; probably he had resented being hampered and had ripped off most of his decorations; but he, too, was gay with colored streamers and a collar of gold beads.

"They have found their Paradise," I remarked, as we watched them.

"And I shall find mine there as well," said Ramon almost reverently.

"Amen…" I said. "I only hope and pray that you may, Ramon." And now we are approaching the end.

I HAVE gone through a great many tense moments in my adventurous life; I have been under many nerve strains, and I have more than once had that strange sensation that is best described as having one's heart in one's throat. But never, in all my years of exploration and of discovery, of venturing among savage tribes, of hunting savage beasts, of running rapids—even of being shipwrecked—have I felt so keyed up, so nervous, so tense, so shaky-kneed, as on that eventful morning when Ramon announced that he was ready for his spectacular experiment.

Everything was in readiness. The new prism had been carefully placed beside the other one, adjusted until we could see the village and the houses through it, although it was not sufficiently powerful to reveal the people plainly. We had sent the Cholos off in order that they might not by any chance see what took place, and in their terror desert me. Ramon had attired himself in his poncho, his sandals and his head-band, and all that remained to be done was for him to take his place behind the prism and draw the bow across the violin strings.

Somehow, I felt as if I was taking part in an execution. And, as is so often the case when one is under the stress of great emotions, I remember the thought crossed my mind that Ramon was about to act as his own executioner, and that I considered it rather humorous. Ramon, however, seemed brighter, happier, more elated than at any time. He was confident, sure, convinced that in the twinkling of an eyelid, he would find himself beside the woman he loved.

Never was a Christian martyr more exalted, more happy at taking the step into the unknown, for, like the martyrs, Ramon believed implicitly that his final step would lead directly to his eternal happiness.

And seeing him thus, knowing how he felt, realizing how much it meant to him, and remembering the reward that awaited him if he was successful, I could not be sorry for him and could not be selfish enough to grieve at the thought of losing him.

"I'd better say *adios,* Don Alfeo," he said, as he took his place, violin in hand. "If all goes well, as I know it will, you'll see me down there in the village within a few seconds. And," he laughed boyishly, "don't forget what I promised you—a kiss blown to you from the loveliest, most adorable lips on earth. You don't know how you are being honored and rewarded, my friend. The kiss of a princess—of the *Sumak Nusta,* is a most precious thing, a priceless gift, even if it is thrown to you and not bestowed in person. But, seriously, *amigo mio,* my very dear good friend, the one and only regret I have is that I must bid farewell to you. It is not yet too late. Will you not alter your decision? Will you not go with me? It was for that I made this prism of such size—because I hoped that, at the last moment, you might join me. It is large enough to transform us both, my friend."

I shook my head and I fear my eyes were wet. I loved Ramon deeply, and now that I was about to lose him, I fully realized how much I valued his companionship and friendship. But even so, I could not accept his offer; I had no beautiful woman awaiting me in the village. Though I might, though I knew I would, find it intensely interesting and of the greatest scientific value, I also knew, however, that I would never be happy unless I could publish my discoveries to the world, that to live the rest of my days among Indians would be most unpleasant.

And—I am almost afraid to admit it, for it was a rather childish and unworthy attitude—I knew I should be miserable in the presence of the consummated love and happiness of Ramon and Kora. To be near such complete happiness, to see them, watch them, hear them, would, I knew, make me very lonely, very miserable, very blue, for I would continually be mentally comparing their state with my own solitary, loveless condition.

So, with an unsteady but determined voice, I again refused to join Ramon, and grasped his outstretched hand. He gripped my hand firmly. Then, in a sudden impetuous movement, drew me to him, threw his arms about me, patted me on the back and kissed my unshaven cheek in the fervent Spanish salute of farewell.

"Now, *amigo,* will you please do me the last favor?" smiled Ramon, though I noticed a suspicious moisture in his eyes. "Take a peep through the prism, and watch for the coming of Kora. When she appears, let me know. Are you ready?"

I nodded and glanced into the crystal. The people were dispersing from their morning sun-dance, the musicians were leaving. Then I saw the Indians gather, their eyes turned toward the palace. My heart beat hard and fast. I felt weak, cold, almost ready to scream. Then from the palace door Kora appeared. I hardly recognized my own voice as I turned toward Ramon. "She is coming!!" I said hoarsely. "She—"

"*Adios,* then, my beloved friend!" cried Ramon joyously. "Go thee with God always. I go—I go to my beloved!"

I saw the flash of his bow through mist-dimmed eyes. As if in a trance I heard the swiftly rising, wailing note of his violin. As from a vast distance I heard the sonorous twang from the prism. And then I seemed to be losing consciousness; I felt smothered, blinded, and as if sinking into a bottomless abyss.

SLOWLY I opened my eyes. My head reeled, my eyes burned, every muscle of my body ached. Then full consciousness swept over me. I remembered Ramon, the sound of his violin's note, the twang of the agonized prism. What had happened? What had rendered me insensible? With an effort I raised my head and glanced about. From head to foot I was covered with a fine white powder. Coughing, sneezing, tears streaming down my cheeks from my irritated eyes, I stared. Ramon had vanished! There, where he had been standing, lay his violin and its bow. He had gone! What had been his fate? I leaped to my feet, scarcely aware of the agonies the movement cost me. I must look through the prism, must see if he was with Kora.

The next instant I staggered back. The prism had vanished! There was its stand; there was the metallic adjusting device. But not a trace of the prism remained! Dazed, uncomprehending, realizing only that I could not see my friend, could not learn his fate, I cursed, raved, groaned. Then slowly, gradually, my brain began to function properly. With a great effort I controlled myself, calmed myself. What had happened? What had become of the prism? Why had I lost consciousness?

Then it came to me, dawned upon me! Ramon's prism, the one he had used, had been too close to the other. What short-sighted, stupid fools we had been! The note from the violin had affected both prisms. By the narrowest of margins, by the sheerest piece of good luck, I had not been in line with the prism. Had I remained looking at the village, had I not stepped aside, I, too, would have been transformed, utterly destroyed or reduced to a microscopic being! I had come within a hair's breadth of joining Ramon, despite my own wishes. And no doubt it was my proximity to the line of activity that had resulted in my being bereft of my senses temporarily. Or again, it may have been the choking, irritating cloud of dust that had enveloped me. Probably I shall never know.

But of one thing I was certain. I could never learn how Ramon had fared, I could never see him beside Kora; I could never see her blow that promised kiss to me. But they would never know it. They would be unaware that I could not fulfill my promise.

Then I laughed hoarsely, hysterically, as I thought of that other pledge I had given Ramon, of my promise to destroy all vestiges of the Manabinite. I had no need to do that now. The matter had been taken from my hands. As far as I knew, not a fragment of the mineral larger than a pea existed.

Almost reverently, I picked up Ramon's violin and bow. As I did so I saw that the strings had vanished from both. They, too, had been of animal matter; they, too, had been reduced.

Slowly, with bowed head, I stumbled to my hut. It was all over. Ramon had gone. Never would I see him, never would I hear his voice again.

And never would I know his fate. Never would I be certain whether he had been utterly destroyed or whether he still lived, supremely happy, with his beloved Kora, his *Sumak Nusta*.

THE END

If you've enjoyed this book, you will not want to miss these terrific titles…

ARMCHAIR SCI-FI & HORROR DOUBLE NOVELS, $12.95 each

D-121 **THE GENIUS BEASTS** by Frederik Pohl
       THIS WORLD IS TABOO by Murray Leinster

D-122 **THE COSMIC LOOTERS** by Edmond Hamilton
       WANDL THE INVADER by Ray Cummings

D-123 **ROBOT MEN OF BUBBLE CITY** by Rog Phillips
       DRAGON ARMY by William Morrison

D-124 **LAND BEYOND THE LENS** by S. J. Byrne
       DIPLOMAT-AT-ARMS by Keith Laumer

D-125 **VOYAGE OF THE ASTEROID, THE** by Laurence Manning
       REVOLT OF THE OUTWORLDS by Milton Lesser

D-126 **OUTLAW IN THE SKY** by Chester S. Geier
       LEGACY FROM MARS by Raymond Z. Gallun

D-127 **THE GREAT FLYING SAUCER INVASION** by Geoff St. Reynard
       THE BIG TIME by Fritz Leiber

D-128 **MIRAGE FOR PLANET X** by Stanley Mullen
       POLICE YOUR PLANET by Lester del Rey

D-129 **THE BRAIN SINNER** by Alan E. Nourse
       DEATH FROM THE SKIES by A. Hyatt Verrill

D-130 **CRY CHAOS** by Dwight V. Swain
       THE DOOR THROUGH SPACE By Marion Zimmer Bradley

ARMCHAIR SCIENCE FICTION CLASSICS, $12.95 each

C-55   **UNDER THE TRIPLE SUNS**
       by Stanton A. Coblentz (single) 1950s, Fantasy Press

C-56   **STONE FROM THE GREEN STAR**
       by Jack Williamson, Amazing 10 & 11/31, (cleared by Eli)

C-57   **ALIEN MINDS**
       by E. Everett Evans

ARMCHAIR SCI-FI & HORROR GEMS SERIES, $12.95 each

G-13   **SCIENCE FICTION GEMS, Vol. Seven**
       Jack Vance and others

G-14   **HORROR GEMS, Vol. Seven**
       Robert Bloch and others

If you've enjoyed this book, you will not want to miss these terrific titles…

ARMCHAIR SCI-FI & HORROR DOUBLE NOVELS, $12.95 each

D-131 **COSMIC KILL** by Robert Silverberg
BEYOND THE END OF SPACE by John W. Campbell

D-132 **THE DARK OTHER** by Stanley Weinbaum)
WITCH OF THE DEMON SEAS by Poul Anderson

D-133 **PLANET OF THE SMALL MEN** by Murray Leinster
MASTERS OF SPACE by E. E. "Doc" Smith & E. Everett Evans

D-134 **BEFORE THE ASTEROIDS** by Harl Vincent
SIXTH GLACIER, THE by Marius

D-135 **AFTER WORLD'S END** by Jack Williamson
THE FLOATING ROBOT by David Wright O'Brien

D-136 **NINE WORLDS WEST** by Paul W. Fairman
FRONTIERS BEYOND THE SUN by Rog Phillips

D-137 **THE COSMIC KINGS** by Edmond Hamilton
LONE STAR PLANET by H. Beam Piper & John J. McGuire

D-138 **BEYOND THE DARKNESS** by S. J. Byrne
THE FIRELESS AGE by David H. Keller, M. D.

D-139 **FLAME JEWEL OF THE ANCIENTS** by Edwin L. Graber
THE PIRATE PLANET by Charles W. Diffin

D-140 **ADDRESS: CENTAURI** by F. L. Wallace
IF THESE BE GODS by Algis Budrys

ARMCHAIR SCIENCE FICTION CLASSICS, $12.95 each

C-58 **THE WITCHING NIGHT**
by Leslie Waller

C-59 **SEARCH THE SKY**
by Frederick Pohl and C. M. Kornbluth

C-60 **INTRIGUE ON THE UPPER LEVEL**
by Thomas Temple Hoyne

ARMCHAIR SCI-FI & HORROR GEMS SERIES, $12.95 each

G-15 **SCIENCE FICTION GEMS, Vol. Eight**
Keith Laumer and others

G-16 **HORROR GEMS, Vol. Eight**
Algernon Blackwood and others

If you've enjoyed this book, you will not want to miss these terrific titles…

ARMCHAIR SCI-FI & HORROR DOUBLE NOVELS, $12.95 each

D-141 **ALL HEROES ARE HATED** by Milton Lesser
AND THE STARS REMAIN by Bryan Berry

D-142 **LAST CALL FOR DOOMSDAY** by Edmond Hamilton
HUNTRESS OF AKKAN by Robert Moore Williams

D-143 **THE MOON PIRATES** by Neil R. Jones
CALLISTO AT WAR by Harl Vincent

D-144 **THUNDER IN THE DAWN** by Henry Kuttner
DR. VARSAG'S EXPERIMENT by Craig Ellis

D-145 **A PATTERN FOR MONSTERS** by Randall Garrett
STAR SURGEON by Alan E Nourse

D-146 **THE ATOM CURTAIN** by Nick Boddie Williams
WARLOCK OF SHARRADOR by Gardner F. Fox

D-147 **SECRET OF THE LOST PLANET** by David Wright O'Brien
TELEVISION HILL by George McLociard

D-148 **INTO THE GREEN PRISM** by A Hyatt Verrill
WANDERERS OF THE WOLF-MOON by Nelson S. Bond

D-149 **MINIONS OF THE TIGER** by Chester S. Geier
FOUNDING FATHER by J. F. Bone

D-150 **THE INVISIBLE MAN** by H. G. Wells
THE ISLAND OF DR. MOREAU by H. G. Wells

ARMCHAIR SCIENCE FICTION CLASSICS, $12.95 each

C-61 **THE SHAVER MYSTERY, Book Six**
by Richard. S. Shaver

C-62 **CADUCEUS WILD**
by Ward Moore & Robert Bradford

ARMCHAIR MYSTERY-CRIME DOUBLE NOVELS, $12.95 each

B-1 **THE DEADLY PICK-UP** by Milton Ozaki
KILLER TAKE ALL by James O. Causey

B-2 **IF THE COFFIN FITS** by Day Keene
HIGH HEEL HOMICIDE by Frederick C. Davis

B-3 **FURY ON SUNDAY** by Richard Matheson
THE AGONY COLUMN by Earl Derr Biggers

STRANDED IN THE WASTELANDS OF TITAN

The Carefree was an outstanding space yacht—the owner J. Foster Andrews had spared no expense. It had all of the finest equipment and amenities. Unfortunately warp eddies and space vortices weren't concerned by such things and the Carefree soon found itself plummeting toward a crash-landing. Shipwrecked on Titan, their radio busted, and most of the survivors having never done an honest day's work in their lives, the only person who seemed capable of leading the castaways to their survival was a mild mannered and dedicated male secretary.

For a time life became easier—even comfortable. They'd found warmth and safety in a series of caves. But a planetary darkness soon threatened their lives, and before long an alien menace reared its ugly head. Could they somehow transmit an interplanetary S.O.S. before it was too late?

CAST OF CHARACTERS

GREGORY MALCOLM
Once a secretary, Malcolm discovered he was the only man among the shipwrecked that could lead them to survival.

"SPARKS" HANNIGAN
This outspoken radioman was Malcolm's right-hand man. But how could he get the radio to work with no glass tubes?

CRYSTAL ANDREWS
This gorgeous creature was the desire of many—Malcolm included—but she was already spoken for.

"AUNT MAUD" ANDREWS
She was once a pampered spinster, but she overcame her high society ways to be a matronly provider to her cave-mates.

RALPH BREADON
Sure, he was a strong guy, and a trained pilot, but he didn't have a lick of sense needed to lead his fellow castaways.

TOMMY O'DOUL
Trust a child to turn a catastrophe into an adventure. Due to this young cabin boy's resourcefulness, the survivors had livestock.

MARBERRY
Having crash landed nearby, he was near death when he ran into the survivors, and he brought a warning of dire threat with him.

WANDERERS OF THE WOLF MOON

By NESLON S. BOND

Illustrated by
Ingels

ARMCHAIR FICTION
PO Box 4369, Medford, Oregon 97504

*The original text of this novel was first published
in* Planet Stories *by Love Romances Publishing*

Armchair Edition, Copyright 2015 by Greg J. Luce
All Rights Reserved

*For more information about Armchair Books and products, visit our
website at…*

www.armchairfiction.com

Or email us at…

armchairfiction@yahoo.com

CHAPTER ONE

SPARKS snapped off the switches and followed him to the door of the radio turret. Sparks was a stunted, usually-grinning, little redhead named Hannigan. But he wasn't grinning now. He laid an anxious hand on Greg's arm. "If I was you—" he said, "—if I was you, Malcolm, I don't think I'd say nothing to the boss about this. Not just yet, anyhow."

Greg said, "Why not?"

Sparks spluttered and fussed and made heavy weather of answering.

"Well, for one thing, it ain't important. It would only worry him. And then there's the womenfolks, they scare easy. Which of course they ain't no cause to. Atmospherics don't mean nothing. I've rode out worse storms than this— plenty of times. And in worse crates than the *Carefree.*"

Greg studied him carefully from behind trim plasta-rimmed spectacles. He drew a deep breath. He said levelly, "So it's that bad, eh, Sparks?"

"What bad? I just told you—"

"I know, Sparks. I'm not a professional spaceman. But I've studied astrogation as few Earthlubbers have. It's been my hobby for years. And I think I know what we're up against.

"We hit a warp-eddy last night. We've been trapped in a vortex for more than eight hours. Lord only knows how many hundreds of thousands of miles we've been borne off our course. And now we've blasted into a super-ionized belt of atmospherics. Your radio signals are blanketed. You can't get signals in or out. We're a deaf-mute speck of metal being whirled headlong through space. Isn't that it?"

"I don't know what—" began Sparks hotly. Then he stopped, studied his companion thoughtfully, nodded. "O.Q.," he confessed, "that's it. But we ain't licked yet. We

got three good men on the bridge. Townsend…Graves… Langhorn. They'll pull out of this if anybody can. And they ain't no sense in scaring the Old Man and his family."

"I won't tell them," said Greg. "I won't tell them unless I have to. But between you and me, what are the odds against us, Sparks?"

The radioman shrugged.

"Who knows? Vortices are unpredictable. Maybe the damn thing will toss us out on the very spot it picked us up. Maybe it will give us the old chuckeroo a million miles the other side of Pluto. Maybe it will crack us up on an asteroid or satellite. No way of telling till it happens."

"And the controls?"

"As useless," said Sparks, "as a cow in a cyclone."

"So?"

"We sit tight," said Sparks succinctly, "and hope."

Malcolm nodded quietly. He took off his spectacles, breathed on them, wiped them, replaced them. He was tall and fair; in his neat, crisply pressed business suit he appeared even slimmer than he was. But there was no nervousness in his movements. He moved measuredly. "Well," he said, "that appears to be that. I'm going up to the dining dome."

Sparks stared at him querulously.

"You're a queer duck, Malcolm. I don't think you've got a nerve in your body."

"Nerves are a luxury I can't afford," replied Greg. "If anything happens—and if there's time to do so—let me know." He paused at the door. "Good luck," he said.

"Clear ether," said Sparks mechanically. He stared after the other man wonderingly for a long moment, then went back to his control banks, shaking his head and muttering.

GREGORY MALCOLM climbed down the Jacob's-ladder and strode briskly through the labyrinthine corridors that were the entrails of the space yacht *Carefree*. He paused once to peer through a *perilens* set into the ship's port plates. It was a weird sight that met his gaze. Not space, ebony-black and bejeweled with a myriad flaming splotches of color; not the old, familiar constellations treading their everlasting, inexorable paths about the perimeter of Sol's tiny universe, but a shimmering webwork of light, so tortured-violet that the eyes ached to look upon it. This was the mad typhoon of space-atmospherics through which the *Carefree* was now being twisted, topsy-turvy, toward a nameless goal.

He moved on, approaching at last the quartzite-paned observation rotunda which was the dining dome of the ship.

His footsteps slowed as he composed himself to face those within. As he hesitated in the dimly-lighted passage, a trick of lights on glass mirrored to him the room beyond. He could see the others while they were as yet unaware of his presence. Their voices reached him clearly.

J. Foster Andrews, his employer and the employer of the ten thousand or more men and women who worked for Galactic Metals Corporation, dominated the head of the table. He was a plump, impatient little Napoleon. Opposite him, calm, graceful, serene, tastefully garbed and elaborately coiffured even here in deep space, three weeks from the nearest beauty shop, sat his wife, Enid.

On Andrews' right sat his sister, Maud. Not young, features plain as a mud fence, but charming despite her age and homeliness simply because of her eyes; puckish, shrewdly intelligent eyes, constantly aglint with suppressed humor at— guessed Greg—the amusing foibles and frailties of those about her.

She gave her breakfast the enthusiastic attention of one too old and shapeless to be concerned with such folderol as calories and dietetics, pausing only from time to time to share smidgeons of food with a watery-eyed scrap of white, curly fluff beside her chair. Her pet poodle, whom she called by the opprobrious title of "Cuddles."

On J. Foster's left sat his daughter, Crystal. She it was who caused Gregory Malcolm's staid, respectable heart to give a little lurch as he glimpsed her reflected vision—all gold and crimson and cream—in the glistening walls. If Crystal was her name, so, too, was crystal her loveliness.

But—Greg shook his head—but she was not for him. She was already pledged to the young man seated beside her, Ralph Breadon. He turned to murmur something to her as Greg watched; Greg saw and admired and disliked his rangy height, his sturdy, well-knit strength, the rich brownness of his skin, his hair, his eyes.

The sound of his own name startled Greg.

"Malcolm!" called the man at the head of the table. "Malcolm! Now where in blazes is he, anyhow?" he demanded, of no one in particular, everyone in general. He spooned a dab of liquid gold from a Limoges preserve jar, tongued it suspiciously, frowned. "Bitter," he complained.

"It's the very *best* Martian honey," said his wife.

"Drylands clover," added Crystal.

"It's still bitter," said J. Foster petulantly.

His sister sniffed. "Nonsense. It's delightful."

"I say it's bitter," repeated Andrews sulkily. And lifted his voice again. *"Malcolm!* Where *are* you?"

"You called me, sir?" said Malcolm, moving into the room. He nodded politely to the others. "Good morning, Mrs. Andrews...Miss Andrews...Mr. Breadon..."

"Oh, sit down!" snapped J. Foster. "Sit down here and stop bobbing your head like a teetotum. Had your breakfast? The honey's no good; it's bitter." He glared at his sister challengingly. "Where have you been, anyway? What kind of secretary are you? Have you been up to the radio turret? How's the market today? Is Galactic up or down?"

Malcolm said, "I don't know, sir."

"Fine. Fine," Andrews rattled on automatically before the words registered. Then he started, his face turning red, "Eh? What's that? Don't know. What do you mean, you don't know? I pay you to—"

"There's no transmission, sir," said Greg quietly.

"No trans—nonsense. Of course there's transmission. I put a million credits into this ship. Finest space-yacht ever built. Latest equipment throughout. Sparks is drunk, that's what you mean. Well, you hop right up there and—"

MAUD ANDREWS put down her fork with a clatter. "Oh, for goodness sakes, Jonathan, shut up and give the boy time to explain. He's standing there with his mouth gaping like a rain-spout, trying to get a word in edgewise. What's the trouble, Gregory?" She turned to Greg, as Jonathan Foster Andrews wheezed into startled silence. *"That?"*

She glanced at the quartzite dome, beyond which the veil of iridescence wove and cross-wove and shimmered like a pallid aurora.

Greg nodded. "Yes, Miss Andrews."

Enid Andrews spoke languidly from the other end of the table.

"But what is it, Gregory? A local phenomenon?"

"You might call it that," said Greg, selecting his words cautiously. "It's an ionized field into which we've blasted. It—it—shouldn't stay with us long. But while it persists, our radio will be blanketed out."

Breadon's chestnut head came up suddenly, sharply.

"Ionization? That means atmosphere!"

Greg said, "Yes."

"And an atmosphere means a body in space somewhere near—" Breadon stopped, bit his lip before the appeal in

163

Malcolm's eyes, tried to pass it off easily. "Oh, well—a change of scenery, what?"

But the moment of alarm in his voice had not passed unnoticed. Crystal Andrews spoke for all of them, her voice preternaturally quiet.

"You're hiding something, Malcolm. What is it? Is there—danger?"

But Greg didn't have to answer that question. From the doorway a harsh, defiantly strident voice answered for him. The voice of Bert Andrews, Crystal's older brother.

"Danger? You're damn right there's danger! What's the matter with you folks—are you all deaf, dumb and blind? We've been caught in a space-vortex for hours. Now we're in the H-layer of a planet we can't even see—and in fifteen minutes or fifteen seconds we may all be smashed as flat as pancakes!"

The proclamation brought them out of their chairs. Greg's heart sank; his vain plea, "Mr. Andrews—" was lost in the medley of Crystal's sudden gasp, Enid Andrews' short, choking scream, J. Foster's bellowing roar at his only son.

"Bert—you're drunk!"

Bert weaved precariously from the doorway, laughed in his father's face.

"Sure I'm drunk. Why not? If you're smart you'll get drunk, too. The whole damn lot of you." He flicked a derisive hand toward Greg. "You too, Boy Scout. What were you trying to do—hide the bad news from them? Well, it's no use. Everybody might as well know the worst. We're gone gooses...geeses...aw, what the hell. Dead ducks!" He fell into a chair, sprawled there laughing mirthlessly with fear riding the too-high notes of his laughter.

J. Foster turned to his secretary slowly. His ire had faded; there was only deep concern in his voice.

"Is he telling the truth, Malcolm?"

Greg said soberly, "Partly, sir. He's overstating the danger—but there is danger. We are caught in a space-vortex, and as Mr. Breadon realized, the presence of these ionics means we're in the Heavisidelayer of some heavenly body. But we may not crack up."

Maud Andrews glanced at him shrewdly.

"Is there anything we can do?"

"Not a thing. The officers on the bridge are doing everything possible."

"In that case," said the older woman, "we might as well finish our breakfast. Here, Cuddles! Come to momsy!" She sat down again. Greg looked at her admiringly. Ralph Breadon stroked his brown jaw. He said, "The life-skiffs?"

"A last resort," said Greg. "Sparks promised he'd let me know if it were necessary. We'll hope it's not—"

But it was a vain hope, vainly spoken in the last, vain moment. For even as he phrased the hopeful words, came the sound of swift, racing footsteps up the corridor. Into the dining dome burst Hannigan, eyes hot with excitement. And his cry dispelled Greg's final hopes for safety.

"Everybody—the Number Four life-skiff—*quick!* We've been caught in a grav-drag and we're going to crash…"

CHAPTER TWO

THOSE next hectic moments were never afterward very clear in Greg Malcolm's memory. He had a confused recollection of hearing Sparks' warning punctuated by a loud, shrill scream which he vaguely identified as emanating from Mrs. Andrews' throat…he was conscious of feeling, suddenly, beneath his feet the sickening, quickening lurch of a ship out of control, gripped by gravitational forces beyond its power to allay…he recalled his own voice dinning in his ears as, incredibly, with Sparks, he took command of the hasty flight from the dining dome down the corridor to the aft ramp, up the ramp, across girdered beams in the superstructure to the small, independently motored rocket-skiff cradled there.

He was aware, too, of strangely disconnected incidents happening around him, he being a part of them but seeming to be only a disinterested spectator to their strangeness. Of his forcing Maud Andrews toward the door of the dome...of her pushing back against him with all the weight of her body...of her irate voice, "Cuddles! I forgot him!" Then the shrill excited yapping of the poodle cradled against her as they charged on down the corridor.

J. Foster waddling beside him, tugging at his arm, panting, "The officers?" and his own unfelt assurance. "They can take care of themselves. It's a general 'bandon ship." Enid Andrews stumbling over the hem of a filmy peignoir...himself bending to lift her boldly and bodily, sweating palms feeling the warm animal heat of her excited body hot beneath them. Crystal Andrews stopping suddenly, crying, "Tina!"...and Hannigan's reply, "Your maid? I woke her. She's in the life-skiff." Bert Andrews stopping suddenly, being sick in the middle of the corridor, his drunkenness losing itself in the thick, sure nausea of the ever-increasing unsteadiness beneath their feet.

Then the life-skiff, the clang of metal as Hannigan slammed the port behind the last of them, the fumbling for a lock-stud, the quick, grateful pant of the miniature hypos, and a weird feeling of weightlessness, rushingness, hurtlingness as his eardrums throbbed and his mouth tasted brassy and bloody with the fierce velocity of their escape.

Sense and meaning returned only when all this ended. As one waking from a nightmare dream, Greg Malcolm returned to a world he could recognize. A tiny world, encased within the walls of a forty foot life-skiff. A world peopled too scantily. Andrews, his wife and sister, his son and daughter;

Tina Laney, the maid; Breadon, Hannigan, young Tommy O'Doul, the cabin-boy (though where he had come from, or when, Greg did not know). And himself. In a life-skiff. In space.

Somewhere in space. He looked through the *perilens*. What he saw then he might better never have seen. For that shimmering pink-ochre veil had wisped away, now, and in the clean, cold, bitter-clear light of a distant sun he watched the death-dive of the yacht *Carefree*.

Like a vast silver top, spinning heedlessly, wildly, it streaked toward a mottled gray and green, brown and dun, hard and crushing—brutal terrain below. Still at its helm stood someone, for even in that last dreadful moment burst from its nose-jets a ruddy mushroom of flame that tried to, but could not, brake the dizzy fall.

For an instant Greg's eyes, stingingly blinded and wet, thought they glimpsed a wee black mote dancing from the bowels of the *Carefree;* a mote that might be another skiff like their own. But he could not be sure, and then the *Carefree* was accelerating with such violence and speed that the eye could see it only as a flaming silver lance against the ugly earth-carcase beneath, and then it struck and a carmine bud of flame burst and flowered for an instant, and that was all…

And Greg Malcolm turned from the *perilens,* shaken.

Hannigan said, "It's over?" and Greg nodded.

Hannigan said, "The other skiffs? Did they break free, or were they caught?"

"I don't know. I couldn't see for sure."

"You must have seen. Are we the only ones?"

"I couldn't see for sure. Maybe. Maybe not."

Then a body scrambled forward, pressing through the tightness of other huddled bodies, and there was a hand upon his elbow. "I'll take over now, Malcolm."

IT WAS Ralph Breadon. Gregory looked at him slowly, uncomprehendingly at first. His hand was reluctant to leave the guiding-gear of the small ship which was, now, all that remained to them of civilization and civilization's wondrous accomplishments. He had not realized until this moment that for a while…for a short, eager, pulse-quickening while…on his alertness, in his hands, had depended the destinies of ten men and women. But he knew, suddenly and completely, that it was for this single moment his whole lifetime had waited. It was for this brief moment of command that some intuition, some instinct greater than knowledge, had prepared him. This was why he, an Earthlubber, had studied astrogation, made a hobby of the empire of the stars. That he might be fitted to command when all others failed. And now—

And now the moment was past, and he was once again Gregory Malcolm, mild, lean, pale, bespectacled secretary to J. Foster Andrews. And the man at his side was Ralph Breadon, socialite and gentleman sportsman, trained pilot. And in Malcolm the habit of obedience was strong…

"Very well, sir," he said. And he turned over the controls.

What happened then was unfortunate. It might just as well have happened to Malcolm, though afterward no one could ever say with certainty. However that was, either by carelessness or malfortune or inefficiency, once-thwarted disaster struck again at the little party on the life-skiff. At the instant Breadon's hand seized the controls the skiff jerked suddenly as though struck with a ponderous fist, its throbbing motors choked and snarled in a high, rising crescendo of torment that lost itself in supersonic heights, and the ship that had been drifting easily and under control, to the planet beneath now dipped viciously.

The misfortune was that too many huddled in the tiny space understood the operation of the life-skiff, and what must be done instantly. And that neither pilot was as yet in control of the ship. Breadon's hand leaped for the Dixie rod, so, too, did Malcolm's—and across both their bodies came the arm of Sparks Hannigan, searching the controls.

In the scramble someone's sleeve brushed the banks of control-keys. The motors, killed, soughed into silence. The ship rocked into a spin. Greg cried out, his voice a strange harshness in his ears; Breadon cursed; one of the women bleated fearfully.

Then Breadon, still cursing, fought all hands from the controls but his own. And the man was not without courage. For all could see plainly, in the illumined *perilens*, how near to swift death that moment of uncertainty had led them. The skiff, which an instant before had been high in the stratosphere of this unknown planet...or satellite or whatever it might be...was now flashing toward hard ground at lightning speed.

ONLY a miracle, Greg knew, could save them now. An impulse spun his head, he looked at Crystal Andrews. There was no fear in her eyes. Just a hotness and an inexplicable anger. Beside her was the other girl, the maid, Tina; she was frankly afraid. Her teeth were clenched in her nether lip, and her eyes were wide and anxious, but she did not cry out.

Only a miracle could save them now.

But Breadon's hands performed that miracle; his quick, nerveless, trained hands. A stud here...a lever there...a swift wrenching toss of the shoulders. His face twisted back over his shoulder, and his straining lips pulled taut and bloodless away from his teeth. "Hold tight, folks! We're going to bounce—"

Then they struck!

But they struck glancingly, as Breadon had hoped, and planned for, and gambled on. They struck and bounced.

The frail craft shivered and groaned in metal agony, jarred across harsh soil, bounced again, settled, nosed over and rocked to a standstill. Somewhere forward something snapped with a shrill, high *ping!* of stress; somewhere aft was the metallic flap-clanging of broken gear trailing behind them. But they were safe.

Breath, held so long that he could not remember its inhalation, escaped Greg's lungs in a long sigh. "Nice work, Mr. Breadon!" he cried. "Oh, nice work!"

But surprisingly, savagely, Breadon turned on him.

"It would have been *better* work, Malcolm, if you'd kept your damned hands off the controls. Now see what you've done? Smashed up our skiff. Our only—"

"He didn't do it," piped the shrill voice of Tommy O'Doul. "You done it yourself, Mr. Breadon. Your sleeve. It caught the switch."

"Quiet!" Breadon, cheeks flushed, reached out smartly, stilled the youngster's defense with a swift, ungentle slap. "And you, Malcolm—after this, do as you're told, and don't try to assume responsibilities too great for you. All right, everybody. Let's get out and see how bad the damage is."

Instinctively Greg had surged a half step forward as Breadon silenced the cabin boy. Now old habit and common-sense halted him. He's overwrought, he reasoned. We're all excited and on edge. We've been to Bedlam. Our nerves are shot. In a little while we'll all be back to normal.

He said quietly, "Very well, Mr. Breadon." And he climbed from the broken skiff.

HANNIGAN said, "Looks bad, don't it?"

"Very," said Malcolm. He fingered a shard of loose metal flapping like a fin from the stern of the skiff. "Not hopeless, though. There should be an acetylene torch in the tool locker. With that—"

"You ought to of poked him," said Hannigan.

"What? Oh, you mean—?"

"Yeah. The kid was right, you know. He done it."

"His sleeve, you mean. Well, it was an accident," said Greg. "It could have happened to anyone. And he made a good landing. Considering everything. Anyhow—" Again he was Gregory Malcolm, serious-faced, efficient secretary. "Anyhow, we have been thrust into an extremely precarious circumstance. It would be silly to take umbrage at a man's nervous anger. We must have no quarreling, no bickering—"

"Umbrage!" snorted Sparks. "Bickering! They're big words. I ain't sure I know what they mean. I ain't exactly sure they mean *anything.*" He glanced at Greg oddly. "You're a queer jasper, Malcolm. Back there on the ship, I figured you for a sort of a stuffed-shirt. Yes-man to the boss. And then in the show-down, you come through like a movie hero—for a little while. Then you let that Breadon guy give you the spur without a squawk—"

Malcolm adjusted his plasta-rimmed spectacles. He said, almost stubbornly, "Our situation is grave. There must be no bickering."

"Bickering your Aunt Jenny! What do you call that?"

Sparks jerked a contemptuous thumb toward the group from which they were separated. Upon disembarking, only Greg and Sparks had moved to make a careful examination of their damaged craft. The others, more or less under the direction of Breadon, were making gestures toward removing certain necessaries from the skiff. Their efforts, slight and uncertain as they were, had already embroiled them in argument.

The gist of their argument, so far as Greg Malcolm should determine, was that everyone wanted "something" to be done, but no two could agree as to just what that something was, and no one seemed to have any bursting desire to participate in actual physical labor.

J. Foster Andrews, all traces of his former panic and confusion fled, was planted firmly, Napoleonically, some few yards from the open port of the life-skiff, barking impatient orders at little Tommy O'Doul who—as Greg watched— stumbled from the port bearing a huge armload of edibles.

Tina, the maid, was in a frenzy of motion, trying to administer to the complaints and demands of Mrs. Andrews (whose immaculate hair-do had suffered in the frenetic minutes of their flight) and Crystal Andrews (who knew perfectly well there were sweaters in the life-skiff) and Miss Maud (who wanted a can of prepared dog food and a can-opener immediately, and look at poor Cuddles, momsy's 'ittle pet was *so* hungry).

Bert Andrews was sulkily insisting that it was nonsense to leave the warmth and security of the skiff anyway, and he wished he had a drink, while the harassed, self-appointed commander of the refugee corps was shouting at whomever happened, at any given moment, to capture his divided and completely frantic attention. His orders were masterpieces of confusion, developing around one premise that the castaway crew should immediately set up a camp. Where, how, or with what nonexistent equipment, Breadon did not venture to say.

"You see what I mean?" demanded Sparks disgustedly.

GREG MALCOLM saw. He also saw other things. That their landing spot, while excellent for its purpose, was not by any manner of means an ideal campsite. It was a small, flat basin of sandy soil, rimmed by shallow mountains. His gaze sought these hills, looked approvingly on their greenness, upon the multitude of dark pock-marks dotting them. These caves, were they not the habitations of potential enemies, might well become the sanctuaries of space-wrecked men.

He saw, also, a thin ribbon of silver sheering the face of the northern hills. His gaze, rising still skyward, saw other things—

He nodded. He knew, now, where they were. Or approximately. There was but one planet in the solar system which boasted such a phenomenon. The apparent distance of the Sun, judged by its diminished disc, argued his judgment to be correct. The fact that they had surged through an atmospheric belt for some length of time before finally meeting with disaster.

"Titan," he said. "Hyperion possibly. But probably Titan."

Sparks' gaze, following Greg's upward, contracted in an expression of dismay.

"Dirty cow! You mean that's where we are?"

"I believe so. There's Saturn, our mother planet, looming above us as large as a dinner plate. And the grav-drag here is almost Earth norm. Titan has a 3,000 mile diameter. That, combined with the Saturnian tractile constant, would give us a strong pull."

Sparks wailed, "But Titan? Great morning, Malcolm, nobody ever comes to Titan. There ain't no mines here, no colonies, no—" He stopped suddenly, his eyes widening get farther. "And, hey—this place is *dangerous!* There are—"

"I know it," said Greg swiftly, quietly. "Shut up, Sparks. No use telling the others. If they don't guess it themselves, what they don't know won't alarm them. We've got to do something, though. Get ourselves organized into a defensive community. That's the only way—"

Ralph Breadon's sharp, dictatorial voice interrupted him. "Well, Malcolm, stop soldiering and make yourself useful."

And J. Foster, not to have his authority usurped, supplemented the order. "Yes, Malcolm, let's get going. No time for daydreaming, my man. We want action."

Sparks said, "Maybe you'll get it now, fatty." under his breath, and looked at Malcolm hopefully. But his companion merely nodded, moved forward toward the others, quietly obedient to the command.

"Yes, sir," he said.

Hannigan groaned and followed him.

CHAPTER THREE

BREADON SAID, "All right, Tommy, dump them here. I have a few words to say." He glanced about him pompously. "Now, folks, naturally we want to get away from here as soon as possible. Therefore I delegate you, Sparks, to immediately get a message off. An SOS to the nearest space cruiser."

Hannigan grinned. It was not a pleasant grin He took his time answering. He spat thoughtfully on the ground before him, lifted his head. He said, "A message, huh?"

"That's what I said."

"And what'll I send it with?" drawled Sparks. "Tom-toms?"

Breadon flushed darkly.

"I believe the life-skiff was equipped with a radio? And theoretically you are a radio operator?"

"Finest radio money can buy," interpolated J. Foster Andrews proudly. "Put a million credits into the *Carefree*. Best equipment throughout."

Sparks looked from one to another of them, grinned insolently. "You're both right. I am a radio operator, and there was a radio. But we crashed, remember? On account of some dope's sleeve got caught in the master switch—"

"That will do!" snapped Breadon angrily. He stared at the bandy-legged little redhead. "You mean the radio was broken?"

"It wasn't helped none. The tubes was made out of glass, and glass don't bounce so good."

Greg Malcolm said thoughtfully, "Sparks, can't you fix it?"

"Well, mebbe. But not in five minutes. Maybe not in five years. I won't know till I get going on it."

Breadon frowned.

"I'll handle this, Malcolm," he crisped. Again to the radioman, "Well, you get to work on it immediately. And as soon as you get it fixed, send out an SOS advising the patrol where we are—"

"Speaking of which," insinuated Sparks, "where are we?"

Breadon glared at him wrathfully.

"Why—why on one of the satellites of Saturn, of course. Any fool can see that."

"O.Q. But does any fool know which one? Or shall I tell you it's Titan? And when you know that, then what? Titan wasn't named that on account of it was a pimple. It's a big place. What'll I tell the Patrol? *SOS. Stranded in the middle of we-don't-know-where, somewhere on Titan, maybe.* They'll be hunting for us till we've got whiskers down to our knees."

Breadon's irate look vanished. He looked stricken. He said, "I—I don't know. We have a compass—"

Once again it was Gregory Malcolm who entered into the conversation. He had been toying, almost absentmindedly, with a funnel taken from the skiff's stores. Into this he had poured a small portion of water; his right forefinger was pressed to the bottom of the tube, closing it. He said, "I can answer part of that question now. Enough to cut the search in half, anyway. We're in the northern hemisphere of the satellite. "

Maud Andrews looked at him sharply as if noticing him for the first time in her life.

"How," she asked, "did you know that, Malcolm?"

GREG SAID, "Watch this." He released his finger at the base of the funnel gently, carefully, taking care not to shake it. The captured water swirled and trickled through the opening. Greg said, "Notice the direction in which the water whirlpools? Clockwise. On the northern hemisphere of any normally revolving heavenly body, water released from a basin, funnel, container of any sort, swirls in that direction. In the southern hemisphere it swirls counter-clockwise. Maybe you've noticed in bathtubs, or—"

Breadon said impatiently, "Never mind the speeches, Malcolm. A very clever bit of reasoning—if it's true. Do you think you can figure out our exact latitude and longitude from that?"

Greg met his gaze levelly.

"Not from that," he said, "nor from anything else. Perhaps you've forgotten that latitude and longitude are artificial inventions of man's, based in one case on an imaginary 'equator,' and in the other on an arbitrarily appointed 'line,' like Greenwich.

"But I believe I can approximate our position and state it in such a way as to cut to a minimum the time of any search that might be made for us. That is, if a space patrol ever comes close enough to get within range of Sparks' radio."

"When," said Sparks, "and if I get it fixed."

"When," said Malcolm confidently, "you get it fixed."

Breadon gave in with as good grace as he could muster.

"Well, all right," he conceded grudgingly. "We'll let that rest for now. Meanwhile, it is apparent that we can't escape Titan—or wherever we are—immediately. That being the case, our first task will be to set up a camp. This is as good a spot as any. We'll stay right here by the ship. We'll use the ship to sleep in at nights—"

Greg coughed apologetically. "Mr. Breadon—"

"Well, what now? More funnels, Malcolm?"

"If you'll excuse me, sir—I don't believe it wise to make camp here. Nor to use the skiff for sleeping purposes."

"And why not, my man?" That was J. Foster.

"The conservation of what little fuel and power, we have, for one thing," said Greg. "Mr. Breadon's idea of using the skiff to sleep in was undoubtedly based on the plan of using the heating units. That we must not do. The time may come when we will need the skiff again, badly. We must save its fuel and electro-motors.

"And as for making camp here beside the ship—"

He hesitated. Crystal Andrews, her voice a trifle edged, as had been that of her father, prodded him for reply.

"Well?" she demanded. "Go on, Malcolm…"

"It wouldn't be safe, Miss. This is an exposed and vulnerable spot. Titan has—dangerous denizens." The words came reluctantly. "It would be much safer to take refuge in the hills. In one of those caves up there."

Crystal gasped, "Caves? Us—living in a cave. Ridiculous!" J. Foster echoed her words vehemently. Breadon laughed curtly; Mrs. Andrews made a gesture of repugnance with a slim, pale, exquisitely manicured hand. Bert Andrews snorted. Of the tycoon's family, only Maud Andrews showed any inclination to heed the secretary's suggestion. Her old eyes glinted shrewdly; her head made the ghost of a pleased nod.

BUT OTHERS more openly approved his plan. The maid, Tina, watching Malcolm with curious attentiveness, nodded and said, "That is wise. I have heard tales about Titan and its—its denizens." Tommy O'Doul grinned delightedly. He said, "Caves! Boy, caves! Old-time stuff, huh, Greg?" And Sparks Hannigan had said, "That's right, folks. And it's past noon now. Might as well get going right away so's we can get settled before dark. Right, Greg?"

And yet again there was the counter-play, the balance of Breadon's wealth, Breadon's name and Breadon's accustomed authority to the calm, sane logic of the slim young secretary. Breadon's curt laugh changed to something definitely antagonistic; his words sheered the muttering like a keen blade.

"Very interesting, Malcolm. But wholly impractical and completely absurd. We will remain here. And now—" He glanced at the high-riding sun. "And now I think we should eat before setting up our camp. Tommy, Hannigan—bring the electro-stove from the skiff. Tina, prepare lunch. We'll pursue a more intelligent discussion of our situation on full stomachs. Malcolm, bring cases from the skiff. We'll build a rough table out here in the open."

He scowled impatiently, authoritatively about the strangely silent group.

CHAPTER FOUR

AT THAT MOMENT Gregory Malcolm realized what he must do. It was not a pleasant realization. Greg Malcolm was an easy-going, a peaceful, a placid man. The secretarial type. Sparks had called him a—what was it?—a "stuffed shirt." Never, save in rare moments of dreamful imagining, had Greg ventured to impress his opinions, his will, upon the desires of fellow men.

But he, of all those now surrounding him, seemed to understand, fully and completely, the crisis which now faced their refugee group. And he—it was made apparent to him by the pompousness of J. Foster Andrews, by the mulish petulance of Bert Andrews, by the aloof hauteur of Crystal and Mrs. Andrews, by the suicidal "orders" just given by Ralph Breadon—he alone was, in this moment of need, capable of deciding the destinies of the Earth-exiles.

J. Foster Andrews had the acumen and common-sense to lead them—but he had not the requisite knowledge. Breadon had the training, the space-experience—but he lacked solid horse-sense, and his decisions were too strongly flavored by his own savor of self-importance. Yet if they, ten humans, were to exist for a week…a month…a year…until help reached them, someone must command And he, Gregory Malcolm, was the only one capable of taking into his hands the reins of rulership.

It was a knowledge at once heady, intoxicating and frightening. But—there it was. It had to be faced. And Greg moved, grimly but methodically, to the accomplishment of that which he deemed necessary. He halted the radioman with a gesture.

"Wait a minute, Sparks. Tommy, wait. Tina!" And he faced Breadon firmly. "We are not going to do that, Mr. Breadon," he said. "It would not be wise. We are not going to do it."

Breadon's brown features darkened with swift anger.

"What? What's this?"

And J. Foster Andrews waddled forward, puffing irate astonishment. "Here, here, Malcolm. What in the world do you mean? This is—hrrumph!—blasted impertinence, sir. Insubordination."

Malcolm held his ground, his pale cheeks oddly flushed.

"We are not going to do these things," he repeated slowly, definitely. "Breadon—" It did not occur to him that unconsciously he had abandoned the respectful, formal "Mr." which heretofore he had never omitted. "Breadon, your orders clearly indicate that you have not in any way grasped the full implications of our plight.

"I have already warned that we should not make needless use of our limited fuel and power reserves. Yet you've told Tommy to bring the electro-stove. I have hinted that there are dangerous antagonists on Titan, yet you wish boldly to tempt attack by cooking and eating here on this exposed plain in broad daylight. Common sense should advise you of the folly of eating what few food stores we hold in reserve, yet you calmly command the preparation of a full and wasteful meal."

He did not make mention of the other, perhaps irrelevant but nonetheless rankling detail. That never once had Breadon offered to help in these doings, nor had any member of the Andrews clan volunteered to assist; that the physical labor had arbitrarily been assigned to those of lesser caste— himself, Hannigan, young Tommy, Tina.

"Therefore," he continued doggedly, "I, for one, am refusing to obey your orders. I do so because I must. Call it 'insubordination' if you wish, Andrews—" The older man spluttered incoherently, mauve-jowled. "—but I would call it the, 'will-to-exist.' The law of survival. I mean to survive on this unknown, hostile planet. That can't be done if we squander resources as Breadon apparently means to.

A MOMENT of tight silence answered his outburst. A slow, awkward movement stirred through the little group. It was, Greg sensed, a movement of alignment. He could sense, rather than see, the unconscious coalition of his sympathizers behind him; could see, without sensing, the outraged drawing-together of the Andrews husband and wife, *fille* and *fils,* beside Breadon. One there was whose bright, intent eyes were clouded with uncertainty...Maud Andrews. Then, as if irresistibly drawn by the bonds of blood, she too looked to Breadon as her spokesman.

Breadon's voice was a thick flame of wrath.

"So that's the way it is, eh, Malcolm? Well, this had to come sooner or later. Might as well have it over with right now. Get the glasses off, my pale young friend. One leader is all we'll have around here."

He stepped forward, bigger, browner, heavier than Malcolm. There was a rustle behind Greg; Sparks had stepped to his side, was pressing something into his hand.

"This'll make him behave, Greg."

"Put it away," said Greg coldly. "We'll have better use for firearms later on. I'll handle this the way Breadon wants." Slowly, painstakingly, he removed his plasta-rimmed glasses, slipped them in a Lucite case, slid the case into a pocket, removed his trimly cut double-breasted business coat, handed it to the grumbling little redhead.

"But look—" growled Sparks. Then stopped. There was a newness about Greg Malcolm that stopped him. With the goggles removed, he thought dimly, Malcolm's eyes looked different. Less soft and meeky-mosey. They were like—sort of like chunks of grey flint. And Greg wasn't as skinny as he had looked, now that you saw him with his coat off. He was lean, yes—but there was a greyhound whippiness to his leanness; a tight, spring-coiled sort of strength.

"Well?" said Greg. "You're ready, Breadon?"

Breadon's answer was a sudden, rushing charge. One of the women gasped; there came the whipping splat of flesh striking flesh, then all noises muted save the sound of two men meeting in face-to-face conflict. Breadon's left jarred Greg back, his right swung wide and hard to put a swift end to the dispute—

But found no target. For leanly, deftly, with pantherlike swiftness, Greg was out from under the blow; his own left, probing sharply, flicked once…twice…again into his antagonist's face, jarring Breadon, shocking, stunning him, halting his bull-like rush and jolting him back on his heels.

Maddened, Breadon whirled, seeking this will-o-the-wisp whose jabbing lefts stung like salt in an open wound. He growled something that was never completed, for knuckles bruised the word against his lips. Blood sprang, saline and hot in his mouth; the taste of it edged his rage to inchoate blindness, he flailed out recklessly, forgetful of anything he had previously known about fighting.

And that was his undoing. Against his bulky charge, Greg could do nothing but fight the kind of fleeting defensive battle he had learned in long hours at the gymnasium. A maddened warrior like this was a different matter, though; he was a vulnerable fighter.

Calmly and with infinite assurance, Greg stepped inside Breadon's swinging arms, beneath his faulty guard. His right hand came up once, sharply, to Breadon's jaw. The big man spluttered pink spray, lifted his arms. Again Greg lashed out with his left, this time to the belly; Breadon gasped and his mouth remained open, sagging.

Like the whipping length of a python, Malcolm threw that lean, deadly-sure right again—this time squarely to the other man's jaw at the spot where jawbone meets the ear. The blow cracked in the dull, astonished silence like the chunk of a heart-biting axe on timber. Breadon straightened slowly, numbly, in a meaningless reflex. The fire went out of his eyes; their brownness dulled like sun-faded velvet. Then he fell. As a tall building might fall. Crumpling...the knees folding first, the body sagging, the shoulders, the head helpless and rolling. In sections. He rolled once and lay still.

Sparks Hannigan said, "Gawddlemighty..." His voice was feeble, awestruck.

Greg Malcolm's fists, falling to his sides, uncoiled reluctantly. As if they had gripped the fiery baton of his anger, the battle-urge slipped from him with their unclenching. He drew a deep breath to steady his ragged breathing, nodded to the wide-eyed Tina.

"Take care of him," he said. "Water. He'll be all right in a minute." He faced the others, his manner an odd mixture of apology and aggressiveness. "Breadon said there could be but one in command," he said. "Let us hope that is definitely settled. For all time. And now I will ask all of you to help. Our first step will be to strip the skiff of the equipment we may need and carry it into the hills. In one of those caves we will make our headquarters."

But the fight was to have its aftermath. Crystal Andrews it was who burst from the little knot before him to kneel at her fiancé's side, taking Breadon's head in her arms, glaring rage and hot defiance at Greg.

"With you?" she cried. "With *you,* you—cheap, upstart bully? Not in a million years. Ralph—Ralph, dear, are you all right? Did he hurt you?"

She jerked the water-soaked handkerchief from the maid's hands, pressed its coolness to Breadon's sand-bruised forehead. Breadon's eyes opened, dazed at first, then full of awareness, sultry, indignant, incredulous. He moved to get on his feet again. Greg stared at him coldly.

"Get up if you want to, Breadon. But don't get up fighting..."

Hannigan chuckled, "He ain't hurt much. Just his conceit. It's punched full of right and left hand wallops."

"That will do, Sparks!" snapped Greg. He looked at the others, replacing his glasses carefully, a vague sorrow in his eyes, defeat in his voice despite his victory. "You all feel that way? You still refuse—?"

Crystal Andrews cried out, "Talk! Talk! Will you stop talking and go? Go to the hills if you want to. Leave us in peace. We don't want you and don't need you. Go to the hills—and good riddance to you..."

The tiny gimlet of hurt that lay somewhere deep inside of Greg twisted once more at her words, snapped, became suddenly cold and bitter. His jaw set. He nodded to Sparks.

"Very well. If that's your desire. Sparks, there are four of us, six of them. Take an inventory of all equipment and supplies in the skiff. We will take exactly four-tenths of everything...fuel, power units, food, water...everything. Get going. I'll help you directly."

Sparks said, "The radio?"

"We'll take that. You're the only one capable of repairing it. We'll save them in spite of themselves. If we can."

Sparks said, "Aye, sir. Come on, Tommy, Tina." He started toward the crashed skiff; Greg hesitated, feeling the desire to say something, to make one final plea, not knowing what to say or how to say it, restrained by the yet cold anger etched on his heart by Crystal's scorn. Then he too turned to help. A strident voice halted him.

"Just a moment, young man..."

"Yes, Miss Andrews?"

Maud Andrews, Cuddles firmly cradled to her ample bosom, left her brother's side and marched toward the life-skiff. "Tell Sparks to make that a fifty-fifty division," she said. "There will be five of us in the hills."

ENID ANDREWS bleated faintly. Crystal, still kneeling, stared at her aunt incredulously. J. Foster Andrews vented his indignation in a sudden, blustering roar. "Maud. Don't be a blasted idiot. Come back here this minute."

Maud Andrews continued to surge inexorably forward.

"I'm not," she grunted, "being an idiot. It's you who are, my dear, fat, dimwitted brother. I'm a selfish, pampered old fool, but I know common-sense when I hear it, and I know a man when I see one. Furthermore, silly as you may think it, I have a ridiculous desire to keep on living. I may have to work to do that, and I'm not, overly fond of work, but if Mr. Malcolm will have me—?"

"Just plain 'Malcolm,' Miss Andrews," said Greg gravely, gratefully. "And I'm happy you see it my way."

"Tut... I'm not doing you a favor, Malcolm. I'm just looking out for myself, as I always do. Well, Sparks, don't stand there yawping like my thick-pated brother. What can I do to help?" She waddled away.

Greg glanced hopefully at those still waiting, immobile. "Won't you—" he began. "Won't the rest of you—"

The eyes that met his were glacial. Bert Andrews, thick-lipped and bridling, snarled disdain. "The hell with you, Malcolm. The sooner you get out of here, the better."

Greg said, "We'll let you know where to find us. If you should—should need us, just call."

"We won't need you." That was Crystal, coldly.

"I hope you won't," said Greg. "I sincerely hope you won't..."

CHAPTER FIVE

SPARKS HANNIGAN came out grinning. He said, "This one looks like the business, Greg. Plenty of room. Dry and warm. It's even got a natural flue-vent so's we can have a fireplace inside."

Greg nodded, pleased.

"Sounds good. I was beginning to think we'd never find a suitable cave. This one's within easy reach of that spring, too; that solves the fresh water problem. Well, we might as well get settled. Getting toward evening."

Tina glanced at the sky, surprised. "So soon? I didn't know it had taken us so long. It seems as if only a few hours ago it was noon."

"It was," grinned Greg. "Titan's days are shorter than Earth's. Its diameter is only about 3,000 miles. By Earth measurements you'd say Titan had a sixteen hour day."

"And the 'day,'" grumbled Sparks, "ain't none too bright at that. On account of—we're so far from the Sun."

"You haven't seen the worst of it. Right now we're on the Sun side of Saturn. We revolve about our primary once every 500-odd hours. Since Saturn is so large, when we are to the lee of it, it eclipses us entirely. So for about five days every Titan 'month' we suffer a complete blackout."

"And that—" Greg sobered. "That is another reason the others should dig into a good warm cave. It gets plenty cold during that eclipse period. An open camp on an exposed plain—" He shook his head.

Maud Andrews said, "I can't understand why this satellite is habitable at all. I was under the impression that Saturn is a frozen planet."

"It is. Its surface temperature is approximately 300° below zero, Fahrenheit. But the warmth of its numerous satellites is one of the astonishing discoveries made by the early space explorers, fifty or sixty years ago. Scientists have not yet explained the matter satisfactorily. Some say the tremendous mass of Saturn, the waves of atmospherics set up by its swirling motion and the 'grindstone' of its ring, form an electronic barrier-shield for the satellites. Still others believe that frigid Saturn acts as a gigantic mirror or solar reflector for its children."

"But Greg—" That was Tommy O'Doul. "Why ain't there any colonies here if the climate's O.Q.? Men live on Venus, where it's hot as billy-be-hanged, and on Uranus, which is nothing but a ball of ice, and on a bunch of cold, airless asteroids—"

"Economics, Tommy. The simple, single dictator of mankind's every venture. Venus has valuable vegetation.

Uranus and the asteroids have important metals that can't be duplicated in Earth's laboratories, the asteroids have rare ore deposits. There is not—or at least there has not as yet been discovered—anything native to Titan that cannot be mined or made elsewhere more cheaply, more easily. Someday man's ever-expanding frontiers will claim this satellite as a colony, too. But now that the entire universe is open to man, the human race can increase a million fold and still allow every soul more lebensraum than he can possibly use."

Sparks Hannigan gazed at him admiringly.

"It's stoo-pendous," he said.

"Titan? Not any more so than—"

"Not Titan. You. You know everything, don't you? Pal—" Sparks shook his head. "I sure had you figgered wrong. I thought you was a soft-soaping dope. So then you got us off the *Carefree* onto the skiff, cooled Breadon like a herring, declared yourself *It* and made us like it—"

Greg said, "Nonsense. I just happened to— Oh, nonsense! Shall we go into our new home?" But he flushed.

By evening—Titan's short, grey shadowed evening, the only logical unit of duration by which they could live so long as they remained captive here—their new cave home began to take on some semblance of lived-inness.

Vegetation was abundant on the hillsides. Sparks and Tommy had gathered heaps of dry faggots while Greg built a crude stone fire place underneath the flue-vent Sparks had reported; shortly thereafter the women had a cheerful blaze crackling on the hearth, and mingled with its grateful warmth was the odor of a savory stew, welcome scent to the nostrils of five who had worked long and hard in gathering the vegetables that had gone into that potage.

"Eat nothing," Greg had warned, "dig nothing that does not show signs of having been eaten, dug or picked by wild animals. Later we can make chemical analysis of dubious foods to determine their edibility. For the present we will depend on the most certain test, the acceptance by other flesh-and-blood creatures."

He had also permitted that a single can of bouillon concentrate be used in the stew. "For flavoring. There is so little food in reserve that we must save it against the cold, dark days when we can't get out to gather supplies. Later on we'll have fresh meat."

He looked thoughtfully at Cuddles, sniffing, yapping excitedly by the fireplace, and Maud Andrews, with a swift, maternal gesture, swept the poodle into her arms and glared at him belligerently.

"Oh, no you don't. You'll eat me first!"

"I wasn't thinking of that," said Greg indignantly. "I had something else in mind. A poodle, eh? Hmmm…"

Tina and young Tommy came into the cave, arms full of fresh and fragrant ferns which they dumped beside a wall. Greg, glancing at them, could not curb his astonishment at the overwhelmingly sudden change that had come over Tina. During the *Carefree's* cruise, during the years he had worked for old J. Foster, he had seen the girl a thousand times—but never, he discovered now, really *seen* her before! Always she had been a dim, dusty figure in the background. A foil for the spoiled, immaculate perfection of Enid Andrews, the glittering, heart-stopping beauty of Crystal.

Now, viewed as a woman and a comrade, he was aware that she was lovely herself. Slim as a rush, and yielding strong as that same wild water-flower; dark-eyed; hair as the Martian midnight with live lights glinting in it, too, as the stars glinted over the Martian deserts; soft, white hands, graceful but capable—

But here! he thought, what nonsense was this? He had work to do. And this was no time for weaving poetic cadences about a girl who was practically a total stranger I

Now she laughed, gaily, her very laughter seeming to burst from a heart happy with newfound freedom. And she said, "It was just as you said, Greg. We found the ferns down by the spring. Did we bring enough of them?"

Greg said, "Enough for tonight. They'll make comfortable beds. Later on Sparks and I will build real beds for all of us. Thank goodness there was a tool-chest on the skiff. You folks ready to eat?"

Hannigan lifted his nose from the fireplace.

"Ready? *I* been ready for a half hour, and my stummick's been ready for a week…"

And somehow it didn't seem at all surprising to Greg that Maud Andrews should be the one who, sleeves rolled up, face flushed with hearth-heat, warmth and good fellowship, seized the ladle, beat on the side of the pot vigorously and bawled, in what was far from a wealthy socialite's cultured tone, "Come and get it! Come and get it!"

SO, SOMEHOW, the first day was over…and the second day, too…and a week of Titan's sixteen hour days slid past so quickly that Greg could not truly say where they had disappeared.

Duties, chores, at first chaotic became matters of mere routine as one or another of the little band took them on his own shoulders. Maud Andrews, who on the second day bluntly and surprisingly startled everyone with the pronunciamento that henceforth there would be, "—no more of this 'Miss Andrews' stuff; call me Aunt Maud; I'm old enough to have mothered every last one of you," set herself up as cook, thus freeing Tina to take care of the multitude of other household—or cave-hold—duties. And an excellent cook she turned out to be, performing miracles with the odd, variegated samples of produce brought to her by the rest of the group.

Her once-aroused suspicion flared again when Greg casually requested, one day, permission to take Cuddles for a little run in the woods. She clucked to her pet, turned him over to Greg, but watchfully.

"I don't know what you have in mind, Greg Malcolm. But if you come back here with any sinister looking pieces of meat and no Cuddles—"

"I'm hoping to come back," confessed Greg, "with both meat and Cuddles. He's a poodle, isn't he? Well, he's always been a lap-dog to you, but I have an idea maybe his heritage will overcome his habits when I get him out into the woods. The poodle, in its earliest beginnings, used to be a hunting dog, you know. It was bred and trained especially for that purpose. Of course his nose may have been ruined by being pampered, but—"

"My Cuddles," exclaimed Aunt Maud, "a hunting dog?" She looked horrified.

Greg said slyly, "I hope so. He wouldn't be the first member of this party to prove his true worth beneath a thin veneer of civilization."

Aunt Maud's cheeks were red, but it might have been the warmth of the fire. And maybe the wood-smoke made her eyes shine like that, too. She pushed Greg roughly.

"Oh, run along," she ordered. "But mind you bring him back unchanged."

"Okay, Auntie," Greg said.

Greg brought him back, but not unchanged. For the poodle had, amazingly, reverted to type, once set on the trail of wild game. Greg carried back to the dinner table two small creatures, one vaguely resembling a squirrel, one definitely allied to the rabbit family, plunked them proudly before his companions.

"Don't give me credit. It was the purp. He's a humdinger. You should have seen him tree that squirrel—or whatever it is. And that rabbit-thing—he went scrambling halfway down a warren after it. Didn't you, Slewfoot?"

The dog yerped happily. Aunt Maud moaned.

"Slewfoot? Oh, my gracious! Cuddles, come here to momsy-womsy right away. Did nassy-mans call him—"

Cuddles made no move to obey. Greg whistled, and the dog looked up. "Okay, Slewfoot. Go to momma…" And the dog pranced over to Aunt Maud. Greg grinned. "I think he likes his new name better," he said.

Slewfoot yerped again in an ecstasy of approval.

AND SO, gradually, life became easier and smoother and happier for the quintet of cave-dwellers. Beds took the place of piled ferns, the woodpile towered toward the cove roof against the days of dark and cold which, according to Greg's computations, might be expected within the next week or so, food was varied and plentiful, and a needed food was supplied when Tommy O'Doul marched triumphantly home with a bawling kid in his arms.

Sparks glared at him.

"Hey, youngster, what did you tote that home for? We ain't got no room for pets. And that thing ain't ripe to be et yet."

Tommy said, "I had to bring it. It was the only way I could make its mom follow me. See?"

And sure enough, a few yards away, anxiously eying its captive offspring, was a mother goat. Or something like a goat, anyway. Sparks caught on then. A flying tackle and the camp had corralled its first head of livestock. And from then on there was milk.

And there were songs in the evening, and card games and stories and compensations for the long, hard tasks of the daytime. Sparks labored on his radio set, though without too much hope. "Smashed to hell and gone, Greg. The tubes is the wust part. I could jockey the wires around. But glass—"

Greg looked thoughtful. "I wonder," he said. "I wonder? Well—do what you can with the metallic parts."

So they waited and worked, and in some dim corner of their minds continued to hope for the release which all in some vague fashion expected might come "someday." And their camaraderie was great and wholesome, but there was a single subject they never mentioned. The other quintet on the plain below. From their hillside eyrie they could see the other camp, but by common consent they, made no effort to approach Breadon's followers. They had offered assistance and it had been refused. They could do nothing more, now, unless—

The unless came sooner than they expected. In the still of the night it came in the dark, multi-mooned Saturnian night, when Greg and his comrades were all asleep in their bunks.

Greg woke with a strained feeling that he could not at first identify. He only knew, as a newly awakened sleeper dimly knows, that something was amiss.

Then, as he listened, he heard it again. The sound of a firing rifle. And the thin, muted whisper of a cry from the clearing below. A voice lifted in dismay.

With a start he was on his feet.

"Sparks!"

Hannigan bounced from his blankets like a redheaded ball of rubber. He was on his feet, scrubbing his eyes with the backs of his hands, even before he knew he was awake.

"Smatta? Whuzzup, Greg? Smatta?"

"Below!" roared Greg. "The party in the valley—they're in trouble of some kind. Get your gun and come on..."

CHAPTER SIX

THE OTHERS were awake now. Young Tommy was aquake with excitement. He made a headlong dash for the dry niche wherein were stored the arms of the cave-dwellers, came back dragging three rifles, handed one to Greg and another to Hannigan.

"Let's get going, Greg!" he yelped. "Golly Moses, what do you think it is? Animals, maybe? Or people? Damn, let's get going…"

Greg took the spare rifle from him firmly.

"*We'll* go; *you* stay." Then, in swift contrition as the lad's face fell measurable inches, "Someone must guard the cave while we're gone, Tommy. Tina, build up the fire and put a kettle on. Aunt Maud—"

The old woman nodded grimly.

"I know. We'll have hot water ready. And bandages if you need 'em. Run along…"

How they ever got down that mountainside so quickly was ever afterward a mystery to Greg. It was not exactly a painless descent; their progress was a series of runs, falls and buttock-bruising slides. The footing, in broad daylight, was precarious at best; with only sallow Saturn and the aura of the Rings to illumine their way, it is a wonder they ever reached the plain whole, in a single piece.

To add to their frenetic haste, in their ears there rang the constant challenge of gunfire. Crimson flashes lit the flatsward below, once a whining slug, miserably aimed, made both of them duck instinctively as it shrilled somewhere over their heads, *spanged!* against a rock behind them, went ricocheting off into the darkness.

For now they were on level ground, and mingled with the rattle of arms there was another sound, the purling whimper of tongueless, inhuman things astir and hungry. Greg had once heard, on Earth, the furtive night-passage of a jackal tribe; the soft, half plaintive mewlings, the incessant scrape of scrabbling paws, the ammoniac stench of unwashed bodies. He thought of this now, sharply, as he heard these mutterings, smelled these rank odors, strained his eyes to determine contours in the darkling night.

Hannigan complained, "You see 'em, Greg? It's dark as a whale's gut. I can't see nothing. What'll we fire at? Are our folks out in the open or in the skiff? We might hit them if—"

Greg said, "We'll know in a minute." As they moved forward he tugged from his belt the weapon he had been holding in reserve; the one such weapon found amongst the stores of the life-skiff; one he dared use but infrequently because once its charge was exhausted he had no way of replenishing it. "We should be near enough now. Spot 'em quick and fire while there's light."

He jerked the trigger of the Haemholst flame pistol. A writhing streamer of ochre speared from its muzzle, lighting the plain with a hot and eerie effulgence. Like a fiery dart it blazed into the heart of the pack surrounding the life-skiff. By its lingering gleam Greg saw, with stomach-churning repulsion, the creatures which attacked.

Neither men nor wolves were they, but a cruel parody on each. Lean, hair-matted beast-things running on four legs, semi-human of feature but with loose lips snarling back from yellow fangs; fingered paws long-clawed; indescribably evil and filthy; the more inhuman because they embodied so many physical attributes of Man.

Their pack must have numbered three score, ranging from gray-pelted old ones to skinny, ragged pups. Apparently they had surprised the plateau party in the open, allowing them no time to remove their precious campstuffs, because the ground about, around and before the skiff was littered with a refuse of clothing, blankets, supplies and equipment, cases and scraps of food.

It was for this last that the wolf-men had attacked, because even as the ochre beam found their midst, they were scrambling hungrily about the campsite, avidly gobbling all edible scraps they could nose out. A few more aggressive ones scented richer victuals; these it was who, despite the sporadic fire from within the skiff, snuffled, clawed and clamored at the port.

UNTIL the heat-beam struck them. That put an end to their hunger and their blood-lust. Like any wild woodland animal, they had no fear of firearms; they had no experience with them. Bullets that struck, killed; wolf-men untouched by bullets had no way of associating hurt with a sharp burst of sound and a strange, unfamiliar powder-scent.

But light—light that burned the hair and scorched the flesh; light that spared not one of them, but spread to dose all with its heatful pain—that was something different. As the beam struck and spread, snuffings changed to bestial screams of fear and pain. Those nearest the beam's focal point felt no pain; they died instantly, charred hulks that crisped and sank, shapeless, to the ground. And from these strangely altered, swiftly dead companions the others fled, howling in shrill alarm. Their footsteps were the dry patter of leaves on shale; they broke and ran wildly for the nether hills, tonguing shrill ululations of hurt.

Then the door of the skiff opened cautiously; dim light was a sliver, a crack, an oblong. And the voice of J. Foster Andrews quavered through the darkness to their ears. It sounded shrill and afraid.

"Malcolm—is that you?"

Sparks snorted derisively. "Ain't that awful?" he demanded. "Is that you?" He raised his voice, "Hell, no, it ain't him. It's the Gray Lensman. Who'd you think?"

"Shut up, Sparks," Greg said, "Hold your fire, the wolf-things are gone. We're coming in…"

A few moments later, he and Hannigan were standing within the life-skiff.

GREGORY MALCOLM was twenty-six years old. For more than eight years he had been training himself to undergo any and all emotions without change of expression. That was, in his opinion, a prime requisite for a man whose vocation lay in a subordinate position. Now he was grateful for learning that self-control, and hoped his features were as granite-like as he tried to make them. He hoped his eyes did not mirror the astonishment, the shock, the numb dismay he felt when he first glanced about the interior of that cabin, and at those who stood before him.

It was incredible that in one short week—one very short Titanian week—so great a change could have been wrought in this haughty quintet. *His* followers were weathering the storm of catastrophe without faltering, without any relaxation of civilized standards. But Breadon's—

He studied them, his quietude concealing the sudden heartsickness he knew, his spectacles hiding the swift light of horror in his eyes. The men had not shaved, it was clear, since their crash-landing. Five day stubble lay frostily on the jowls of J. Foster Andrews, blackly on the cheeks of his son and son-in-law to-be.

Nor did slovenliness end there. Beneath the beard-growth, the skin of the men looked dirty, dingy, sallow, as if they had not washed for days. Their clothes were equally soiled and sorry. Greg saw that J. Foster's nails were dull and broken and grubby as the nails of a stevedore.

He rallied himself with an effort. These were men. They had been working hard, laboring. They could not stay immaculate. They had been in a fight.

Then he looked at the women, and knew that he made excuses vainly. It was even more disillusioning to see what had happened to Mrs. Andrews and Crystal in so short a time.

Enid Andrews, fashion-plate of two continents, one of Earth's smartest-dressed women, thrice-named by fashion authorities as Best Dressed Woman in the Solar Confederation, hobbled sloppily about on scuffed slippers, the heel of one of which had broken off and not been replaced, so that her posture sagged like a bag of meal, split at a side-seam and sifting awkwardly away" Her once elaborate coiffure was a bird's-nest of tangled braids which hung unbraided, curls that sagged limply; hastily adjusted pins and combs clung insecurely to locks that, once pearl-silver, were now day-crusted gray.

Crystal—glamorous, pulse-stirring Crystal—was in no better plight. Her gorgeous ash-gold hair was pulled severely back from a forehead which, Greg discovered, was not nearly so broad and smooth and high as he had imagined; the artificial color had rubbed from her cheeks, leaving them lustreless and sullen; her lips—ever rich, ripe, full—were pale and harsh-thin and her mouth had tight, argumentative lines at the corners. Her eyes were dark-rimmed, weary, haggard. She was, thought Greg with shocked comprehension, a tired girl.

They were all tired. Tired and beaten and dejected. All but Breadon who, even now, was eyeing Greg defiantly, as if challenging him to comment on their condition. He said, bitterly, "Thank you, Malcolm. It was a most magnanimous gesture, coming down from your hilltop castle to rescue us."

GREG said nothing. He was looking about the interior of the cabin, noticing with incredulous disfavor the way it had been abused, littered, left uncleansed. Ashes, dirty dishes, scraps of cloth and paper, fragments of cartons and dirt tracked in from outside...

But Hannigan was not bound by Greg's compunctions. He spoke his mind frankly, staring at the five skiff-dwellers with obvious contempt in his eyes.

"If you'd ask me," he said, "it's damn near time somebody come down and rescued you. Not from wolves, neither. From yourselves. You all look like you'd been drug through the butt end of a wringer."

"Well, we have," began Bert Andrews savagely. "We have been through—"

"Shut up, you fool," Breadon cut short his plaint viciously; blustered defiance that was in itself an apology. "We've been busy making a camp around here. We haven't had time to—"

Sparks drawled, "Bud, we been busy making a camp, too, in a place which wasn't already equipped with furnishings, like your'n. And I think we done a better job of it. And in between times, we found time to shave and bathe once in a while."

Andrews flushed and said stiffly, "There is a need of being provident with water. Our supply is limited—"

Greg said, "What? You mean you've been using the water reserve from the life-skiff?"

Enid Andrews answered. Excitedly. Volubly. Almost at the point of tears. She wrung her hands, and Greg could not help noticing the anomaly of those at once dirty and gem-bedecked fingers.

"We have. Oh, we have. There's no other water anywhere around here. Nor food. We've been living on concentrates...sickening, horrible stuff..."

"That's not true," flamed Breadon. "We did have other food. I made bread. I caught small game. I put out traps. There would have been plenty of food except for the wolf-men who raided tonight. They broke our stove...stole my reserves..."

"Which," mocked Sparks, "you conveniently left out for them to sniff and come a-running after? Why don't you call it a day, Breadon? Admit you're nothing but a cocky Earthlubber at heart and—"

"Why, you little whippersnapper!" Breadon took a swift step forward. But Greg had heard enough. He laid a re-straining hand on the socialite's arm. His voice was as soothing, as pleading, as he could make it.

"Haven't we had enough of that already? Look here, Breadon, let's let bygones be bygones. We've had our little quarrel, now let's act like sane and sensible humans.

"You're not situated here any too well. You've admitted you're not near a water supply. The terrain is open to attack, as is proven by tonight's incident. You've been, well—let's say 'unlucky.'

"On the other hand—we've been lucky. We've got a nice, warm cave large enough to house all ten of us easily. We have soft beds and good food and fresh milk; safety and good fellowship. With some of the things you have in here—those upholstered chairs, for instance; what remains of your equipment and supplies, we could make a veritable paradise of our cave.

"So what do you say? Let's cast in our lots together. Make it one big, happy family?"

J. FOSTER looked at him thoughtfully. Enid Andrews began to cry softly. Crystal glanced at Ralph, then at Greg, than at Breadon again. Bert Andrews stroked his chin. He said, "It sounds good—"

Breadon interrupted.

"There's just one thing, Malcolm," he said curtly. "We'll accept your—your overtures of friendship on one condition. That you'll step down from the high horse you've been riding lately, come to the realization that you're not cock-o'-the-walk around these parts."

Greg said gravely, "If you mean that our community shall be a society in which all share and share alike, I am in complete agreement with you."

"That's what I mean," said Breadon. "Of course, we all recognize that there must be leadership. As our oldest man, our most important member, Mr. Andrews is that logical leader. I can assure you, acting as his lieutenant—"

"No!" said Sparks loudly. "It's the same old thing in a different package, Greg. He wants to be boss, else he won't play. The answer is—comets to you, Breadon. We're doing all right the way we are; you're making a mess of your affairs. As far as I'm concerned, you can stay here and stew in your own gravy."

He turned toward the door. Greg said, "Wait, Sparks, I'll be right with you." And he, too, nodded at Breadon. "I fear Sparks is right, Breadon. You haven't learned your lesson yet. We're going back where we belong. We're glad to have been of some small service to you. If you ever need us again, just call. Meanwhile, my offer remains open. If you should ever decide to join us on *our* terms—"

A loud and cheerful voice interrupted him. A voice from outside, bellowing gay greeting, "Ahoy, you in there! Open the door!"

Sparks said, "Aunt Maud... What's she—?" and pulled the door open. In the oblong, against the slow gray dawn now crawling above the hilltops, stood Aunt Maud, a huge grin on her face, a tremendous bowl in her stalwart arms.

From the bowl rose a tantalizing aroma. She waddled in, plunked it on the nearest desk.

"Thought you folks might be sort of hungry after a scrap," she grinned. "Watched it from the cave. Nice, cozy place to watch a fight from. Saw morning was coming on, so I brought you down some breakfast.

"Sister—" She glanced at the sallow-cheeked Enid shrewdly. "You look sort of peaked. You too, Crystal. You look older, honey. Well, Greg—ready? We'd better be running along. Tina's got our breakfast almost ready. Fruit juice and porridge and pancakes with butter and sugar-syrup. Sounds good, eh? Well, 'bye, folks…"

And by main force she herded the two men swiftly out of the skiff. Outside, moving toward the hill, Sparks turned on her pettishly.

"Now, what did you go and do that for, Aunt Maud— you've gummed up everything. Greg was telling 'em off; just beginning to make 'em listen to reason—"

Aunt Maud grinned and winked broadly at Greg.

"Sparks, are all radiomen as dumb as you, or do you hold the championship? Greg could talk from now to doomsday and not get anywhere with that outfit. I know. They're my own haughty, independent, pigheaded flesh and blood.

"But that stew I brought them—" She chuckled and rolled her eyes delightedly. "Now, that's a real argument. The best their bellies ever listened to. Just wait and see…"

CHAPTER SEVEN

THE TRUTH of her statement was exhibited very soon. That very afternoon, in fact. The dim Titanian sun was settling toward the westward hilltops, and Greg was just putting the finishing touches to a crude grist-mill he was rigging for the women, when there came the scrape of hesitant footsteps up the rocky pathway.

Hannigan had been away since breakfast time, making a survey of the natural resources within easy distance of their cave, Greg thought it was the radioman returning.

"Hi!" he shouted over his shoulder, without looking back. "Any luck? What did you find?" Then, as no voluble, profane, fantastic answer was forthcoming, he turned around. His eyes momentarily betrayed his astonishment. "Oh... Hello, Andrews," he said.

Bert Andrews shuffled uncomfortably. His gaze held a curious mixture of wistfulness, reluctance and expectancy. He said, in a voice that was a trifle too breathlessly nonchalant, "Hello, Malcolm. Just taking a little stroll, so I thought I might drop up and see—see how you're making out." He glanced about him, obviously impressed. "Not so bad," he said. "Not bad at all. That's the cave, I suppose? See you have things pretty well straightened out. What's that?"

Greg's gaze followed his nod to the crosswork which was suspended directly above the cave-mouth; a latticework of steel, firmly wire-lashed, secured by a rope, the stretch of which dipped into the cave itself.

"Barrier-shield," explained Greg. "Hangs on a pulley. We can drop it from inside. In case of attack, you see. Slides down that groove into the channel cut in the ground, holds tight there." He grunted. "That's one of the reasons we don't have any honest-to-John furniture in our home. We had too many other important uses for the metal."

"Clever," said Andrews. "Ingenious. I—er—got to thinking over what you said this morning, Malcolm, after you left. You were right. For a group of civilized people we let ourselves get into sorry shape."

He rubbed his chin reflectively, Greg noticed for the first time that his face was no longer dark with beard; that though his clothes were still dirty, he had made an effort to straighten them, dust them. The skin of his face, though, was pink and sore; chafed.

Greg said, "What in the world did you shave with, Bert? A cross-cut saw?"

Andrews said defensively, "The electric razor won't work. The dry-cells are exhausted, and we can't use D.C. without wasting fuel. There wasn't a honed blade aboard the skiff. I used my pocket-knife. It—" he confessed ruefully, "—it wasn't very sharp."

Greg said, "Hannigan mounted carborundum sheets on a lathe wheel and put edges on a couple steak knives for us. I'll let you have one before you go back. Hey, there he is now. What's the story, Sparks?"

Hannigan came into the clearing at a trot. He was excited. He said, "Sweet Christmas cow, Greg, you know what I run across? A—What's this? Company?"

The eager, interested look fled from Bert Andrews' eyes. He said stiffly, "I—I guess I'll be running along now, Malcolm. See you again."

HE TURNED, his shoulders very stiff. Too stiff to be convincing. Greg glanced at him appraisingly, motioned the radioman to keep his mouth shut, called after the young Andrews.

"Don't go yet, Bert. We're just getting ready for dinner."

"Dinner?" The young man spun like a top. Then he recalled his dignity. "Oh—dinner. Why, I guess ours is almost ready, too. 'Bye—"

We'd be glad to have you stay," said Greg levelly, striving to keep the amusement out of his voice. "I think there's a roast tonight. Something that looks like a young suckling pig can't exactly tell, though, till we taste it. These Titanian animals are different. Then there's a salad and potatoes and beans, a fruit compote, and I think Tina baked a pie today."

Andrew's eyes widened as his lips twitched. "I—I wouldn't want to be any trouble," he said faintly.

"No trouble at all," said Greg. Then, unable longer to restrain himself, "But of course if you think they'll be expecting you—?"

"No, I'll stay," blurted Andrews hastily. "Thanks, I can wash up somewhere?"

"Inside. Ask Aunt Maud for soap. She's the custodian of that." Then, as the young man disappeared into the cave hurriedly, Greg grinned at Hannigan. "One," he said.

"You want to hear about what I seen?" demanded the redhead. "Listen, it was terrific. Great big marsh, full of the damnedest life-forms and craziest vegetation anybody ever met up with. Hot, too. Steamy, like the Grand Marshes of Venus, only not quite as stinking—"

He stopped, annoyed. "One what? You ain't listening to a word I'm saying. Don't you want to hear?"

"Later, Sparks," said Greg. "Right now I'm wondering how long it will take the others to fall in line."

IT DIDN'T take long. The citadel of stubbornness had been undermined the night of the attack, it toppled with Bert Andrews friendly visit—from which, sometime later, he staggered home glassy-eyed with an overdose of wild roast, hot vegetables, crisp greens and luscious fruits, succulent berry pie—and it crashed, violently, the next day.

Bert Andrews brought his dad up the hill, presumably to confer with Malcolm on a future mutual defensive system; the two of them lingered for lunch—and after lunch old J. Foster, with the blunt directness which accounted for his success in Earth's business world, sat back, grunted comfortably, and said, "That's the first meal I've enjoyed since I was a pup in the Service. Malcolm, you win. I'm sick and tired of this squabbling, and of our hand-to-mouth existence down there. Is there room for me in this cave of yours?"

It was no moment for gloating triumph. Greg said, "Yes, sir."

"Then I'm moving in. And so is my wife. What do you want me to do?"

Greg said, "Hannigan and I were planning to break ground for a small farm this afternoon, but this is more important. We'll go down with you and help you move up your personal things. How about..." he hesitated briefly. "How about Crystal? And Breadon?"

"I don't know," said J. Foster unhappily. "But if they're smart, they'll quit kicking against the pricks, too."

They were smart. When Andrews and his son, accompanied by Hannigan, Tommy and Greg, appeared at the skiff to move the Andrews' property, when Andrews told them bluntly that he and Enid and Bert were casting their lot in with the cave-dwellers, there was a moment of sultry silence, fraught with reluctance, anger, recrimination—then Breadon bowed to the inevitable. Not with good grace, but with grudging agreement he said, "Very well. If that's the way you want it, Mr. Andrews. If we're welcome up there, Malcolm—?"

Greg said, "You are welcome, Breadon. I told you that a week ago." And promptly forgot Breadon and Breadon's surliness as he realized that Crystal, too, had been shamed into a recollection of her feminine duty to herself. Somewhere she had found cosmetics, and somehow she had managed to clean and press out a fawn-colored desert sun-suit. Once again, ash-blonde hair combed back to a shoulder-length veil of shimmering loveliness, pale golden skin fresh and creamy and fragrant beneath the sheer silk of her abbreviated costume, she was the glamorous, crystal—lovely Crystal of more leisured days. A woman at once lovely, challenging and—desirable.

Thus the nation divided against itself was united. And thus began the second phase of the refugees' struggle to exist against staggering odds on the lonely, hostile moon of Saturn.

CHAPTER EIGHT

AMAZINGLY, the period of readjustment was not long, nor was it arduous. It was accomplished briefly, surely, in a series of emphatic object lessons. There was Enid Andrews, for instance. On her first afternoon in the cave she called Tina to her side, ordered the beautification of her face, her hair, her nails, and with a sigh of relief surrendered to the ministrations of the younger girl.

Greg, witness to this, frowned. But he motioned for silence when Aunt Maud would have made some irate comment.

That evening, by former agreement, Enid washed the dinner dishes. When Tina stepped forward to dry them, Greg stopped her.

"Sit down, Tina. Mrs. Andrews will dry them."

Enid started, gasped, stared at the huge pile appalled. Tina said, "But there are so many of them, Greg. Ten of us—"

"You have done extra work today." said Greg suavely, "to earn your rest. Mrs. Andrews is in your debt. She must work out her obligation. We have," he continued pointedly, "no servants or masters here. Courtesies must be repaid in kind."

Only twice more did the lessons have to be repeated; once when Bert Andrews gluttonously devoured an entire berry pie and was made to spend the next lunch hour picking fruit for another; again when Breadon carelessly fouled the spring by washing in it, and in penance was required to construct a clay-and-stone dam below the spring, that in the future the community might have adequate bathing facilities; after that everyone understood that he had his allotted share of work, that the work must be done, that meals, warmth, comfort and safety could be earned only by sweat and toil.

And gradually the rude cave dwelling began to take on the semblance of a home. During the short days at their disposal before Titan, pursuing its cosmic rounds, plunged into the umbra of its gigantic mother planet, every member of the refugee corps worked feverishly to prepare and fortify for the dark days to come.

It was well that they did so, for when the darkness descended, ensued a bleakness even more terrifying than Greg had anticipated. The eclipse of Titan by its parent was no mild, momentary phenomenon like the eclipsing of Earth by Luna; it was a five day cessation of all heat and light.

With the darkness came sweeping, icy winds, gales monstrously violent, and incredible cold. From a sky black and terribly came the snow, five inches of it in an hour, eight feet of it in a day. It was alarming at first. Then Greg and all of them realized that the very ferocity of the storm was their salvation. Were there to be this frightful cold *without* snow, not all the fires of Gehenna, not all the clothing and blankets in the universe, could have protected them. But the snow, dropping like a sodden, white blanket, choked and filled the mouth of their cave, piled thicker and thicker, enswaddling them in a fleecy comfort that kept out the bone-brittling blasts.

Then they thanked the foresight that had led them to build up a roof-touching fuel reserve, a store of fresh produce and game, for they could not leave their refuge. They were snowbound until Titan left the shadow of Saturn and the warmth should again melt their prison walls.

But those days were not days of idleness; they were days of accomplishment. The women, under Tina's guidance, ripped apart unneeded goods salvaged from the skiff's stores—tarpaulins, extra bedding and napery, carpeting, drapes—and restitched them into more needed, more practical articles of wearing and household apparel.

BREADON and Greg, laying aside a mutely-acknowledged hostility, pooled their knowledge and ingenuity in an effort to ascertain their whereabouts on the satellite. Neither had studied mathematics closely, a fact each now bewailed. But they had a few books on astrogation, taken from the skiff, and they had determination and intelligence. Utilizing some of their precious, dwindling store of forged metal, they constructed a crude but—they believed—reasonably accurate sextant with which, when the darkness was gone, they hoped to take celestial readings that would aid their computations.

In the making of this, Greg was forced to sacrifice something that had been for almost ten years as much a part of him as his arms and legs. His spectacles. Strangely, he did not miss them much after the first day. Their purpose had been mainly to protect him from eyestrain and headaches in a confined vocation that required much reading. But here on Saturn's satellite, health improved by hard labor, Greg had experienced no headaches. He was, in fact, almost disgustingly healthy. He could tell by the straining of his clothes at throat and chest and waistband that he was gaining weight; his appetite had improved and when night came, he did not have to read himself to sleep.

Young Tommy took upon himself the task of chronicling their exile. His method, though extravagantly romantic as befitted his years and enthusiasm for this adventure, was nonetheless efficient. He laboriously scraped smooth a wide portion of the cave-wall; on this he inscribed a calendar, a log, and a map of such portions of the satellite as they had so far explored.

Meanwhile Sparks Hannigan fretted over his damaged radio set. An accomplished bug-pounder, he took little time to get the wiring rearranged. The replacement of metal parts was a tougher problem, but it, too, he solved with the aid of their acetylene torch.

One final job, however, stopped him cold. He shook his head when he spoke of it to Malcolm.

"The tubes, Greg. It just ain't no use. We can't operate the radio less'n we got tubes, and ours is gone. I guess I'm just wasting my time."

Greg said, "Isn't there a type of radio that works without tubes? Operates on a crystal, or something?"

Sparks said, "Yeah. But it ain't got no power. We got to get a message plumb off the satellite, out into space where it can be picked up by a Space Patrol cruiser. Or the Saturn lightship."

"And that's impossible? Suppose you had glass?"

"Can you make it?" scoffed Sparks.

"Maybe," said Greg. "Glass was accidentally discovered in the first place, you know, by Phoenician sailors who built a fire on a sandy beach wherein was imbedded raw chunks of natron. We might be able to do the same."

Sparks shook his head glumly. "O.Q. So that gives us glass. We still got to blow it, and figger out some way of sucking the air out, and winding filaments. Oh, understand, I ain't saying we can't do it, Greg. But it'll take years."

Greg nodded soberly.

"Well, we'll overlook no bets. Sparks—tell you what to do. You go ahead and build one of those simple "crystal" sets, just in the event that someday a scout ship or exploration plane should come within our range. Andrews is an important man, you know. Earth won't dismiss him casually as 'Lost in Space.' We'll also, as soon as the Sun comes back, clear a wide swath in the plain below us and construct a huge SOS sign of wood and underbrush that will be visible by day and can be set afire by night.

"Then, if we should ever hear the signal of a scout ship, we'll hope they see our marker."

"If!" grunted Sparks.

"What's that?"

"Skip it," said Hannigan. "I was just making book against myself."

SO GREG maintained an optimism before the others, an optimism he did not entirely feel himself. Always he talked of the day they would leave Titan, but sometimes he wondered if that day would ever come.

And truth to tell, there were periods when he almost hoped that day would not ever come. For here, a thousand million miles from the Earth that had borne him, Gregory Malcolm had finally come into the rulership that, on Earth, he could never win, but that here was his by right of greater strength and knowledge.

He gazed about him, musing, and saw a cavern bright with candles that he had taught the womenfolk to render from the fats of wild beasts, warm with a flame he had kindled and nurtured, comfortable with furnishings he had constructed to their purpose. He saw nine men and women, a half dozen of whom had been his "superiors" aforetime, but who now looked to him for guidance, protection and leadership.

His mind's eye pierced the rock walls of the cavern and gazed, marveling, at the cosmos as viewed from desolate Titan. When these snows melted he could stand upon the hillside beneath the flaming moons of Saturn, beneath the never-ending wonder of Saturn's massive, multi-colored

Rings, and say with Defoe's ancient castaway that here he, indeed, was monarch of all he surveyed.

This was his ordained fate; this was his brave, new world; these people were his subjects. And he was, for howsoever brief or long a time, an Emperor. And the white, the whirling stars—these were his empire.

Perhaps he was not the only one of that group who saw this truth. For there was more than mere grudging lip-service in the changed attitude of Andrews and his wife and son. Bert Andrews was a changed boy. His willfulness had vanished; his allegiance to Greg was ardent. Maud Andrews' affection for Greg was an obvious thing. She saw to it that he was first fed, first clothed, first taken care of in all things; hers was an attitude of fierce maternalism, springing from a breast that had never known motherhood.

And—and there was another strange thing, too. A thing of singing glory that Greg could scarce believe, even though it's truth was exhibited to him in a thousand little ways.

Crystal Andrews!

A great change had come upon Crystal Andrews since the loss of the *Carefree*. Of the old Crystal, only one part remained. Her blindingly radiant beauty. Her selfishness, her coldness, had fled, had been banished as her accustomed languidness had been banished by the obligation of labor.

Daily her attitude toward Greg grew more intimate. From aloofness she melted into acceptance, acceptance faded and became approval. Approval waxed as transpiring events proved time and again Greg's wisdom and his right to rule; there came upon the girl an eagerness to be the first to do whatever he suggested.

This was good, and as it should be. But there was something else, too; something deeper. At first Greg could not understand it, then gradually its meaning became clear even to his wholly-masculine mind. The sudden glance…the lingering touch of hand against hand as they chanced to pass one another...the host of unnecessary little questions that brought them into contact a dozen times a day...the sweeping flush when he, looking up unexpectedly, met her gaze. All these and other things. The lithe, sure, free, but overwhelmingly feminine allure of her body, shoulder brushing his as they sat before the fireplace in the long evenings. The slow caress of her voice when she spoke his name. The moment of swift alarm—a torpid snake that had somehow wriggled into the cavern, toward the warmth of the fire—and Crystal in his arms for all too short a moment. And drawing away reluctantly when the "danger" was past.

HE SHOULD have known from these things. Or from the amused glances of Sparks Hannigan, or the increased surliness of Ralph Breadon, or from the sudden loss of gaiety on the part of Tina.

"What's the matter with you, Tina? Don't you feel well lately?"

Her eyes avoiding his. "I'm all right, Greg. It's nothing."

"But you don't sing any more. You're sure you're well? There's nothing I can do for you?"

"No." Her voice low. "No, thank you."

"But I want you to be happy. Look, Tina—let's you and me play cribbage tonight like we used to? We haven't had a game for weeks. How about it?"

"Oh, Greg—would you like to? Really?"

Her dullness slipping away from her like a dropped cape; her voice throbbingly eager. Then another voice at his elbow, a throaty, heart-stirring voice, "Oh, Greg—me, too? May I play? Will you teach me the game?"

Greg turned, smiling. "Why, of course. We'll get Sparks and make it a fourhanded game. Eh, Tina?"

But Tina drew back, her eyes hurt again and distant. Her voice faint. "N—no, Greg. You and Crystal. I don't think I want to…"

Which Greg could not understand. But gradually, out of his confusion and miscomprehension, one truth came clear. And with its coming there was a sudden singing in his heart, a fire in his veins. He loved Crystal Andrews. And Crystal Andrews loved him.

THEN one day they woke to find the floor of the cave glistening darkly with a pool of water. The snow was melting from the mouth of the cave. When they attacked the weakened snowbank with shovels and brooms, laughing and fighting their way clear of the white barrier, they discovered that the dark days had ended, that once again the sky of Titan was silver-blue and bright, that already the warmth had turned the snow mantle to chuckling rivulets that ran merrily down the hills, leaving fresh green in its wake. The miracle of Titan's "winter" had passed, and the land would again be theirs for three warm weeks.

Greg's brain was afire with a hundred projects. A viaduct to carry water into the cavern during the next cold period. They had had to depend on melted snow this time. A study of the stars with their new sextant. The clearing of ground for the gigantic signal. He turned to the others enthusiastically.

"We've got to work now, folks, as we never worked before. Tommy, I want you to get right to work on that new viaduct we were talking about. Andrews, your first job will be to replenish the wood supply. Try the west woods, that's the best timber. Tina, see what these short 'winters' do to the vegetation, will you? I don't imagine they're dead. Nature has ways of counteracting its own excesses. I believe we'll find the vegetation here on Titan is phenomenally hardy. But see, anyway.

"Aunt Maud—you and Enid set out those traps we made during the dark spell. We'll have a hot stew tonight. Breadon, suppose you and Sparks and I go down to the plain and start planning our signal system? Crystal—"

Crystal was at his side, her hand on his arm. "I'm going with you, Greg."

"What? But they need you...oh, all right..."

He smiled. Behind him Aunt Maud snorted and disguised the snort with a rattling cough. Tina looked at him oddly for a moment before she turned obediently toward where last week there had been a vegetable patch. Her eyes were hurt. Greg could not understand why.

It was not until he was halfway down the hill that he remembered he had promised to let her help with the sign project. Of course it was too late to do anything about it then. Besides, Crystal's feet were unsteady on the melting path. She needed his arm about her for support. And her hair had a tantalizing fragrance all its own...

CHAPTER NINE

IT TOOK all of the men, working steadily from dawn to dusk every day, two full weeks to construct the signal. When it was done, Greg looking down upon it from their hilltop eyrie, gazed upon it with approval and found it good.

Across the mile-wide flatness of the plain they had heaped huge piles of branches, faggots, brush, forming the letters "S. O. S." Green, they stood out boldly; withered and faded, their brownness would be equally clear.

Hannigan was pleased with his share of the work, too.

"—wire," he finished, "from the bottom of the 'S' to the cave. We just about had enough, too. Anyhow, if the ship should happen to come at night instead of in the daytime, all we got to do is push the switch, and a spark'll jump in the tinder. Send the whole signal up in flame in less time than you can say 'integral calculus.'" He frowned. "If," he added, "a ship comes at all. Which of course I couldn't say yes or no."

"It will come," said Greg absently. He said it because it was the thing to say; as a matter of habit. He was not even thinking of his words. He was thinking, now that this project had been accomplished, of other things. Of a silo that must be built. They had nine head of livestock now, due to Tommy O'Doul's persistence. The beasts would have to be provided with winter quarters. One goat in the cave had not been so bad, last month. But nine goats— Perhaps, he thought, that small cave next to ours. If we could dig into it through the west wall…make a small opening…

His lack of concentration brought a false conclusion from the third man in the group. Ralph Breadon stirred restively. "You should say," he insinuated, "if Malcolm *wants* a ship to come."

The words penetrated Greg's thoughts of the future slowly. He turned a blank, questioning look on the other.

"Eh?"

"I merely said," repeated Breadon, "that one could not condemn a man in your position for showing lack of enthusiasm in a rescue party."

Greg stared at him thoughtfully.

"Just what do you mean by that, Breadon?"

Breadon shrugged.

"Isn't it fairly obvious? Two short months ago you were a nobody. A secretary without background, position or authority. Today you're the demigod of Titan. Sir Boss. I don't complain; I merely comment. You have everything a man could ask for. Authority…security…a woman…"

The last jolted Malcolm out of his apathy. He took a swift step forward, gripped Breadon's lapels with a fist grown heavier, rougher, with labor.

"If you mean Crystal, Breadon—"

Breadon stood his ground. "Let go of me. Malcolm. I'm not going to fight you again. Of course I mean Crystal. It's perfectly obvious that you and she—Oh, hell, man! Don't be a hypocrite. After all, when people live as intimately as we do, in one little cave..."

GREG felt dark anger welling up within him like a gall-tinctured flood. Rage not that Breadon should say this thing, but that there should be cause for his thinking it. He choked, thickly, "Damn you, Breadon—there's not a thing wrong between Crystal and me. I love her, yes. And Crystal loves me. We've only been waiting till this big job was finished—"

"Then if I were you," retorted Breadon wearily, "I wouldn't wait any longer. Or is it another case of the king being incapable of doing wrong? Anyhow, I think you understand what I mean now. Two months ago a marriage between you and Crystal Andrews would have been ridiculous. Today—"

He shrugged again. Greg glared at him wrathfully, impotently, for a long moment. Then he spun on his heel, led the way down the hill to the cave. Sparks scurried along behind him anxiously. "Now, look, Greg—don't do nothing you might regret—"

"Shut up. I'll handle this."

At the cave he called all the settlers before him. They came from their tasks, surprised, wondering. He wasted no time. He broached the subject boldly.

"Because we ten are marooned here on a desert satellite," he said savagely, "without a clergyman, there is no reason we must abandon all the rights and privileges of civilized society.

Human emotions have a habit of enduring. I think it is no secret that Crystal Andrews and I have fallen in love. I intend, therefore, to marry her as soon as it can be arranged.

"Crystal—" He turned to the girl. "Do I speak for you as well as for myself?"

The girl nodded and stepped forward into the circle of his arm. "You know you do, Greg."

J. Foster Andrews looked pleased. He said, "That's fine, son. But who's going to do the marrying?"

"You are. As owner of the *Carefree,* you were also its commander. I think the space code would permit your acting in capacity of justice." Greg's anger melted. "I'm not being very formal about this, sir. Perhaps I should ask for your permission."

"You have it, my boy. And now—" Archly. "When will the—hrrumph!—happy event take place?"

Greg looked at Crystal questioningly. "Next week?" she said. "I'll have to have a little time, Greg."

"That's it, then," said Greg. "Next week. When the dark period comes."

THE LITTLE group broke up, then. One by one they murmured words of congratulation and approval to their leader and his bride-to-be and drifted away. Finally Crystal went back into the cave, and Greg was left alone with Tina, who alone of all the group, had so far said nothing. He went to her.

"You haven't told me you're happy, Tina."

She turned slowly.

"Shall I say so, Greg?"

"I want you to. Why do you act so strangely toward me, Tina? Do you dislike me? You used to—"

"I'm happy," she cried suddenly. "Now I've said it. You want me to. Are you satisfied? Why don't you let me alone,

Greg? Must I like or dislike you? You have one woman? Must you—" She broke from his side, raced forward to the edge of the hill, stared blindly down into the plain.

Greg moved after her, worried. "What is it, Tina? You're not happy. Are you lonely? Why don't you get married, too? Sparks…or Breadon…"

He stopped, his gaze over her shoulder settling on something in the valley beneath. A thing incredible to behold, but that was…yes, *was*…

"Tina!" he gasped.

At the tone of his voice she spun swiftly, anxiously. "What is it, Greg?"

"Look! Down there… A—a human!"

CHAPTER TEN

"MORE GRUEL, Marberry?" asked Aunt Maud solicitously. "Can you eat another spoonful?" She glared at those who ringed the reclining spaceman belligerently. "Why don't you let him alone?" she demanded. "Greg Malcolm, I thought you had better sense. The man's weak and sick."

Marberry's eyes were like charred pockets, but he summoned a weak smile.

"I'm all right," he said. "There isn't much more to tell. We managed' to cut free from the *Carefree* just before she crashed. Four of us. Lipstead, Hawkins, Craeburn and myself. Our skiff cracked up in a mountain gorge. Craeburn was killed, and Lipstead broke his leg. But we fixed it up in splints, and he got by.

"When the snow came—" He shut his eyes momentarily, as though to rid them of a persistently evil vision. "When the snow came we almost died. We ran short on fuel, and the skiff leaked. Then the electro-stove ran down, and we had to eat cold, canned food.

"Even so, we pulled through. But when it got warm again, Hawkins said we mustn't spend another winter in the skiff. We had to find a cave in the mountains, he said. So we abandoned the ship and started moving. It was then that they caught us."

Breadon, who had entered late, asked, "Who?"

"Natives of Titan," Greg capitulated briefly. "He described 'em to us before you came in. Savages. Cannibals. Humanoid, but no culture. Funny physical make-up, like the Uranians. Don't feel the cold at all. Murdering devils. From what he says, we're lucky they haven't found us before this."

Breadon said, "Cannibals..." and looked sallow. The supine man continued weakly.

"We had to leave Lipstead behind. He couldn't run. He drew a gun on us, threatened to kill us all if we didn't leave him. We heard his gun afterward. He must have got a half dozen of them before—before they got him.

"Then Hawkins and me split up. It was the only way, he said. One of us might be lucky. I—I guess I was. They followed him instead of me. And all the time—" His voice raised feverishly, "And all the time, we was only about ten miles from here. If we'd only known—"

Aunt Maud would stand for no more. She bustled between the invalid and his listeners, shooed them away angrily. "Run along, now. This man needs sleep and quiet. Go away."

BUT LATER, as Marberry slept the sleep of exhaustion, Greg called a council of war.

"Ten miles," he said soberly. "If those creatures are only ten miles from here, we can expect an attack almost any day. Or moment. From now on, we must keep a watch at all times. No one must leave the cave alone."

Hannigan said, "You reckon they'll find us, Greg? Titan's a big hunk of dirt."

"They're savages. Savages can follow the faintest trails of wild animals, let alone the spoor of a frightened, sick man. They'll be here."

Hannigan said, "There's one good hunk of news in the whole sorry mess. Marberry said him and his companions sent out radio SOS calls for three solid weeks. Till their radio run dry. Maybe somebody picked up one of them calls. Maybe there's help on the way right now."

"Radio. Speaking of radio, Sparks, how about that crystal receiving set you were working on? Is it finished?"

Sparks smiled sourly.

"Finished your sainted sandals! It's all washed up. Listen to this…"

He stepped to the hodge-podge of wires and coils on which he had been laboring, adjusted it. From its diaphragm came dismal sounds. Squawks, squeals, quavering vibrations.

"Static," said Breadon.

"Double it," gloomed Hannigan, "and add a thousand. The worst kind of static. An electrical disturbance field."

Greg frowned. "But that can't be, Sparks. There's no electricity around here. No generating plants or—"

"It can't be," snorted Sparks, "but it is. I don't know what makes it act that way. Maybe it's the Hylayer of this cockeyed satellite. Sun spots, maybe. Whatever it is, it sure gums up my machine." He stared at the tiny set helplessly.

Greg stirred himself.

"Well, then we'll have to look forward to fighting this battle without hope of assistance. Andrews, I want you and Tommy to inspect the cave-mouth barrier immediately, see that it's in perfect shape and reinforce it. Ralph, you and Sparks drive the livestock into the small cave so they'll be hidden. Tina, the fuel reserve?"

"Complete, Greg."

"Good. I'm going out to stand the first watch. If you need me, I'll be—"

At that moment a small figure, bristle-haired with excitement, came scampering into the cave.

"Greg!" cried Tommy O'Doul. "Greg—they're down there. On the plain. I seen them. And I—I think they seen me, too. They're heading up this way!"

A HALF HOUR later, Greg, flanked by a tight-jawed little band of compatriots, crouched in the bottle-mouth of an altered cavern.

The short time that had elapsed since Tommy O'Doul gave the alarm had been minutes of swift preparation. What little of water, food and supplies could be brought into the cave had been hustled in by eager hands. The stock had been herded into the small, adjoining cave, and boulders had been rolled against the cave mouth. The metal grill had been dropped before the mouth of their own cage; it was behind this they now crouched, through this that Greg looked out upon a lead-gray sky and green hills.

"There's one thing," said Greg. "One break in our favor. It's starting to get darker, and it's barely afternoon. We must be dipping into the penumbra of Saturn. In a little while the darkness should come, and the gales and the cold."

Hannigan said, "That ain't no break for us. Marberry said they didn't feel heat and cold."

"I know. But they can't prevent the snow falling. If it comes down like it did during the last dark spell, we will have an eight-foot fall of ice between us and our attackers."

Andrews looked at the sky anxiously.

"But until it snows, Greg?"

"We fight," said Greg grimly.

Bert Andrews, who had wriggled forward on his belly to the furthermost ell of the bottle-neck, ducked back hastily, twisted his head over his shoulder.

"Then we fight now," he rasped. "Here they come!"

It was then that the Earth-exiles saw, for the first time, the dominant race of Saturn's sixth satellite. To see was to marvel that Nature had once again—as on Earth, Mars, Uranus and Io—selected the bipedal humanoid form in creating a ruling race. Except for the thick, downy pelts that covered these Titanians' bodies, the low, slanting, bestial foreheads, the depth of breast and rapacious mouth slits, these creatures were the counterparts of man.

But there were other unapparent differences, thought Greg. Marberry had reported the Titanians impervious to heat and cold, which argued a difference in normal body temperature and perhaps a difference in basic metabolism. There must be sharp differences between man's mentality and that of these man-like beasts, as well, else they would not come seeking their interplanetary guests as the huntsman seeks his quarry.

A long, questing, silver-pelted line, they climbed the hillside path to the flat clearing before the cave. They paused there, peering about them suspiciously, nostrils wide and eyes searching. Greg realized, suddenly, that these man-things were far down humanity's scale; so much of the animal was in them that they placed more dependence in their olfactory than in their visual sense. They seemed to catch the man scent, the spoor they had been following. Their leader moved forward to the grillwork. Hannigan's shoulder brushed that of Greg as he wriggled forward.

"Now, Greg? Shall we let 'em have it?"

Greg whispered hurriedly, "When I give the word, all fire at once. Remember, we have very little ammunition. We must make every shot count. Ready?"

He glanced at his all-too-tiny fighting crew. Bert Andrews, old J. Foster, Breadon, Sparks, himself. "Tommy," he ordered, "go back into the cave!"

"Aw!" said Tommy—but obeyed. Greg glanced about him once more. Others of the Titanians had slunk to their leader's side now. Their voices, guttural and monosyllabic, carried plainly over the few intervening yards.

"Now!" cried Greg.

FIVE RIFLES spoke as one. Their conjoined thunder beat deafeningly upon the sweating cavern walls, echoed and re-echoed, ripping at Greg's eardrums. But another sound pierced the roar of gunfire. The shrill, pain-laden screams of stricken man-things. The inquisitive leader fell without ever knowing the cause of his death. A Titanian behind him opened his slit-mouth in a flat, high scream, turned to run, tearing at his gaping chest with claws that crimsoned as he tore. He took three steps, toppled, crashed. Another body was beneath his own; still another fell upon his.

Old J. Foster's lips were white. He turned to Greg, sickened and trembling.

"We can't do this, Greg. It's slaughter…"

A weak voice cackled derision. "Don't feel sorry for 'em. If they get in here, they'll show you what a real slaughter looks like. Malcolm, have you got a gun for me?"

It was the sailor, Marberry. Greg said, "Go back and rest a while longer, Marberry. We have no more guns."

"I'll get Tommy's."

"Rest. This siege may last all day, all night or for a week. You'll get your turn."

Marberry disappeared. Greg said, "Fire! Keep on firing! They're bewildered. Maybe they'll break and run."

Again the salvo of gunfire rocked the corridor, and again foremost figures slumped to the ground, slicing the ranks of the attackers. But now, peering through the grill, Greg saw that he had underestimated the manpower of the attackers. They were not a dozen or two dozen...there were a hundred of them milling, now, in the small clearing, and the path was still clogged with the silvery bodies of others lumbering to the attack.

What happened in the next hour was such stuff as nightmares are made of. At first Greg cautioned himself each time he pulled the trigger of his rifle that he must make his shot count; later he fell into a dull, scarce-comprehending state of monoexistence wherein he was conscious only of the nerveless and repeated movements of his hands. Aim...load...fire! Aim again...load...fire...aim...

And at first there was little need for aiming For the Titanians, savagely prodigal of life, knew only one way of fighting—to press forward in brute force, attempting to crush down the metal grill that stood between them and their vengeance. To fire into that thick press of bodies was sure havoc. The Titanians were weaponless save for the cudgels they whirled about their heads threateningly; nor could they break down the barrier so long as the succeeding hands of all who gripped it became the limp, impotent hands of the dead.

Then at last even their dim, animal intelligence saw that this was a losing battle. A cry rose and was shuttled from mouth to mouth. The silvery figures, now gray in ever-gathering dusk, wisped away from the cave-mouth.

"Licked 'em!" cried Hannigan. "They're running, by Peter. Look at that pile out there..."

There was awe in his voice, distaste in Greg's eyes as he looked on the motionless mound heaped before the cave. But Greg said, "Don't get rash. They may be planning a new attack. Breadon—what's wrong with you, man?"

Ralph Breadon grinned wryly. "Fortune's favored child, that's me. They didn't have any weapons to shoot me with, so I shot myself. Bounced a bullet off the grill. It came back and pinked my arm."

"Go get it dressed. There it comes!" cried Greg.

"The new attack?" Sparks whirled.

"The darkness. And the snow…"

He was right. The threatened period of darkness had descended at last. Once again Titan was within the shadow of its primary. And once again the vast winds were keening from the hilltops, the great flakes of snow were tumbling from a lifeless sky, Greg's voice was exultant.

"Now we're safe. In an hour or so we'll be behind a fortress of ice. And I don't think they'll lay siege to us in a blizzard for a solid week."

His triumph was short-lived. For even as he anticipated victory, disaster beat on the portals of their refuge. From the depths of the cave came a shrill scream, the shout of Marberry, and Tommy's frantic cry—

"Greg! Come over here! They've found the back entrance!"

THE back entrance! Greg's heart lurched. He cursed himself, suddenly, for having tried to accomplish too much in making their cavern habitable. For by so doing, he had rendered them vulnerable in a spot where would be no barrier of ice an hour hence.

The back entrance. The archway they had broken out between their large cave and the smaller one wherein Tommy's livestock was herded. Somehow the Titanians had found the other cave, rolled away the boulders, and were now attempting to get at their quarry from the rear.

Greg shouted, "Andrews, you stand guard here. One man will be enough. The rest of you—come on!"

The first of the Titanians was pushing through the cleft just as he reached the main chamber. There was a look of unholy glee on the manlike creature's thin lips as he attained the cave. But it died there, suddenly, frostily. It was not Greg who dropped him. It was young Tommy, staggering under the recoil of a rifle almost as tall as himself, firing pointblank, bouncing back to reload manfully, bawling with youthful glee, "Got him, Greg."

THEN there was no time for speech, because the Titanians were pouring through the breech in a howling, flame-eyed mob. For a moment Greg, even as he fought, felt despair touch his heart with leaden fingers. There was no grill here to bar the enemy's passage; the cleft was wide enough to admit three at a time. He and his companions were outnumbered ten, twenty to one.

But he did not, could not, take into consideration two vital facts. The first was the indomitable gallantry, of his fellow exiles. He had expected that, in defense of their lives, their possessions, their women, the armed men would fight to the last breath. And they did. Pressing forward on relentless feet. Breadon, Andrews, Bert, Hannigan. But Greg had not realized that the women, too, could fight. As in a smoke-veiled dream he caught glimpses of their activities. Aunt Maud and Tina, armed with huge ladles, dipping their weapons into a massive pot of boiling water, flinging the scalding liquid at the cold-impervious but heat-sensitive invaders. Crystal, no longer a serene and radiant beauty, but a flaming Balkyr whose ash-blonde hair tumbled about her, forgotten, gaining a vantage point at the very lip of the opening, slashing ferociously at the attackers with a monstrous cleaver. Enid Andrews racing to the wall, digging in Greg's duffle, pressing something into his hands.

"Your flame-pistol, Gregory!"

Greg grasped it eagerly. "Stand back, Crystal..."

She turned, and saw, and fled. And the ochre flame mushroomed into the heart of the still-charging Titanians. Their charge stilled, faltered, wavered, died. The stench of charred bodies was nauseous. Then there were screams of fear—and the Titanians were in rout.

Into the small cave they pursued them; from it but a handfull of the silver-pelted savages escaped. And when the last living invader had disappeared, Greg turned to his exhausted followers with a smile of weary triumph.

"We'll see no more of them," he promised. "Already the snow is a foot deep. By morning both caves will be completely walled in. And I think we've taught them to fear us. What, Tina?"

For she was standing before him; her eyes were cool and positive…there was decision in her tone.

"I thought it was all over for us a moment ago," she said. "And I knew, then, Greg, that it was a mistake for me to die without having told you. I promised myself that if a miracle occurred…and we should live…I would tell you."

He said wonderingly, "But what, Tina? I don't—"

"I know you don't, Greg. That is why I must say it. I love you. Have loved you since that first day." Her eyes were grave. Greg's were embarrassed.

He said, "But you—you shouldn't say such things, Tina. Crystal—"

"She is a brave woman, Greg. But she is not your woman. She is his."

His gaze followed Tina's across the room, to where Crystal knelt beside the injured Breadon. She was cleansing his wound, which was as it should be. But there was a softness, a tenderness, to her motions…and a look in her eyes. Greg looked away, suddenly aware that even from the beginning he had felt this barrier between them. Perhaps Crystal had loved him, for a while and in a fashion. But she loved him for his strength, his power, his ability to rule. She was a woman of the ruling class; ever her conscious trend would be toward allegiance with those who led. But in the showdown…when instinct overcame logic…

Hannigan cried across the chamber, "What, Greg?"

"I didn't say anything," said Greg gruffly.

"But you did. I heard you say—*Omigawd!*" Sparks made a sudden leap toward the bench on which rested the forgotten crystal set. "It's this. Listen…"

STATIC still boiled through the speaker of the tiny set. But now, above the static, riding its vibrations, was superimposed the sound of a human voice. And the voice was calling, over and over again.

"Space Patrol Cruiser Orestes…calling survivors of the Carefree. We are looking for you. Where are you…where are you? Come in, Carefree survivors. Space Patrol Cruiser Orestes…calling survivors…"

Greg looked at Tina. Then once again at Crystal, whose face, upturned with sudden, speechless joy, was the radiant vision of unattainable perfection. Then at Sparks, whose gaze met his reluctantly. He said, "Sparks—press the plunger."

Hannigan's hand moved slowly toward the control that would set into flame the gigantic brush-signal on the plain below. With strange reluctance, everything considered. For certainly Sparks realized as plainly as he, Greg, that the snow was falling with increasing rapidity, that the cruiser must be almost directly overhead for its signal to penetrate the raucous interference of static, that if this opportunity were lost it might be years and years before…

Sparks voice was low in his ears.

"Are you sure, Greg?"

And suddenly there was deathly silence in the cave. Never until that moment had Gregory Malcolm realized how completely was he the ruler of this tiny clan. Here, where all life and the future of life and the future of these men and women were concerned, the last great judgment was relegated to him.

He looked about him uncertainly. And what he read in his comrade's eyes surprised him. For there was reluctance in the eyes of Bert Andrews...a vague regret in those of old J. Foster Andrews...hope and pleading in those of the girl Tina...frank disapproval in those of the woman they knew as 'Aunt Maud.'

Only the eyes of Crystal Andrews, who were he to let the cruiser pass might be his wife, was there mirrored fear and apprehension...

He shook himself. And with that small gesture he shrugged from his shoulders an ermine that had lain there all too briefly. Quietly he said the words that stripped him of his sceptre, that swept away his empire of the stars.

"Press it, Sparks," he said.

"A REMARKABLY ingenious device, sir," said Captain Allengrove approvingly. "And you made use of it in the nick of time. We were just about to abandon the search when the snowy waste beneath us blossomed suddenly with that signal. I'm sorry we couldn't get here sooner, sir. But—" And he glanced about the cavern appreciatively. "But you appear to have had matters under control."

J. Foster Andrews said, "Well—er—Captain, as a matter of fact, it wasn't—hrrumph!—altogether my doing, Greg, here—"

Captain Allengrove dismissed Malcolm with a glance.

"Yes, yes, I quite understand. One couldn't expect you to take care of all the minor details. But I must say, Mr. Andrews, you are a fortunate man. Inasmuch as you established residence on Titan, the Federation will be forced to acknowledge your priority claim to the heretofore unknown ore deposit near your cave."

"The—er—ore deposit?" Andrews looked blank.

Sparks hollered, "Oh, my sainted tonsils. The swamp! Of course. Pitchblende! That's why there was so much static interference. Radium…"

The cruiser's commander frowned on him.

"Exactly. Of course, Mr. Andrews, you cannot file a full claim to the property. That requires a full year's residence. And a man as important as yourself—"

Greg Malcolm started. He had said nothing up till now. He had been given an opportunity to say nothing. The captain had addressed himself solely to the one "important" man in their party, the man for whom, primarily, the search had been made, the man to whose "genius" was attributed the existence of the castaways.

Now he spoke up. He said, "But *I* am establishing residence, Captain Allengrove."

Allengrove permitted himself the luxury of a small smile.

"You, Malcolm? But really, my dear fellow, only a spaceman could undertake such a task. A *secretary—*"

Aunt Maud waddled forward belligerently. She said, "Secretary—pah! Fiddlefaddle, Captain! You don't know what you're talking about. And as for you, Brother Jonathan, I'm ashamed of you. Taking credit for all this—arragh!" She turned to Greg. "Gregory, I'm an old woman, and perhaps I'm an old fool, as well. But I've had more fun and excitement in the past month than I've had in the previous forty years. Be—be *damned* if I'll go back to Earth and piddle away my remaining years at operas and pink teas, I'm staying here with you."

Enid Andrews, into whose shoulders had so quickly come the grace and ease of authority that was her charm, looked shocked. "Maud!" she exclaimed.

Sparks Hannigan breathed a sigh of relief. "Then that makes three of us," he said. "Any more takers?"

Tommy O'Doul pushed his way to Greg's side. "Can I stay, too, Greg? Can I, huh? Me, too?"

Greg said gratefully, "If you want to, Tommy. But, Bert—you?"

FOR Bert Andrews had also aligned himself with his aunt and Sparks. Now he said defiantly, "What Aunt Maud says is good enough for me. I'll stick."

Tina was already beside Greg; her gaze was fiercely loyal. She did not need to say anything. Captain Allengrove looked stunned. "But really," he said, "but really, this is most unusual. I mean, we were sent to rescue you. I—er—I don't quite see how you expect to survive without leadership—"

Aunt Maud snorted belligerently. "Leadership? You just leave us supplies and we'll have all the leadership we need. Marberry, you're staying, aren't you? Well, that's seven of us. A lucky number! I don't suppose there are any more?"

She glared at Crystal. Greg, too, was watching the girl. Now before the steadfastness of their combined gazes, her eyes dropped. Her cheeks colored faintly. But she did not move from Breadon's side. She said, "I—I'm sorry. I hope you understand, Greg."

Greg said, "I understand."

"Furthermore," declared Aunt Maud staunchly, "I'm warning you, Jonathan. I know you. If you go home bragging about your part in the colonization of Titan, I'll follow you, so help me! And if you fail to keep us equipped with supplies—"

J. Foster said hurriedly, "Now, Maud..."

Captain Allengrove looked at them all uncomprehendingly. It didn't make sense. But he was a Space Officer—it was not his place to engage in family quarrels; his duty was to rescue what few of this astonishing crew wished to be rescued. He coughed nervously. He said, "Well, Mr. Andrews—if you're ready now?"

"Yes," said J. Foster. "We're ready now. Goodbye, Greg," he said. "And—er—thanks, old boy."

Greg said levelly, "That's all right, Goodbye." He said, less levelly. "Goodbye, Miss Andrews."

But Crystal and Breadon were already turning toward the portal, toward the cruiser that would carry them back to an easier, gentler world. So at the end, there were no last farewells. Just a single word, and silence.

Yet somehow, strangely, Greg Malcolm did not mind too much. For in losing one thing, he had found much more. He was bulwarked with greater, truer friends than most men ever know...he stood in a cave that was his home...on a new world that was yet his shining, unblemished empire.

And there was the touch of a warm hand on his own.

THE END

www.ingramcontent.com/pod-product-compliance
Lightning Source LLC
Chambersburg PA
CBHW050039180626
46810CB00002B/793